A Deadly Entanglement

GENTLEMEN *of* LONDON

Laura Beers

Chapter One

England, 1813

Reginald Heathcote, the Marquess of Haddington, surveyed the filthy hall of The Drunken Sailor with a tankard in hand. An aura of desperation hung in the musty air, despite the tavern being filled with boisterous noise. Someone retching in the corner drew his attention, and Reginald shook his head. The poor man must have tried the cook's special.

Boden leaned closer, an unwashed odor hanging about him like a cloud. "I've heard that the cook will use any carcass he finds on the streets to create his special meals," he remarked.

"That wouldn't surprise me, especially since there is no shortage of those in these parts," Reginald said.

"It only takes one time to learn one's lesson," Boden muttered.

"That it does," Reginald agreed. "Although, I do recall that you recommended the cook's special to me when we first met."

Boden lifted his tankard and laughed. "I had to have some fun with you."

Mellor spoke up from the other side of the round table. "We made a bet to see how long before ye threw it all up."

"Who won?" Reginald asked.

Smith raised his hand proudly. "I did," he announced. "I won enough to buy the next round of drinks."

"I don't fault any of you for it. I would have done precisely the same thing to any of you," Reginald said.

"We know ye would have," Boden responded with a smile. "It's why we continue to let ye drink with us."

"I thought it was because of my stunning conversational skills," Reginald joked.

"That is most assuredly not it," Smith bantered back.

Reginald took a sip of his watered-down ale as he studied these brawny men. He'd known them for a little over a year now, and the information they had let slip while inebriated had been invaluable to his assignments. But he still had to be cautious around them. He had little doubt that they would kill him just as easily as they'd befriended him if they discovered his true purpose in associating with them.

Boden lifted his tankard in the air and shouted, "More ale!"

Mellor chuckled. "I think you've had enough for one evening."

"I disagree," Boden responded, lowering his tankard. "If I can still manage to walk to the hovel I live in, then it is not enough."

"It's still better than my place," Smith said.

"That isn't saying much," Mellor interjected.

A red-haired serving wench walked over with a tankard and plopped it down in front of Boden. "Here ye are," she said. "Now do stop your racket."

Boden reached into his tattered jacket pocket and pulled out two coins. "Thank ye, my love."

The serving wench brushed off his flirting and accepted the coins before walking off.

"Ye sure have made an impression on her," Mellor commented sarcastically as he watched her retreating figure.

"Give it time," Boden said, unperturbed. "I am slowly wooing her with my dashing good looks and charming disposition."

"I daresay it's not working," Reginald joked.

Boden lowered his tankard to the table and grew serious. "I was approached by someone yesterday that's looking to hire some like-minded individuals."

"What kind of 'like-minded individuals'?" Smith asked.

"Someone that doesn't ask a lot of questions," Boden replied. "There's a new weapons smuggler that's set up shop in the rookeries."

Boden had his full attention, but Reginald feigned indifference. "There's always a new dealer in town," he said, bringing the tankard to his lips. "What makes this one different?"

Boden shifted in his seat to face him and lowered his voice further. "There's an insurrection coming soon."

"There's always talk of uprising, but in the end, nothing comes of it," Reginald said. "I don't mean to be a naysayer, but I don't want to set my cap at someone who might be taken down by the end of the week."

"This time is different," Boden pressed.

Reginald put his tankard on the table and rose. "I have had enough of this watered-down ale for one evening."

"The job pays ten pounds," Boden revealed.

Reginald stilled. "Ten pounds?" he repeated. "What exactly does it entail?"

Boden shrugged. "Does it matter?"

"I don't want to do anything that gets me transported," Reginald said, glancing around as he returned to his seat.

"Then don't get caught," Boden advised.

Mellor spoke up. "I'm in. I need the money."

"As am I," Smith said, accentuating his statement with a burp.

Boden lifted his brow at Reginald. "What say ye, Daventry?"

Reginald pressed his lips together as he pretended to consider it. This is what he did as a spy, infiltrating radical groups or any association that was not loyal to the Crown. It was dangerous work, considering he could be outed and killed at any time, but that was a chance he was willing to take.

"I'm in," he said, bobbing his head.

Boden smiled broadly. "I assumed that would be the case. Towle wants to meet in three days at the old wharf near Tooly Street. Come at sundown."

"I'll be there." Reginald rose, then gave a bow with a flourish. "Good evening, gentlemen."

Mellor scoffed. "Ain't no gentlemen here!"

"Speak for yourself," Reginald said with mock indignation, tugging down on his ragged brown jacket. "I could fit into the highest echelon of Society, if I chose to."

Smith shook his head. "Ye have about as much chance of that as Boden does with the woman who brought his drink."

Leaving their guffaws behind as he walked towards the door of the tavern, Reginald glanced over to the corner and saw that the man was still eating the cook's special, despite the poor effect it'd had on his stomach. He wished he could say that he was surprised, but he wasn't. Food was scarce in the rookeries due to escalating prices. People were suffering, and little was being done to help them.

He departed the soot-blackened building and started down the narrow pavement. He had just turned the corner when he saw his friend, Hawthorne, leaning against the wall of a dilapidated brick building.

Reginald glanced over his shoulder to ensure he wasn't being followed before stopping in front of Hawthorne. "What are you doing here?" he asked.

"Merritt sent me," Hawthorne replied, straightening from the wall.

"You're his errand boy now?" Reginald joked.

Hawthorne grinned. "No, but it has been a few days since you last checked in, and he's getting anxious."

"I was just on my way to see him."

Hawthorne turned his attention to the moon, which was high in the sky, and asked, "At this hour?"

Reginald gave him a knowing look. "We both know that he'll be in his office."

"That we do," Hawthorne said. "That man lives and breathes for the Crown."

"As do we."

They had just started walking down the pavement when four men stepped out of an alleyway with daggers raised.

Reginald put his hands up. "We don't want any trouble."

The tallest of the men spoke. "Just give us yer money and ye can pass."

"I'm afraid I am in need of my coins," Reginald said as he patted his jacket pockets. "I can't spare any for you lot."

A man with missing front teeth leered at him. "You're going to lose 'em anyway, old man."

"Old man?" Reginald questioned indignantly. "I'm not even thirty!"

Reginald noted the men's positions as they surrounded them, biding his time before making his move. The men had weapons, but it was evident by the way they held them that they didn't know how to handle them properly. Unfortunately for them, he was in no mood for games.

A side glance at Hawthorne showed that his friend was just as unconcerned as he was.

"It would be best if you walked away and pretended this unfortunate incident never happened," Reginald advised.

The tall man tightened his hold on his dagger. "We aren't

going anywhere, but I might just cut ye for fun even if you ain't got no money."

Reginald tsked. "You need to work on your threats," he said. "I would have said something like, 'I'll gut you like a fish and let you bleed out.' It's much more specific and would invoke more fear."

"I agree," Hawthorne stated. "Your delivery was good, but the message was rather vague."

The tall man's eyes narrowed as he stepped closer. "Enough!" he shouted. "Just give us your purses."

Reginald jabbed his fist into the tall man's throat before he crouched and punched the man with missing teeth squarely in the stomach. Both men fell to the ground, gasping for breath, as Hawthorne dispatched the other two attackers in a similar fashion.

Hawthorne gestured down the street. "Shall we?"

They stepped past the downed attackers and continued along the pavement. As they crossed the street, Hawthorne glanced over at Reginald. "May I ask what has been occupying your time as of late?"

"The usual pursuits, I suppose," Reginald replied.

"You haven't been to White's in a few days," Hawthorne commented.

Reginald half-shrugged. "I've been busy."

Hawthorne gave him a concerned look. "I would be remiss if I didn't mention that you have appeared despondent since Hugh's wedding."

"I don't know what you are speaking of."

"I think you do," Hawthorne pressed.

"I'm happy for Hugh."

"I never questioned that."

Reginald stopped and turned towards his friend. "Then what is it you aren't saying?"

"It makes me wonder if you are feeling left out now that you are the only one of us not married."

Reginald scoffed. "I am a grown man, and I am much too busy to feel sorry for myself," he said. "Besides, I'm glad I haven't fallen prey to the parson's mousetrap."

"Surely you don't mean that."

"But I do," Reginald asserted. "I am free to do as I please, but you have a wife you have to give an account to."

Hawthorne sighed. "Forget I said anything."

"I already did," Reginald said as he resumed walking.

Marriage was the last thing on his mind. Besides, there was only one woman he would ever consider marrying, and she wanted nothing to do with him.

As they neared the unassuming brick building that housed their headquarters, Reginald saw that Talbot and Worsley were each holding a mangy cat.

"What now?" Reginald muttered.

Talbot and Worsley were assigned to guard the building, but they kept coming up with new ruses as to why they were standing out front. It seemed that every venture grew more and more ridiculous.

Talbot held up the black and white cat as they approached. "Would you care to purchase a cat?"

"You're selling cats now?" Hawthorne asked as he stopped in front of them.

Worsley leaned over and placed his orange cat on the ground. "We are," he replied. "It's our best business venture yet."

Reginald watched as the cat hurried away and disappeared down an alley. "It would appear that you lost your cat."

"Not to worry," Worsley said. "It'll return when we feed it."

Hawthorne gave them an amused look. "Has anyone actually bought one from you?"

"We haven't sold any yet, but we have had lots of interest," Worsley replied. "It's genius on our part, really."

"In what way?" Reginald asked.

"There are stray cats everywhere," Worsley said, gesturing widely, "and we are the only ones taking advantage of the opportunity."

Reginald shook his head. "It's a good thing you two are somewhat competent agents."

"That we are," Talbot agreed. "I wouldn't say we were the best agents here, but someone could make a case for that."

Worsley bobbed his head in agreement. "That they could, especially since we both run a business and guard headquarters from threats."

The cat in Talbot's hand meowed and he chuckled. "It would appear that Merritt agrees with you."

"You named it Merritt?" Hawthorne asked.

Talbot smirked. "We thought that Merritt and this cat share a similar disposition."

"You two are idiots," Reginald muttered as he stepped around them to go inside.

Worsley brought his hand up to his chest. "You wound me, sir."

"It pains me to say so, but I do not think you are worthy of one of our cats," Talbot remarked with his nose in the air. "You may move along now."

"I have every intention to," Reginald said, opening the door.

Hawthorne followed him into the narrow hall. Mr. Mostyn sat behind a desk at the near end of it, his eyes following them with mild curiosity from beneath his white hair.

"Good evening, Mostyn," Reginald greeted.

Mostyn tipped his head. "Are those two still selling stray cats?"

"They are," Reginald replied as he walked further into the hall. "I fear they are attracting far too much attention."

"On the contrary," Mostyn said. "People are avoiding this stretch of buildings because of those two fools and their ridiculous antics."

"How is your wife?" Hawthorne asked.

"She is recovering," Mostyn replied. "I should warn you that Merritt is in a foul mood."

"When is he not?" Hawthorne retorted as they approached the door in the back.

The door suddenly opened, and Miss Evie Ashmore stepped through it, a frown etched on her features. She was dressed in a brown, shapeless dress with a matching bonnet, which was a far cry from the fine muslin gowns she usually wore. Even in that horrible ensemble, Evie's comeliness shone through. She was indisputably the most beautiful woman Reginald had ever met.

Evie schooled her features when she saw them. "Good evening."

"What's wrong?" Reginald asked, not fooled in the least by her transformation.

"Nothing that you need to concern yourself with," Evie replied dismissively. "I do wish you luck with Merritt, though, because he is being entirely unreasonable."

Reginald heard the terseness in her voice, although she tried to hide it, but knew she wouldn't confide in him. "You shouldn't be out at this late hour," he chided. "Allow me to escort you home."

"I appreciate your concern, but I will be fine," Evie responded, narrowing her eyes.

"I am just worried about your safety in this section of town, and—"

"My answer is still no," she snapped. "If you will excuse me, I should head home before anyone notices my absence there."

Reginald watched as Evie crossed the hall and stepped out of the building. He had never known a more infuriating woman. She seemed to take great pride in defying him at every opportunity.

"She will be fine," Hawthorne said, "but we won't be if we keep Merritt waiting."

"You're right." Reginald followed Hawthorne through the door and into an adjacent chamber. The room was filled with agents, but it was eerily quiet. Every man appeared to be engrossed in the papers in front of them, and they were studiously ignored as they approached Merritt's office.

Hawthorne stopped in front of the door and knocked.

"Enter," Merritt's gruff voice commanded.

"This doesn't bode well for us," Hawthorne muttered under his breath before he opened the door.

Reginald followed Hawthorne into Merritt's study and closed the door behind him.

Merritt leaned back in his chair with a scathing look. "It appears that Haddington is finally gracing this office with his presence. Where have you been?"

Reginald sat down in a chair in front of the desk, while Hawthorne remained standing in the corner. "I have been rather busy."

Waving his hand over the stack of papers on his desk, Merritt asked, "Aren't we all?"

"I have a lead on a new weapons smuggler in the rookeries," Reginald revealed.

"I'm afraid we have more pressing matters than a smuggler. Turn what you know over to the magistrate and let him handle it," Merritt ordered.

"But they won't do anything about it," Reginald argued.

"Perhaps not, but we don't have the time or resources to pursue every lead we come across," Merritt remarked.

"One of my informants mentioned an 'insurrection was

coming',"Reginald pressed. "I think this has something to do with that."

Merritt didn't look convinced. "You could throw a rock in the rookeries and hit a fanatic saying whatever it took to draw people in. It is a lawless place."

"That it is, but should we not do our due diligence and investigate?" Reginald pressed.

"You have been awfully quiet," Merritt said, turning his attention to Hawthorne. "What do you think?"

Hawthorne stepped forward and claimed the chair next to Reginald. "Radical groups are popping up all over England, and it is only a matter of time before they combine forces," he said. "If Haddington says a possible insurrection is coming, it is worth his time to investigate and shut it down before the movement gains traction."

Merritt considered them both for a moment. "All right. You have a week to determine if this smuggler poses any real threat of rebellion."

"Thank you," Reginald said, rising.

"Before you go," Merritt said, "I have another assignment for you."

Reginald returned to his seat.

Merritt leaned forward. "You've known Agent A since she was young, correct?"

"Agent A?"

"My apologies," Merritt said. "Miss Ashmore. I assigned her the same letter we used to identify her father."

"But I don't even have a code letter," Reginald pointed out.

"Not every agent is assigned one," Merritt said with an unapologetic shrug. "I am working with an abundance of caution where Miss Ashmore is concerned."

"I understand," Reginald said, "and, yes, our parents had neighboring country estates. I essentially grew up with Miss Ashmore."

"Good, good," Merritt muttered. "I need your help, then."

"Whatever you need."

Merritt frowned. "Miss Ashmore has informed me that Rutledge has gone missing—again."

"Again?" Hawthorne echoed. "It might be time to tie a bell around his neck so we know his whereabouts."

Reginald indulged in a chuckle before asking, "How long has he been missing?"

"One day."

It was Reginald's turn to repeat Merritt's words. "One day?" he asked, furrowing his brows.

Merritt nodded. "I tried to convince Miss Ashmore that he is most likely chasing down a lead, but she was adamant that something terrible has befallen him."

"Does she have any proof of that?" Hawthorne asked.

"None," Merritt replied. "She said they were supposed to meet at Dover Park yesterday at noon, but he never showed."

"That doesn't prove anything," Reginald said. "Something more pressing might have come up."

"Precisely, but she doesn't seem to want to believe that," Merritt said. "She asked for permission to search for him."

"Did you grant it?" Hawthorne inquired.

"Not at first, but she can be rather persuasive," Merritt admitted. "I daresay in another life she could have been a barrister."

"What would you like me to do?" Reginald asked.

"I would like for you to partner with Miss Ashmore," Merritt said solemnly.

"She'll be against it."

"I have no doubt, but I fear that she isn't thinking clearly right now," Merritt said. "She has grown rather close to Rutledge over the past few months, and I would hate for her to take any unnecessary risks in her search for him."

"Especially since he might not be missing in the first

place," Hawthorne reminded them. "Rutledge has been known to go undercover and be gone for weeks."

Merritt bobbed his head. "Agreed. I just don't want to lose another agent on my watch. Miss Ashmore hasn't been an agent for long, but she shows great promise, and I don't want that potential to end up wasted."

Reginald rose. "I'll inform her tomorrow of your decision. She's not going to like it."

"Thank you. I'm hoping your personal connection will temper her ire at being partnered up." Merritt picked up a piece of paper from his desk. "You two are dismissed."

Reginald and Hawthorne didn't speak as they exited Merritt's office and headed towards the main door. As they stepped outside, they saw that Talbot and Worsley had been replaced by two other agents, and there were no signs of cats.

"How do you think Evie will take the news that you are to partner with her?" Hawthorne asked, amusement in his voice as he hopped over a pungent gutter and led the way down the pavement.

"I suspect you already know the answer to that."

"I do. She values her independence."

"That she does," Reginald said. "It has been that way since she was a little girl."

Hawthorne glanced over at him. "What's your plan?"

"My plan?"

"To convince her to partner with you?"

"I don't have a plan," Reginald admitted. "I'm just going to inform her that Merritt ordered us to be partners and hope she is sensible enough to go along with it."

"Sensible?" Hawthorne repeated. "Evie is not known to be sensible."

"Don't remind me."

Hawthorne skirted a pile of refuse on the pavement. "Dinah wanted me to invite you to dinner next week."

"Dare I refuse?" Reginald asked.

"And risk Dinah's wrath?" Hawthorne joked.

"Why the sudden interest in me?"

"Dinah is just worried about you since you haven't found a young woman to court yet."

Reginald looked heavenward. "Being unmarried is not a disease," he asserted. "I just haven't found someone who has piqued my interest yet."

"I think we both know that isn't true," Hawthorne said with a pointed look.

"Are you or your wife Cupid?" Reginald asked. "Do you round up unmarried people and force them into unions against their will?"

"I just feel——"

Reginald put his hand up, stilling his words. "I am content with things how they are. I only ask that my friends refrain from matchmaking."

Hawthorne sighed. "As you wish."

Silence descended over them as they walked towards the more fashionable part of town to hail a hackney, which Reginald was most grateful for. It gave him time to think about how he was going to convince the most obstinate woman in London to partner with him.

Chapter Two

Evie reined in her horse near the stable and effortlessly dismounted. After she handed off the reins to the awaiting groom, she started walking towards the townhouse. Her morning ride had gone longer than she'd intended, but she was here now. Hopefully that would be enough for Aunt Nancy.

A footman tipped his head politely as he opened the rear door for her. Evie stepped inside and headed towards the drawing room, her steps faltering when she heard a male voice drifting out into the entry hall. Drat. With any luck, the gentleman was here to call upon her aunt and not her.

She smoothed down her blue riding habit and forced a smile onto her lips. The last thing Evie wanted to do was entertain a gentleman, but her aunt was insistent that she do her duty. She had tried to explain to Aunt Nancy that she had no desire to marry; she would never permit a man to control her or her destiny. But her aunt thought that was just a passing whim and continued to force Evie to meet with potential suitors.

Evie stepped into the room and stifled a groan when she recognized Lord Strathmore. Of all the gentlemen who could have called, why did it have to be him? He was short and red-haired, reminding her of the mythical leprechauns she had read about. His eyes were bland, which was indicative of the person she perceived him to be.

Aunt Nancy gave her a chiding look, but her words were cordial. "You have arrived," she said, "and you have leaves in your hair."

Evie reached up and removed a twig with a cluster of leaves. "I must have acquired them when I rode through the woodlands," she revealed as she set them aside.

"I do hope you weren't going at a breakneck speed," Aunt Nancy remarked with a strained smile.

"I used some restraint," Evie said. She loved nothing more than feeling the wind on her face and the exhilaration of knowing one misstep could be her last.

Aunt Nancy patted the seat next to her. "Come and listen to Lord Strathmore. He was just sharing the most delightful story about his sister, Lady Susan."

Evie reluctantly stepped forward to do her aunt's bidding. She had no doubt that Lord Strathmore was going to share the most boring anecdote, because he was one of the least interesting men of her acquaintance.

Lord Strathmore had stood when Evie entered the room, but he returned to his seat after she sat down. He leaned forward and retrieved his teacup.

"I was just telling your aunt that Susan is thoroughly enjoying her first Season," he drawled, "and we are hopeful she will obtain a match soon."

"Do you not worry that Lady Susan is too young to secure a match?" Evie asked.

Lord Strathmore gave her a baffled look. "I do not," he replied. "My sister is eighteen years old and is in fine condition to bare many healthy boys."

"What if she doesn't give birth to boys?" Evie pressed.

"I have no doubt that her husband will be disappointed,

but I suppose there are worse things than having female children," Lord Strathmore said.

"Yes, like death."

"Pardon?"

Her aunt shot Evie a warning look as she continued. "I just meant death is far worse than giving birth to a girl."

"Quite right," Lord Strathmore said.

"Being attacked by jackals is another example," Evie stated.

Lord Strathmore became very interested in his tea. "Yes, I would imagine so."

Evie arched an eyebrow. "You imagine so?" she questioned. "From what I read, jackals are opportunistic hunters, and they attack anything that encroaches on their territory. I think we both can agree that giving birth to females is preferable to having your skin ripped from your body and—"

"Evie!" her aunt exclaimed, cutting her off. "Your description is far too vivid for the drawing room."

"My apologies." Evie batted her eyes and smiled sweetly at Lord Strathmore. "I hope I did not offend you, my lord."

Lord Strathmore puffed out his chest. "Not at all. I find you to be an absolute delight."

"You are most generous," Evie murmured. She found it unbelievable that gentlemen could be so easily turned by a coy smile or a demure look.

Leaning forward, Lord Strathmore set his teacup and saucer on the table. "Which brings me to a question I have." He hesitated, and Evie had a sneaking suspicion of what he was going to ask, and dreaded the thought of spending any additional time with the pretentious lord.

Evie abruptly rose, causing Lord Strathmore to do the same. "I do apologize, but I fear that I have developed a rash from my ride. I recall now that I brushed up against some baneberry."

"Oh, that is most unfortunate," Lord Strathmore said,

looking unsure. "May I call upon you at a later date to continue this conversation?"

"Yes, that would be preferable, but I am not quite sure how long I will have this rash," Evie said.

Her aunt spoke up. "If it is like your other rashes, I am sure it will be gone within a few hours."

"Or it could go well into the evening and tomorrow," Evie said as she began scratching her arm. "I would feel awful if I wasted Lord Strathmore's time."

Lord Strathmore pulled his lips up in a cloying smiled, making her skin crawl. "I do not mind waiting for you, my dear," he said, "but, if it is preferable, I will wait a few days before I come to call."

"Thank you for your understanding, my lord," Evie said.

"Would you care for me to send my doctor over to examine the rash?" Lord Strathmore asked.

Evie switched the arm she was scratching and replied, "That won't be necessary, since I still have some salve from my last encounter."

"You have had this kind of rash before?" Lord Strathmore asked.

Evie bobbed her head. "I'm afraid so," she replied. "My grandmother's neighbor once fell into a baneberry bush, and she lost an arm because of it."

Lord Strathmore's face blanched. "An arm?"

"Yes, because the resulting infection attached itself to the bone, and it had to be amputated," Evie explained.

She watched as the gentleman started slowly backing away and resisted the urge to smile victoriously.

Lord Strathmore bumped against the wall and stopped. "I, uh, am late for a very important meeting, and I'm afraid I cannot tarry for a moment longer."

Evie's lips formed a pout. "That is most disappointing, but you honored us with your visit, my lord."

Lord Strathmore bowed and departed from the room

without another word. Evie dropped onto her chair and reached for the teapot.

Aunt Nancy shifted in her seat to face her. "Was that truly necessary?" she asked. "Now Lord Strathmore believes you have a rash."

"It is far better than having to reject his offer of courtship," Evie said.

"That is the third suitor you have scared off with your ridiculous antics," Aunt Nancy pointed out. "Don't you want to ever marry?"

Evie poured herself a cup of tea. "I believe I have already made my thoughts on matrimony known."

"You have, but you are wrong to dismiss all callers on a passing fancy of youth."

"It is not a passing fancy," Evie contested. "If I were to marry, I would be at the beck and call of my husband."

"You speak of marriage as though it is an institution to oppress women, but you will have so many more freedoms as a married woman."

"I fail to see how being sold in the marriage mart and devoting my life to creating heirs isn't oppressive," Evie said, bringing her cup to her lips.

Aunt Nancy sighed. "Your sister doesn't seem to be oppressed. In fact, she is blissfully happy with Nathaniel."

Evie lowered the cup and saucer to her lap. "I am happy for Dinah, but we are on different paths."

"And what path are you on, dear?" Aunt Nancy asked. "Because I fear that it is the path to ruination."

"I know how to behave. I take great pains to ensure I will not be ruined."

Aunt Nancy didn't look convinced. "You just chased an eligible lord out the door by feigning a rash."

"I believe I already explained myself."

"It isn't just that. You have been sneaking out of the townhouse at all hours with no explanation at all," her aunt said. "I must wonder if you are meeting someone."

"I am not."

"Then what is so important that you would risk your reputation over?" Aunt Nancy demanded.

Evie pressed her lips together before saying, "I have my reasons, and I assure you that they are good."

"But you never share with me what those reasons are," her aunt said with an expectant look, "do you?"

"It's better if you don't know," Evie murmured.

Aunt Nancy shook her head. "You are on your ninth Season, and well on your way to being on the shelf."

"There are worse things than being a spinster."

"Like death?" Aunt Nancy asked with an exasperated sigh.

Evie laughed. "Precisely," she said.

"This isn't funny."

"It is," Evie said, "just a little bit."

Aunt Nancy's lips twitched. "You are going to be the death of me, child."

"I think not. You are going to live a long, fruitful life, and I will go wherever you are."

"I just worry about you. I won't always be around, and I want to make sure you are taken care of."

"I do not have any qualms about living by myself."

A reflective look came into her aunt's eyes. "You should, because it can be awfully lonely when you find yourself genuinely without companionship."

"Are you lonely?" Evie asked quietly.

"I have been lonely since Andrew died," her aunt replied. "His death left a void in my heart that is so deep that it is a daily struggle to fill it."

"I'm sorry," Evie said, unsure of what to say.

"I want you to find the kind of love that you deserve. Once it's yours, it'll heal every wound you've received along the journey."

Evie took a sip of her drink, then said, "Again, I shall have to decline."

"One day you will see that love is always worth the sacrifice." Aunt Nancy rose. "I just hope the realization won't come too late."

"I know you mean well, but not everyone gets a happily ever after. Some people are destined to be alone."

"You are not one of those people."

Evie gave her aunt a sad smile. "I made my decision long ago, and I have come to terms with it. I hope one day you do, too."

Her aunt cupped her cheek. "I have only ever wanted you to be happy."

"I am happy."

"Are you?" Aunt Nancy asked as she dropped her hand. "Your eyes tell a different story."

Evie lowered her gaze to her teacup.

Her aunt took a step back. "I am going to rest for a spell," she said. "I will inform Barnes to send for me if anyone comes to call."

After her aunt departed from the drawing room, Evie leaned forward and put her empty teacup on the tray.

Why couldn't her aunt understand that she didn't need a man to make her happy? She was doing just fine on her own. She may be lonely sometimes, but that was the plight of any spy—trust no one, rely on no one. That's what Rutledge had told her.

Evie rose and walked over to the window. Where was Rutledge? She knew Merritt thought she was mad for wanting to search for him after only one day, but she knew him. He would never have missed their appointment unless something dire came up.

She would find him. She just hoped he was still alive when she did.

Reginald had just exited his coach when he saw Lord Strathmore rush down the steps of Evie's townhouse with an unusually solemn look on his face.

Lord Strathmore put his hand up as he approached him. "I urge you not to go inside." His voice was insistent and held a note of panic.

"And why is that, exactly?"

Lord Strathmore stopped in front of him and lowered his voice. "It would appear that Miss Ashmore has come down with a rash."

Reginald resisted the urge to laugh, because it was evident that this gentleman believed her tale. What a ridiculous notion! Even if Evie did, in fact, have a rash, she would never have revealed any weakness to Lord Strathmore. So what game was she playing?

With a glance over his shoulder, Lord Strathmore continued. "Miss Ashmore confided in me that her grandmother's neighbor had a similar rash, and she lost her arm because of it."

"Miss Ashmore confided this to you?" Reginald asked.

"She did."

"Yet you are telling me not a moment after you leave her townhouse?"

Lord Strathmore's face blanched. "Only because I am most concerned with your welfare."

"I see, but have you not considered that Miss Ashmore was just having some fun at your expense?"

"Why would she do that?" Lord Strathmore asked with a mystified expression.

Reginald decided that the best course of action was to be tactful. "Miss Ashmore is known to be an incorrigible jokester."

"I had not known that about her."

"She only teases the people she is truly fond of."

Lord Strathmore puffed out his chest, no doubt believing his half-truths. "I believe you are right."

"I am, because I knew Miss Ashmore's grandmother's neighbor, and I never once witnessed her without an arm."

"I shall consider it a grand honor that I saw Miss Ashmore's wit firsthand," Lord Strathmore said.

"As well you should."

Lord Strathmore reached into his waistcoat pocket and pulled out a ring box. He opened it to reveal a gold ring and asked, "Do you think Miss Ashmore will like it?"

Reginald stared at the ring, stunned. "You plan to offer for Miss Ashmore?"

"I am," Lord Strathmore said. "As you know, my wife died two months ago in childbirth, and I have two children who are in desperate need of a mother."

"I had not realized that you held Miss Ashmore in high regard."

"She is quite beautiful," Lord Strathmore said.

"That she is," Reginald readily agreed, "but surely there is something else about Miss Ashmore that intrigues you."

Lord Strathmore gave him a bewildered look, as if he had never considered this before. "Uh, of course. There are many things I am fond of, but that list is too great to divulge now," he rushed out.

Reginald was done with this ridiculous conversation. "Good day to you, Strathmore," he said, tipping his head.

Without waiting for a response, he walked past Lord Strathmore and knocked on the door.

"Lord Haddington," the butler greeted with his usual stoic expression.

"Is Miss Ashmore available for callers?" he asked as he stepped inside and removed his top hat.

"She is," Barnes replied, accepting the hat. "If you wait here, I will announce you."

Reginald turned towards the drawing room. "That won't be necessary. I will show myself in."

"As you wish, my lord."

Reginald crossed the entry hall, stopping in the drawing room doorway when he saw Evie standing at the window. Her hair was pulled back into a tight chignon at the base of her neck, drawing attention to her high cheekbones, and she was dressed in a flattering blue riding habit.

She was undoubtedly beautiful, but he had learned that beauty wasn't just about having a pretty face. One must also have a kind heart, and most importantly, a beautiful soul, to tempt him. And Evie had always tempted him. She was the woman of his dreams—but when he awoke, she was out of his reach.

Evie shifted her gaze towards him and raised an eyebrow. "Did your mother not tell you that it is impolite to stare?" she asked, amused.

"I must have missed that lesson," he joked as he stepped further into the room. "I just had the most informative conversation with one of your suitors."

Evie let out a huff. "I must assume you are speaking of Lord Strathmore."

"I am."

"He is most assuredly not one of my suitors."

"He seems to believe so," Reginald said. "He is also under the impression that you have a rash."

"I do. It would be best if you leave, as well." Her eyes flashed with mirth.

Reginald chuckled. "You will not be getting rid of me so easily."

"Pity."

"Did you know that Lord Strathmore is intent on offering for you?"

Evie bit her lower lip. "I assumed as much," she replied. "That's why I blurted out the first thing that came to mind."

"You might want to work on your excuses, especially since you wouldn't want the *ton* to get word of this 'rash'."

"You are right, of course," Evie said with a wave of her hand. "It was not my finest performance, but it did get the job done."

"Fortunately, no harm was done, since I was able to convince Lord Strathmore that you were only joking," Reginald informed her. "Although, he is now under the impression you favor him."

"Drat," Evie muttered.

Reginald smiled. "A simple 'thank you' would suffice."

"But I am not thankful," Evie said. "Now I must contend with Lord Strathmore again."

"That may be true, but you will have time to think of a better excuse for next time," Reginald said.

Evie gestured towards the settee. "Would you care to sit?"

Reginald glanced at the doorway. "Should we not wait for a chaperone of sorts?"

"I don't think that is necessary. We have known each other since we were children," Evie said as she walked over to the settee. "If you are still worried, I can promise you that I will behave."

Reginald waited until Evie sat down before he claimed a chair next to the settee. He lowered his voice and shared, "I have come at Merritt's behest."

"For what purpose?"

"He's worried about you."

"There is no reason to worry about me," Evie said dismissively. "I'm afraid you have traveled all this way for no reason."

"I disagree. Merritt asked me to help you search for Rutledge."

Evie frowned. "Merritt asked you to watch over me?"

"Assist," he corrected. "There is a difference."

"Not to me," she huffed.

Reginald smiled placatingly. "You must know that it is not uncommon for Rutledge to go missing for days on end," he said. "We might very well find him drinking at a tavern in the rookeries."

"I doubt that. He never would have missed our meeting."

"How well do you really know Rutledge?" Reginald asked. "I've known him for years, ever since he recruited me out of Oxford."

"I know you must think me foolish, but I think I know Rutledge very well. And I am certain that he is in harm's way."

Reginald leaned forward in his seat. "What proof do you have, other than he missed your meeting?" he asked. "I assume you searched his home?"

"I did."

"Was anything out of the ordinary?"

She shook her head. "No."

"I know you are worried, but——"

Evie spoke over him. "Do not attempt to pacify me, Reginald. I may not have been an agent as long as you, but I know what my gut is telling me," she asserted. "I think Rutledge is in trouble."

"But you have no proof." He eyed her with concern. "Perhaps you are just letting your emotions cloud your judgement."

Evie visibly tensed. "And perhaps you are being a jackanapes."

"I meant no offense."

"I did."

Reginald had tapped into Evie's ire, and nothing would be resolved if they continued down this path.

"My apologies," he said. "I do believe I misspoke."

"Yes, you did. Furthermore, you can inform Merritt that I do not require a nursemaid."

"Merritt is the one who gives the orders. He does not take them."

Evie pursed her lips together. "I prefer to work alone."

"As do I, but we have been tasked to work together to find Rutledge."

"I don't need your help."

"But you will have it nonetheless."

Evie looked displeased, but before she could respond, Mrs. Carter stepped into the room and greeted, "Reginald! What a wonderful surprise."

Reginald rose and bowed. "Mrs. Carter."

She gave him a mock chiding look. "I believe I have asked you on multiple occasions to call me Nancy."

"You have, but I'm afraid I am stuck in my ways."

Mrs. Carter walked over and sat next to Evie. Turning towards her niece, she asked, "Did you offer Reginald some refreshment?"

"No, because I did not wish for him to tarry," Evie replied.

"Evie," her aunt admonished. "You are being rude to our guest."

Reginald grinned as he returned to his seat. "I find Evie's bluntness delightful."

"I'm afraid you are the only one," Mrs. Carter said. "Her sharp tongue has sent one too many gentlemen running from our drawing room."

Evie rose. "I'm afraid that Reginald was just leaving."

"Are you trying to get rid of me?" Reginald asked.

"Of course not," Evie replied. "I just assumed that you have more important things to do than engage in idle chit chat."

Reginald held her gaze. "I assure you that there is no other place I would rather be."

Evie slowly returned to her seat. "That is where we differ,

my lord, because I would rather be anywhere but here with you."

Mrs. Carter's mouth dropped. "Evie, you must not say such hurtful things to our dear family friend."

Reginald held his hand up. "You don't need to worry about me, Mrs. Carter," he said. "I have known Evie for far too long to be offended."

"You are too kind," Mrs. Carter said. "I do believe Evie enjoys pushing people away from her."

"It is much easier that way," Evie stated.

Reginald nodded. "True, it may be easier, but it is much lonelier."

"I am not afraid of being alone," Evie said. "Are you?"

"Loneliness is an old friend, I'm afraid," Reginald replied. "It is not something that I wish upon you, though."

Evie watched him for a moment before gesturing towards the teapot. "Would you care for some tea?"

"No, thank you," Reginald responded as he rose. "I have taken up enough of your time."

"It is a shame that you must leave so soon," Evie said as she rose again. Her words were entirely unconvincing.

"Would you care to walk me to the door?" Reginald asked her.

"I would be honored."

They didn't speak as they exited the drawing room. Once they reached the main door, Reginald lowered his voice and asked, "Have you come to terms with the fact that we are partners for the foreseeable future?"

Evie smiled too sweetly up at him. "I am looking forward to it."

Reginald bid goodbye and departed. He wasn't a fool; Evie had no intention of partnering with him.

But he'd anticipated her reluctance. This was one game Evie wasn't going to win.

Chapter Three

Evie did not need a partner, and definitely didn't want one, especially one as vexing as Reginald. He had always unsettled her, which was troubling, since she prided herself on always being in control. She knew it was in her best interest to distance herself from him, but she could never seem to be rid of the man. He was a nuisance.

A deucedly handsome nuisance.

Her aunt's voice reached her from the doorway of the drawing room. "You mustn't be so rude to Reginald."

"Why is that?" Evie asked, feigning ignorance.

"He is your friend."

Evie turned towards her aunt. "He *was* my friend," she said. "As we've gotten older, we have come to realize that our differences are too vast to ignore."

"That is a shame. You two were once thick as thieves."

"We were, but we grew up."

"I wouldn't be so quick to dismiss him. True friends are hard to come by," her aunt counseled.

Evie was tired of talking about Reginald. She had made her decision long ago, and she wouldn't second guess herself now. Quite frankly, she *couldn't.* Her heart had been breaking ever since she'd decided to walk away from him. She could feel it now, aching deeply in her chest, and knew that the pain would never cease. It would always beat at a desperate rhythm as long as Reginald was around to remind her of what could have been.

Her aunt stepped closer to her. "Did you hear me, Evie?"

"I did, but I do not wish to speak about Reginald," Evie replied, tilting her chin. "I think I need a distraction."

"Do I want to know what this distraction is?" Aunt Nancy asked with a resigned sigh.

"Do not be so dramatic, dear aunt," Evie teased, "I believe shopping on Bond Street would help with my humdrum."

"What about suitors who may come to call?"

Evie waved her hand dismissively. "Barnes will inform them that I am not home to receive callers."

"How do you intend to marry if you aren't here to greet your suitors?"

"If a gentleman is so easily turned off by my mere absence, then I hardly think we would suit," Evie said.

Her aunt looked displeased. "You make no effort to secure a suitor."

"Yet you still press the issue," Evie remarked. "I have my own future. Why would I give up my freedom to be shackled to a husband?"

"Marriage can be a wonderful thing."

"Or the precursor to a life of misery," Evie asserted.

"I have never met a person who was so contrary when it came to matrimony," her aunt said with a shake of her head. "Be sure to take along a maid with you when you go shopping. I would accompany you, but one of us has to remain here for callers."

"If I never marry, then just think of all the fun we can have together!" Evie said cheerily.

"I would rather play with your children."

"You will have to be content with Dinah's," Evie said as she walked to the stairs, "because I never wish to have children underfoot."

"You say that now, but things can change. There is no shame in that."

Evie just shook her head as she walked up the stairs. The idea of her having children was preposterous. She loved spending time with the girls at the orphanage, but at the end of the day, she was not bogged down with the responsibility of rearing a family. She wanted her freedom—craved it, in fact.

She hurried down the hall and opened the door to her bedchamber. Her lady's maid was sewing up her buff trousers in the corner.

Abigail looked up when she came into the room, a flummoxed look on her face. "Would you care to explain how you ripped your trousers this time?"

"They got stuck on a nail when I was climbing through a window," Evie explained as she closed the door.

"Could you try to avoid the nails next time?" Abigail asked. "I fear you will need to commission a new pair if you keep getting holes in them."

"That's why I have an extra pair."

"Those aren't in much better shape than these," Abigail said as she pulled the needle through the fabric.

Evie walked over to the wardrobe and removed a pink gown. "I need to dress to go shopping at Bond Street."

Abigail lowered the trousers to her lap. "May I ask where your real destination is?"

"The market."

"I wish you wouldn't go to the market," Abigail said. "It is an unruly place that invites miscreants and people who are just as willing to kill you as sell you their goods."

"I daresay that you exaggerate."

"I know what I am speaking of. Tom robbed people of their hard-earned coins every opportunity he got."

Evie put the gown on the bed. "I believe this is the first I have heard you mention Tom since..."

"Since he sold me," Abigail said, finishing her thought. "It's all right for you to say so."

"I just didn't wish to bring up those painful memories for you."

Abigail rose and draped the trousers over the back of the chair. "I never thought Tom would rid himself of me, but I'm glad that he did. If he hadn't, I would never have met you," she said. "He was cruel and treated me awfully. I am thankful that I'm not under his thumb anymore."

"Do you ever wonder what happened to him?"

Abigail shook her head. "I do not," she replied. "Nor do I care. He lost that right when he sold me at the market."

"It was a terrible thing to do."

Abigail was silent for a moment. "That was Tom," she said. "He didn't care about anyone other than himself. He probably spent all the money you gave him on ale."

"Most likely."

Abigail walked over to the bed and picked up the gown. "I would much rather talk about pleasant things."

"Such as?"

"I am wondering which maid you are going to force to go with you today," Abigail mused.

Evie smiled. "I was hoping to convince you to go with me."

Abigail gave a firm shake of her head. "I am happy here, far away from anyone who can hurt me. There is nothing for me outside of these walls."

"Wouldn't it be a nice change of pace to breathe fresh air?" Evie encouraged.

"There is nothing for me at the market, I can promise you that." Abigail gave her a curious look. "Am I to assume you are meeting Mrs. Taylor at the market?"

"If she is there," Evie replied.

"Why risk going if she might not be there?"

"Because I am looking for information that I'm hoping she has," Evie informed her.

"Is it really so important that you are willing to risk your life for it?"

Evie nodded. "It is," she replied. "Someone must know what happened to Rutledge, and I'm hoping Mrs. Taylor can point me in the right direction."

"But he's only been missing for two days now," Abigail said. "Isn't it a little early to start searching for him?"

Evie sat down on the bed. "I know that he would do the same thing for me," she said. "I don't know what I would do if something happened to him."

"You mustn't think that way."

"How can I not?" Evie asked. "Rutledge has been the one constant in my life since he recruited me. He has taught me so much, and we have grown rather close." A sad smile came to her lips. "He reminds me of my father in so many ways."

Abigail sat down next to her. "Then you must find him."

Lowering her gaze to her lap, Evie asked the one question that had plagued her since Rutledge hadn't shown up to their meeting. "What if I fail to find him?"

Abigail's brows knitted into a frown. "You aren't one to second guess yourself."

"You must think me terribly foolish."

"No, but I am concerned," Abigail said. "You must promise me that you will be careful."

"I will."

Abigail rose and held the dress up. "Then we must dress you before it grows too late to visit the market."

As Evie dressed, she said, "Lord Haddington came to call. He had the ridiculous notion that we should search for Rutledge together."

"He wishes to be your partner?"

"For this assignment, yes."

Abigail shrugged her shoulders. "I don't think it is a terrible idea."

"Well, I think it is," Evie said.

"Is it because you fancy Lord Haddington?" Abigail asked.

Evie's eyes grew wide as she tried to pretend to be outraged by such a ridiculous notion. "I do not fancy Lord Haddington," she stated. "I can hardly stand the man."

Abigail gave her a knowing look. "Is that why you blush when you talk about him?"

"I do no such thing."

"It hardly matters to me, but I do think you should stop lying to yourself," Abigail said as she took a step back.

A knock came at the door, and Evie was grateful for the intrusion. Abigail walked over to the door and opened it, revealing a dark-haired maid.

The maid walked into the room and dropped into a curtsy. "I have been tasked with accompanying you this afternoon."

"That is wonderful, Jenny," Evie responded as she smoothed down her pink gown. "I do hope you will be discrete."

"Of course, miss," Jenny said.

Evie walked over to the dressing table, opened a drawer, and removed a pistol. While she slipped it into a pocket in the folds of her gown, she said, "You will remain in the coach while I run an errand."

Jenny pressed her lips together, clearly displeased by her order. "I was told by your aunt that I was to remain with you at all times."

"That will not be necessary."

Abigail removed a bonnet from the wardrobe and approached her. "This should match your gown splendidly."

Evie took a moment to arrange the bonnet on her head. "If all goes according to plan, I will be back well before it is time to dress for dinner."

"Are you not attending Lady Cadogan's ball?" Abigail asked.

Evie groaned. "I forgot all about that," she said. "I suppose my aunt will not be pleased if I feign a headache… again."

"Your aunt is not a simpleton."

"No, she is not," Evie remarked as she walked over to the door. "I will attend, and I would like to wear my new ballgown."

"Very good, miss."

Evie departed from her bedchamber with the maid trailing behind her. She truly hoped this wasn't a fool's errand.

———————————

Evie exited the coach and stood near the edge of the market. Vendors were lined up next to one another, hawking their goods. She felt curious eyes on her as she adjusted the reticule around her wrist. Most of the people were harmless, but she would be a fool to dismiss everyone.

A footman came to stand next to her. "Would you care for me to escort you?"

"That won't be necessary," she replied. "Remain by the coach, and I will be along shortly."

The footman looked unsure, but he tipped his head in acknowledgement. "Yes, miss."

Evie started down the center of the square, ignoring the shouting as vendors vied for her attention. The smell of freshly baked bread wafted through the air. She saw a young boy in tattered clothing standing a short distance off, eyeing the table where the bread was being sold with a crestfallen expression.

She approached and crouched down in front of him. "Are you hungry?"

He nodded slowly.

Rising, Evie turned towards the vendor. "I would like some bread, please."

The man frowned. "I do hope you don't intend to give it to that street urchin."

"What business is it of yours if I do?"

"You will only encourage him to beg more," the man said as he extended her a loaf. "He should be in a workhouse, working for his food."

Evie accepted the bread and handed him a coin. "A workhouse is no place for a child."

"Neither is the street."

She turned back to the boy and handed him the bread. His eyes lit up as he eagerly accepted it.

"Do you have any family?" Evie asked.

The boy took a bite of the bread before answering, "I do. My mother works in a shop, but she's gone all day."

"I am sorry to hear that," she said. "Do you live close by?"

"Yeah," he replied in between bites.

Reaching into her reticule, Evie removed gold coins and handed them to the boy. "I want you to give these to your mother."

The boy clutched the coins. "Thank you, miss!"

Evie gave him an encouraging smile before she resumed walking through the market. Up ahead, she saw Mrs. Taylor behind a table with fabric of all colors on display.

She was about to put her hand up in greeting when a dark-haired man stepped in front of her. He smiled, revealing a mouth full of missing teeth.

"What do we have here?" he asked as two other men came to stand behind him. They were all of similar height and their skin was darkened by layers of dirt.

Evie met the man's gaze. "Let me pass," she commanded.

The man smirked. "I saw you with that worthless street urchin," he said. "You gave him two coins."

"I did."

Holding up his hands, the man said, "We would like some coins as well."

"Unfortunately, I do not have any more coins," Evie said.

The man pointed to her reticule. "I will gladly take whatever you have in there." He stepped closer to her and held his hand out.

Evie smiled. "You are welcome to my reticule, but first you have to take it from me."

The man let out a bark of laughter. "You cannot be serious, little lady," he mocked. "You do not stand a chance against me, let alone all of us."

"We shall see," Evie said as she squared her shoulders.

All humor fell from the man's face, and he growled, "Very well, then."

Evie slipped her hand into the folds of her gown and gripped the butt of the pistol. As she went to remove it, a familiar voice came from the crowd that had formed around them.

"Leave her be!"

Evie inwardly sighed as she saw Reginald emerge from the crowd. What was he doing here?

Reginald came to stand next to her, still dressed in a bright purple jacket and yellow waistcoat, looking very much the part of a dandy. "I thought you could use some help," he said in a hushed voice.

"You were wrong. I am doing just fine on my own," Evie responded.

He gave her a look that implied he didn't believe her. "Well, I am here now." He turned towards the men threatening her. "The lady asked nicely to pass."

"And we asked nicely for her reticule," the man spat back, "and there is nothing you can do about it."

The man advanced towards Reginald, and he ducked as

the man swung at him. Reginald pulled back and punched the man in the jaw, watching as he dropped to the ground.

The other two men looked down at the unconscious man before staring at Reginald, surprise etched on their faces.

Reginald waved them forward. "Come now," he said. "Who is next?"

Evie rolled her eyes. "I've had enough of this." She pointed her pistol at the men and ordered, "Grab your companion and leave us be."

The two men bobbed their heads before scrambling away with their unconscious companion.

After the men retreated, Evie turned towards Reginald and asked, "Why are you following me?"

"What? Do I get no appreciation?"

"For what?"

"Saving you from those men."

Evie held up her pistol. "I believe I was the one who ended the fight."

"Only after I rendered the leader unconscious."

"I had the situation well in hand."

Reginald huffed. "It didn't appear that way to me."

"Perhaps you need spectacles, then."

"Why are you at the market?" Reginald asked, looking over their surroundings.

"Again, I must pose the question, why are you following me?"

Reginald brought his gaze to meet hers. "We are partners, are we not?"

"No, we are not."

"Merritt ordered us to be partners while you search for Rutledge," Reginald said. "Do you truly wish to disobey his orders?"

Evie slipped the pistol back into the folds of her gown. "I don't need a partner."

"Neither do I," he responded. "As I mentioned before, I prefer to work alone—but here we are."

"All right," Evie said reluctantly. "You may stay, but you mustn't say anything to anyone."

"My lips are sealed."

Evie waved him forward. "Follow me, then." She didn't bother to wait as she approached Mrs. Taylor in the corner of the square.

Mrs. Taylor rose from her seat behind her table. "Evie!" she exclaimed. "How is my favorite customer?"

"I am well," Evie replied as she fingered the material on the table. "Do you have anything new?"

Mrs. Taylor eyed her curiously. "What exactly are you looking for?"

Evie leaned forward and lowered her voice. "Information."

With a curious glance over Evie's shoulder, Mrs. Taylor asked, "Who is your very handsome friend?"

Reginald stepped forward and bowed. "I am—"

"This is my cousin, William," Evie interrupted. "You do not need to concern yourself with him."

"Will he be joining us?" Mrs. Taylor asked.

"No."

"Yes," Reginald interjected.

Mrs. Taylor lifted her brow and glanced between them. "Which one is it?"

Evie rubbed her temple. It would save a considerable amount of time and effort if she just conceded. "I suppose he can join us, but only this once."

Mrs. Taylor pointed towards a cart behind the table. "Why don't you come and take a look?" she encouraged.

Evie stepped around the table and walked the short distance to the cart, barely acknowledging that Reginald was close behind her.

Mrs. Taylor pulled out some blue fabric with gold trim and asked, "What are you seeking?"

"We are looking for someone who went missing in the rookeries," Evie said.

"People go missing all the time in the rookeries," Mrs. Taylor responded. "What makes this one so special?"

"He's my friend," Evie revealed.

Mrs. Taylor pursed her lips. "I may have heard some disturbing chatter about a man who was taken from the Odd Blokes pub."

Evie felt her heart drop. Rutledge was known to frequent Odd Blokes pub. "What happened to him?" Evie asked.

"No one knows," Mrs. Taylor said, "but the rumor is that he was poking his nose into someone else's business."

Reginald spoke up from behind her. "Do you know what kind of business?"

"Rumors say a new weapons smuggler in town is removing any and all opposition to his business," Mrs. Taylor replied. "From what I've heard, he's ruthless."

"Do you know where we can find this smuggler?" Evie asked.

Mrs. Taylor shook her head. "I don't, and even if I did, I wouldn't tell you," she said. "It's far too dangerous for someone like you."

Evie opened her mouth to object, but Reginald placed his hand on her arm. "She's right," he said. "You have no business going after a smuggler."

Mrs. Taylor bobbed her head in approval. "You should listen to your cousin, dear."

Reaching into his pocket, Reginald removed some coins and extended them to Mrs. Taylor. "Thank you for your time."

Mrs. Taylor smiled. "Thank you, kind sir."

Evie grew increasingly infuriated as she allowed Reginald to lead her away from Mrs. Taylor. How dare he take control of the conversation and not let her press Mrs. Taylor for additional information about the smuggler!

Reginald led her a short distance away and turned to face her. "I know you are angry, but hear me out."

Evie crossed her arms over her chest and gave him an expectant look.

"I know how to find this smuggler."

Evie blinked in surprise. "You do?"

"I have a meeting with him in two days," Reginald revealed.

"I'll go with you."

Reginald shook his head. "I don't think that is wise," he said. "I will go and report back to you what I discover."

"So you want me to sit back and do nothing while you assume all the risk?"

"Precisely."

Evie uncrossed her arms and started walking back towards her coach. Reginald easily caught up to her.

"You are upset."

"Is it so obvious?" she mocked.

"We don't know if Rutledge is the man who was abducted," Reginald said. "We don't want to go under potentially false assumptions, or we might miss a good opportunity to learn more about this criminal."

"What if Rutledge was abducted and they have already killed him?"

"Then one day won't matter, will it?"

"Do be serious."

"I am," Reginald said. "You must have faith in Rutledge, at least for a little while longer."

"I'm just worried about him."

"As am I, but he is a seasoned agent."

"I'm afraid that patience is not one of my virtues," Evie said, glancing at her awaiting coach.

Reginald smirked. "I would never have guessed."

Evie allowed herself to smile. "You aren't being very gentlemanly."

"My apologies," Reginald said as he offered his arm. "May I escort you to your coach?"

As she accepted his arm, Evie asked, "Will I be seeing you at Lady Cadogan's ball this evening?"

"You shall," Reginald replied. "My mother and I will both be in attendance."

Evie tensed, but she hoped Reginald hadn't noticed. She was not particularly fond of Lady Haddington. "Wonderful," she muttered.

Reginald stopped next to the coach and dropped his arm. "I hope you have not planned any more clandestine meetings for today."

"I have not." Evie cocked her head. "How did you know that I would be going to the market?"

Reginald reached for her hand and brought it up to his lips. "You seem to forget that I know you, my dear."

His words unsettled her, and not for the first time. He seemed to know more about her than she did about herself.

When Reginald dropped her hand, she turned and entered the coach, sitting across from her maid.

"Did you find what you were looking for?" Jenny asked.

Evie's eyes shifted towards the window, and she watched Reginald's retreating figure. "I did," she replied.

"Can we go home now?"

Evie closed the drapes. "I think that is a brilliant idea."

Chapter Four

Reginald put the quill down and leaned back in his chair. He finally finished signing the last of the documents his man of business had left for him. He had been sitting in this chair for what felt like hours, and was tired of the endless circles of work that needed to be done to run an estate from afar.

His mother stepped into the room. "The coach is being brought around front," she informed him.

Reginald pushed back his chair and rose. "Very good," he said. "I find that I am in desperate need of a distraction."

His mother perused his clothing. "I am pleased to see that you are not dressing as flamboyantly as you usually do."

Tugging down on his black jacket, he replied, "There is nothing wrong with how I usually dress."

"So you say," his mother said lightly.

Reginald came around his desk and approached his mother. Her once-vibrant blonde hair had faded and the lines around her face were starting to deepen. "You look lovely," he said as he kissed her cheek.

"I am growing too old for my liking," she replied.

"It is better than the alternative."

His mother smiled. "That it is."

"May I ask what occupied your day?" he inquired as he led her towards the entry hall.

"Not much, really," she replied. "I must admit that it was a rather uneventful day."

"Are those not the best days?"

"It was entirely too dull for my tastes."

Reginald stopped in the entry hall to collect his gloves from the butler. "Did you go shopping?"

"I did, but I found nothing of note."

With a tip of his head, Reginald acknowledged the butler before he stepped outside. He assisted his mother into the coach before he claimed the seat across from her.

The coach jerked forward as his mother smoothed down her dark blue gown.

"What occupied your time today?" she asked.

"In between meetings, I called on Evie and Mrs. Carter," he revealed.

"I do not know why you insist on spending time with Evie," his mother said with a frown. "She is entirely beneath your notice as a marquess."

"She is the daughter of a viscount, and we've known each other since childhood."

"That is true, but she is well on her way to spinsterhood," his mother pressed. "You wouldn't wish her to have any false hope of setting her cap at you."

"There is no chance of that."

"I should hope not," his mother huffed. "Just think of the scandal if you married Evie. You would be a laughingstock!"

"And why, pray tell, would that be the case?"

His mother gave him a knowing look. "I have it on good authority that Evie is a bluestocking of the highest order."

"I didn't know that bluestockings were ranked," Reginald teased.

"Do be serious," his mother admonished. "You must think of our family's reputation."

"I do, every single day. It occupies my thoughts constantly."

"Then we are in agreement?" his mother asked. "You will stay away from Evie?"

Reginald shook his head. "I have no intention of staying away from Evie. She is my friend."

"Some friendships aren't worth saving," his mother counseled.

Reginald glanced towards the window, hoping to end this futile conversation. He had no intention of ending his association with Evie, whether Society approved of it or not.

"You must think me heartless," his mother continued. "It is not as if I do not care for Evie, but she is in her ninth Season. Surely, she would have been married by now if she had made any effort at all."

"Not all women wish to marry."

"What foolish talk," his mother said. "Men may have the luxury of marrying for love, but women must marry for security. It is a simple fact."

"Evie is an heiress," Reginald reminded her. "There is no reason for her to settle on an unworthy suitor."

"I don't believe Evie even knows what she wants."

Reginald lifted his brow. "And you do?"

"Women like her are all the same," his mother replied. "They have false expectations and ideas that are contrary to what the *ton* deems acceptable."

"Perhaps the *ton* is wrong."

His mother looked stunned. "Surely, you do not mean that," she said. "One cannot fall out of line and not expect some repercussions for their actions."

"I would prefer to speak of something else; anything else, really," Reginald said.

His mother gave him a look that was hard to decipher, but it almost appeared pitying. "I know you favor Evie, and you always have, but—"

"You need not worry," Reginald interrupted, "because Evie does not hold me in high regard."

"But what if she did, son?"

He grew silent. He knew that his mother disapproved of Evie, but it wouldn't change the fact that he had loved her since her hair was in braids.

His mother was still waiting for a response when the coach came to a stop in front of a three-level brown brick townhouse. It dipped to the side as a footman stepped off the perch to open their door.

Reginald exited first and then assisted his mother out. As he led her towards the ballroom, she patted his arm and said, "This conversation is far from over."

"I would prefer if it was."

His mother brought a smile to her face as she acknowledged the other guests. "You are stubborn just like your father was," she said.

"I do not see an issue with that."

"You only seem to focus on what you cannot have."

They stepped into the ballroom and were promptly greeted by Lady Cadogan. The white-haired countess smiled kindly at them. "I am so pleased you were able to join us this evening."

Reginald bowed. "We wouldn't miss it, my lady."

"Perhaps a young lady will capture your attention." Lady Cadogan turned and swept her hand over the room. "There are many lovely young women in attendance this evening."

Reginald's eyes roamed the ballroom until they landed on Evie. She was dressed in a pale yellow gown with a net overlay that highlighted her comely figure. Her hair was piled high atop her head and small curls framed her face. She smiled at something her sister said, and he couldn't help but wonder if maybe, just maybe, she would fall for his smile, just as hard as he had fallen for hers.

Lady Cadogan's voice broke through his musings. "Do you not agree?"

Embarrassed that he had been caught woolgathering, Reginald glanced at his mother, who was giving him an encouraging nod. He wanted to bring this conversation to an end and go speak to Evie.

Reginald smiled at the hostess and replied, "I do."

A bright smile came to Lady Cadogan's lips before she swiftly turned around to address her guests. "May I have your attention?" she said loudly.

The guests all quieted down and turned towards Lady Cadogan.

Lady Cadogan gestured towards him and announced, "Lord Haddington intends to take a wife this Season."

Reginald watched as all of the patrons in the room shifted their gazes towards him and knew he was in trouble. Several young women started batting their eyes at him, and he could practically see the calculations behind the eyes of the scheming matchmaking mothers.

His mother leaned closer to him and whispered, "This situation was entirely of your own making, since you were too busy staring at Evie to acknowledge Lady Cadogan."

Reginald stifled a groan. How had he gotten himself into this situation? His mother was right; he had allowed himself to get distracted by Evie. And why not? She was the most lovely distraction. Regardless, he did not see a way out of his situation. He was stuck in a room full of young women who viewed him as nothing more than a means to an end.

"Enjoy yourself," his mother said as she patted his arm, "but do remember that you are already betrothed."

"I am not betrothed," he replied.

Lady Cadogan turned back from the person she'd been greeting and faced him. "It is my greatest wish that you shall find your bride this evening."

Before he could reply, Lady Cadogan went to greet another guest. Reginald led his mother further into the room. All eyes were on him, and it was making him deucedly uncomfortable.

His mother leaned towards him and said, "I need to go speak to my dear friend Lady Washburn. You will be all right for a moment, won't you?"

"I will be."

As his mother walked away, he saw a few young women, and their mothers, approaching him. This was going to be a long night. He braced himself for the inevitable, but was surprised when Evie broke through the crowd.

She came to a stop in front of him and dropped into a curtsy.

He bowed and asked, "What are you doing?"

"I was hoping you would ask me to dance, my lord," she said with mirth in her eyes.

Reginald extended his hand. "I would like nothing better."

"Thank you for saving me," he added as he led her to the dance floor.

"You would have done the same for me."

"Yes, I most assuredly would have."

Evie glanced over at him. "What on earth possessed you to allow Lady Cadogan to make such an announcement on your behalf?"

"I'm afraid I got distracted."

"That doesn't sound like you."

Reginald stepped onto the chalked floor as the music started. They didn't speak much during the set, but he was grateful for the opportunity to collect his thoughts. He no more wanted a wife than he wanted to chew glass.

The music came to an end and he escorted Evie back to Lord and Lady Hawthorne. As he approached Hawthorne, his friend asked, "What in the blazes were you thinking?"

"I wasn't," Reginald replied, dropping his arm.

Lady Hawthorne offered him a smile. "I do not envy you,"

she said. "With Lady Cadogan's announcement, you have just become the most eligible bachelor of the Season."

"That was not my intention," Reginald groaned.

"Then what was?" Hawthorne inquired.

Evie spoke up. "Reginald said he got distracted."

Hawthorne looked at him inquisitively. "You never get distracted."

"Regardless, how am I going to get myself out of this situation I now find myself in?" Reginald asked.

"You don't," Hawthorne said.

"That's what I was afraid of," Reginald muttered.

A voice cleared their throat behind them. He turned and saw Mr. Stephen Wymond standing behind them, his eyes set determinedly on Evie.

"I do apologize for the interruption, but I was hoping Miss Ashmore would do me the grand honor of dancing the next set with me," Mr. Wymond said.

Evie tipped her head graciously. "I would be honored."

Mr. Wymond smiled broadly. "Wonderful," he replied as he extended his arm. "I shall return her shortly."

Reginald's eyes remained on Evie as she disappeared into the crowd. It shouldn't bother him that she was dancing with other gentlemen, but it did. Greatly.

Hawthorne leaned closer and lowered his voice. "I think I know what distracted you."

Reginald dropped his gaze but remained silent. He didn't want to dignify Hawthorne's words with a response, but his friend was right. Evie was, and always had been, a distraction.

Evie was not one to get nervous, but she was something akin to that as Mr. Wymond escorted her to the dance floor. He was a handsome man, with his dark hair, broad shoulders, and square jaw. His commanding presence made her uneasy —or it could have been that his eyes seemed to bore into hers, as if he could see all the way to the depths of her soul where her secrets were hidden.

Mr. Wymond glanced over at her and asked, "Are you enjoying yourself this evening?"

"Very much so." She paused. "And are you? Enjoying yourself?"

"I am."

Their conversation came to a halt as they lined up to dance the quadrille. Evie noticed that Mr. Wymond appeared rather tense as he acknowledged the other dancers. The music started up and they began to dance. Every time they came together, Mr. Wymond would offer her a private smile, though it appeared strained.

The music came to a stop and Mr. Wymond offered his arm to her. "You dance superbly," he complimented.

"As do you," she graciously replied.

Mr. Wymond's lips twitched. "We both know that is far from the truth," he said. "I'm afraid I did not participate in much dancing on my ship."

"I would assume that you had other duties to attend to."

"That I did. I'm afraid there is an endless amount of work aboard a warship." Mr. Wymond glanced towards the rear of the townhouse where the veranda was situated. "Would you care to step outside for a moment for some fresh air?"

"That sounds like a fine idea."

Mr. Wymond led her through the crowd, and they exited through the french doors. He stopped at a bench that was still in sight of the ballroom before he dropped his arm.

"Would you care to sit?" he asked.

Evie sat down, but Mr. Wymond remained standing. Silence descended over them, and before it grew awkward, she asked, "How is Marielle?"

That was apparently the right thing to say, because Mr.

Wymond's face softened. "I haven't heard from her since she left on her wedding tour with Lord Hugh, but she appeared very happy on her wedding day."

"That she did," Evie agreed.

"I must admit that I had been half-hoping she would call off the wedding, but she was too much in love to ever consider such a thing. Frankly, I would take issue with anyone my sister married, but Lord Hugh was the last man I wanted her to end up with."

"I would imagine so," Evie said. "I hope you do not mind, but Marielle told me the reasons behind the animosity between you and Lord Hugh."

Mr. Wymond clasped his hands behind his back. "Just the mention of his name used to make my blood boil."

"And now?"

"I am learning to accept him for who he has become rather than what he was," Mr. Wymond replied.

"I do not know Lord Hugh well enough to pass judgement, but he appears to make Marielle happy."

"That he does," Mr. Wymond said. "I just hope he won't be foolish enough to do anything to jeopardize that, because I would hate to have a reason to challenge him to a duel."

"Do you often find yourself in duels?" she teased.

"Only when the situation warrants it."

His words were spoken curtly, and Evie couldn't help but assume there was more to the story. As she opened her mouth to prod, he spoke first. "Have you enjoyed yourself this Season?"

"I suppose so."

He looked at her curiously. "Forgive me, but you do not sound very convincing."

"It is my ninth Season, and I am tired of all the endless formalities that one must participate in to not bring scandal to one's name."

"I imagine it can be rather tiresome."

"It is, but that is the plight of being a woman of Society," Evie said. "You must think me terribly ungrateful, considering all the opportunities I have been given."

Mr. Wymond shook his head. "Quite the opposite, in fact," he said. "From a young age, I was told that I would one day run my father's shipyard, but I was determined to join the Royal Navy. I wanted my own adventure before I settled down."

Evie smiled. "You do understand."

"Life is a funny thing," Mr. Wymond said. "Some people are content with a simple existence, but I want to live such that I have no regrets." He paused. "At least, no more regrets."

Her smile dimmed. "Regrets can be a terrible thing."

"That they can."

Evie was quiet for a moment, and she decided it would be best to speak about something much more pleasant. "Are you and your sister close?"

Mr. Wymond nodded. "Marielle is the only family I have left, and I will do anything to ensure she is happy."

"I feel the same way about my sister, Dinah," Evie shared.

"The bond between siblings is a powerful thing."

"That it is," Evie agreed.

Mr. Wymond looked reflective. "I remember the day Marielle was born," he shared. "She was so little, and a surge of protectiveness came over me, even so young. I just knew that I was meant to protect her."

Mr. Wymond unclasped his hands and continued. "Although, I have come to recognize that Marielle does not need me as she once did. She has grown into a formidable woman."

"That she has, but it doesn't mean she doesn't need you in her life," Evie said. "One cannot have too many people who love and support them."

"I agree, especially since she was forced to experience

much heartache." He sighed. "I wish I could have saved her from that."

"If you had, then she wouldn't have grown into the person she is today, and I am rather fond of Marielle just as she is."

"As am I." Mr. Wymond glanced back towards the ball-room. "Would you care for me to return you to Lord and Lady Hawthorne?"

"I take it that you are done with our conversation?" Evie said lightly.

Mr. Wymond chuckled. "Far from it," he replied. "I just assumed that another gentleman has requested to dance the next set with you."

"I am not the belle of the ball; at least, not anymore," Evie said. "I am content with staying in the shadows and letting the other girls shine."

"Then I'm afraid you have failed," he said, his voice growing hoarse as it took on a more serious tone, "because you are by far the most beautiful woman in attendance tonight."

Evie fought the blush she could feel forming on her cheeks. "That is kind of you to say." Why was she behaving like a love-craving debutante? She had been complimented by handsome men before, but it was different with Mr. Wymond. His words appeared to be genuine, not just passing flattery.

"There is nothing kind about it," he replied. "It is merely the truth."

She decided to take hold of the conversation. "You should save your flattery for another woman, because I have no desire to wed."

"I have said nothing of marriage."

"That is a relief," Evie said, rising. "I do not think I could take another botched marriage proposal."

Mr. Wymond grinned. "Do you often get proposed to?"

"I am an heiress, sir," Evie replied. "Men look at me as if I am a trophy to be won. By marrying me, they can save their floundering estates from ruination."

"It is most unfortunate that you are treated so distastefully. Is that why you are against matrimony?"

"I do not wish to give up my freedom."

"Are you not afforded more freedoms when you have the protection of another's name?"

"Not in my case," Evie responded.

Mr. Wymond considered her for a moment. "I find you intriguing, Miss Ashmore. Would it be acceptable if I called upon you?"

Evie lifted her brow. "For what purpose?" she asked. "Nothing will come from it."

"Perhaps, but Marielle speaks very highly of you," he replied. "I think it would be in my best interest to form a friendship with you."

"I could always use another friend."

"As could I."

There was a slight lull in the conversation before Reginald stepped out onto the veranda. He tipped his head at Mr. Wymond before turning his attention towards Evie.

"Your sister wanted me to inform you that the next set is about to begin," he said.

"Thank you," Evie replied. "I will be along shortly."

Reginald nodded as he glanced up towards the moon. "It is a beautiful night, is it not?" he asked. "There is not a cloud in the sky."

"There is not," Evie agreed.

"It reminds me of the night we searched for truffles and you hurt your foot." Reginald turned towards Mr. Wymond and explained, "Miss Ashmore was insistent that she could walk back on her own even though she was in pain."

"I was able to manage on my own," Evie said.

"That may be true, but it would have been much easier if you had let me help you," Reginald pointed out.

"Most likely, but then who would have held the basket of truffles?" Evie asked. "After all, we had to hurry so as not to disturb the magical woodland creatures."

Mr. Wymond furrowed his brow. "Magical woodland creatures?" he repeated.

Reginald chuckled. "Miss Ashmore had read about magical creatures in a book, and she was adamant that they guarded the woods from people stealing their truffles."

"True," Evie responded. "I assumed the ideal time to search for truffles would be when the creatures were asleep, so we snuck out of our country homes when the moon was high in the sky. There was enough light that we were able to search the woodlands, but it wasn't until I fell and hurt my foot on a tree root that we found them."

"We had been hoping that our absence would go unnoticed, but we were not so fortunate," Reginald said.

"My parents were furious that I had snuck out of the nursery," Evie shared. "They forbade me from playing in the woods until my foot properly healed, but that didn't stop Reginald and I from getting into more trouble."

"I do not believe I have ever met a more mischievous girl," Reginald said. "At one point, Evie was determined to fly, so she crafted a large contraption with bedsheets and jumped off the rafters of the barn."

Mr. Wymond stared at her in disbelief. "You're lucky you didn't kill yourself."

Evie shrugged. "The first attempt didn't go as planned, but I was smart enough to jump over a pile of hay."

"The first attempt?" Mr. Wymond repeated. "You did it more than once?"

"I did," Evie replied, unabashed. "One does not give up after merely one failed attempt."

"How many times did you try?" Mr. Wymond inquired.

"I do not believe there was a day that went by that Evie

didn't have some type of straw in her hair," Reginal interjected.

"I do believe flying is entirely possible," Evie said. "After all, no one believed flying in a hot air balloon was possible until the Montgolfier brothers accomplished the feat."

Mr. Wymond glanced towards the ballroom as the orchestra started playing. "I believe it is time that I return Miss Ashmore to her sister," he stated.

"Do not concern yourself with that," Reginald said brusquely. "I shall ensure she is returned to Lady Hawthorne."

"It isn't necessary to trouble yourself," Mr. Wymond pressed.

"I insist," Reginald asserted.

Mr. Wymond frowned. "Perhaps we should leave it up to Miss Ashmore to decide," he said, turning his gaze towards her.

Evie glanced between the men, both of whom had determined looks on their faces. She knew she had only one true option, or else she feared that the two men might resort to blows. "I find that I would prefer to walk alone, but I do thank you both for your consideration."

Without waiting for any response, Evie walked into the ballroom without looking back and headed towards her sister.

Dinah's face lit up when she saw her. "Did you enjoy your conversation with Mr. Wymond?"

"I did; at least, until Reginald interrupted us," Evie replied.

"That was for the best. You don't want to spend too much time with Mr. Wymond and get the gossips' tongues wagging," Dinah noted.

"You make a good point."

"I usually do." Dinah smiled at her husband. "What do you make of Reginald's behavior?"

Nathaniel shrugged. "I do not try to think too much about

Reginald." He glanced over Evie's shoulder. "Speak of the devil…"

Reginald spoke up from behind her. "You should have allowed me to escort you."

Evie turned to face him. "Pray tell, why is that?"

"It is the proper thing to do," Reginald replied. "Besides, there is something about Mr. Wymond that I do not trust."

"He is harmless," Evie said.

Reginald didn't look convinced, but thankfully he let the matter drop. "If you will excuse me, my mother is summoning me from across the room."

Chapter Five

Evie fiddled with the skirt of her pale green dress as she descended the stairs of her townhouse. She'd had a restful night of sleep, but waking had immediately opened her mind to thoughts about Rutledge. She hated that she didn't know what had become of him. She wanted to find him, and she did not like feeling so helpless.

At the base of the stairs, Barnes greeted her with his usual small smile. "Good morning, miss."

"Good morning," she replied as her eyes landed on the four bouquets on the side table. It was customary for a gentleman to send flowers to a woman he had danced with the night before, but she thought the gesture was wholly unnecessary. Flowers were beautiful to look at for a time, but then they wilted, reminding her of all the arrangements she'd received after her parents died.

She walked over to the table and reached for the first card. It was from Mr. Wymond and promised that he would call upon her shortly. She had to admit that she did look forward to seeing him again. He wasn't boring or pretentious like many of the men of her acquaintance. The fact that he wanted to pursue friendship despite knowing she was unwilling to marry was a point in his favor.

Evie retrieved the card from the next bouquet. She resisted the urge to roll her eyes as she read Reginald's message: *Do try and remember that we are partners for the foreseeable future.*

She crumpled the card and dropped it onto the table. Why was Reginald so exasperating? He could hold her captive in one breath, and in the next, he was the most vexing creature she'd met.

A knock came at the door, and the butler crossed the hall to open it. As he stood to the side, he greeted, "Good morning, Lady Hawthorne."

Evie smiled at her sister, who had stepped into the entry hall. "What brings you by today?"

Dinah removed the straw hat on her head and extended it to Barnes. "Nathaniel has a meeting this morning, so I was hoping to join you for breakfast."

"That would be wonderful."

They headed towards the dining room, where they each filled a plate at the buffet before sitting at the table together.

After a long sip of chocolate, Evie placed her cup back on the saucer and turned towards her sister. "Do you want to tell me the real reason why you are here?"

Dinah gave her an innocent look. "Can't I visit my sister with no ulterior motive?"

"At this hour?" Evie asked. "Ever since you married, you have opted to sleep in and have a tray brought to your room."

"That is true, but today is different."

"And why is that?"

Dinah glanced over at the empty doorway. "I wanted to ask you about your dance with Mr. Wymond."

"What about it?"

"After your dance, you spoke with him for quite some time on the veranda," Dinah pointed out.

"That I did." Evie did not like the direction this conversation was headed in.

"Did you speak of anything interesting?"

"We mostly spoke of Marielle."

Dinah reached for her fork. "I just found it promising that you spent some time with him."

"And why is that?"

"Your eyes lit up when you saw him, and I haven't seen you show interest in someone since Reginald."

"I was not showing interest in Mr. Wymond." Evie frowned. "He is a pleasant enough man, but I've told you repeatedly that I have no desire to ever wed."

"So you say."

Evie didn't know why she tried to argue with her sister about matrimony. Dinah was so ridiculously happy in her marriage with Nathaniel that she was clouded to the realities that most people dealt with in theirs.

Dinah took a bite of her eggs, then asked, "Did you tell Aunt Nancy that you danced four sets last night?"

"I have not had the opportunity."

"She will be thrilled."

"It meant nothing," Evie said. "I knew it would be impolite to refuse their requests."

"That it would." Dinah set her fork down and reached for her chocolate. "I want you to get married so our children can grow up together."

"I'm afraid you will be sorely disappointed."

Dinah arched an eyebrow. "Do you take issue with Mr. Wymond?"

"I have no issue with the man."

"He seems to fancy you," Dinah said, hiding a smile in her cup.

Evie turned her attention towards her plate, hoping her sister would drop the subject. She had no desire to talk about Mr. Wymond.

Dinah returned the cup to the saucer. "I've upset you, haven't I?"

"You have not upset me, but I would prefer to talk about something else. Frankly, anything else would be better."

"Would you care to talk about Reginald?"

Evie shook her head. "Heavens, no!"

"You seem to be spending a lot of time with him lately," Dinah commented.

"How do you know that?"

Dinah grinned. "Aunt Nancy told me he came to call."

"Of course she did," Evie sighed. "If you must know, Mr. Rutledge has gone missing, and Reginald is helping me find him."

Dinah gasped. "Oh no! How long has he been missing?"

"For three days now."

"Pardon me for sounding insensitive," Dinah said with furrowed brows, "but that doesn't seem like a long enough time to be concerned, especially since Mr. Rutledge is a spy."

"He missed a meeting with me, and I know something must have happened to him," Evie revealed.

"Then you must do something about it."

"I am trying, but it is proving to be much more difficult than I anticipated."

"You could always hire a Bow Street Runner," Dinah joked. "It worked well for me."

Evie laughed. "That it did. I have never seen you so happy before."

"Nathaniel completes me in a way that I never knew was possible," Dinah said. "He is my match, my other half."

"I am glad to hear it."

Dinah gave her a pointed look. "That's what I want for you."

"Some people don't get a happily ever after," Evie said.

"You are not one of them."

Before she could reply, their aunt glided into the room

with a small box in her hand. "A gift just arrived for you, Evie," she said.

"Who is it from?" Evie asked.

"I'm not quite sure, since there was no note attached," Aunt Nancy replied as she extended the box to her. "I would like to remind you that it is wholly inappropriate to receive a gift from a gentleman you aren't in a courtship with."

"I am well aware." Evie removed the top, revealing a worn pocket watch, and her breath hitched on her throat.

Dinah leaned closer. "What's wrong?"

"This is Rutledge's watch." Evie put the box down and picked up the watch, revealing a small slip of paper in the bottom

Evie picked up the paper. "*Bring one thousand pounds to Hyde Park at noon if you want to see Rutledge ever again*," she read. "*Go to the iron bench near the south entrance.*"

"Good heavens!" their aunt exclaimed. "We should contact the constable at once!"

"That isn't necessary," Evie said. "I will go to the bank to acquire the money and then go to Hyde Park."

Dinah looked at her in concern. "Not to be a naysayer, but how do you know Mr. Rutledge is still alive?"

"I don't have any proof, but I have to try."

"A thousand pounds is a lot of money if you aren't sure," Dinah pressed.

"I'll do anything to save Rutledge," Evie said as she fingered the pocket watch. "He would do the same for me."

Aunt Nancy exchanged a worried glance with Dinah. "I know you must be fond of this Mr. Rutledge, but I fear that you are risking your reputation by traveling to Hyde Park on your own. Do consider your actions before you do something that you may come to regret."

"I care little of the repercussion of my actions if it means that I am able to save Rutledge," Evie said.

"Surely, you don't mean that."

Evie bobbed her head. "I do, wholeheartedly." She pushed back her chair and rose. "If you will excuse me, I need to depart at once for the bank."

"Evie—" Aunt Nancy started.

Evie put her hand up, stilling her words. "I know there is some risk associated with going, but I don't intend to stand by and do nothing."

"There must be another way," Aunt Nancy pressed. "Perhaps you can persuade Nathaniel to accompany you."

"I'm afraid there isn't time. I am to secure the money and arrive at Hyde Park at noon," Evie pointed out.

Their aunt tossed up her hands. "This is foolhardy. What if *you* get abducted?"

"If that had been the intent, the meeting place wouldn't have been Hyde Park," Evie reasoned. "It is much too busy to abduct someone in broad daylight."

"I'll go speak to Nathaniel," Dinah said, rising. "He will know what to do."

"I know you are trying to help, but it is unnecessary," Evie stated. "I am more than capable of handling this situation."

Dinah didn't look convinced. "I believe you're being foolhardy."

Their aunt nodded her agreement. "You must think of this family's reputation before you go traipsing about."

"I will be discreet," Evie promised.

"Why must you do things that threaten to bring down ruination upon us?" Aunt Nancy asked in an exasperated voice.

"I am sorry that I am a disappointment to you, but I need to do this." Evie walked over to the door and stopped. "It will be all right. You must trust me."

Evie departed from the dining room and headed towards the entry hall. "Bring the coach around front," she told Barnes. "I have an important errand I need to see to."

"Yes, miss."

As Evie hurried up the stairs, her mind whirred with questions she didn't have answers to. Who had Rutledge? Where were they keeping him? And how had they connected him to her? But her steps didn't falter. She'd meant what she said earlier—she would do anything to save Rutledge.

"Good morning, my lord," the butler said as he opened the door wide. "Lord Hawthorne is in his study and is expecting you."

"Thank you," Reginald said as he headed towards the rear of the townhouse.

He found Hawthorne in the study as promised, his shoulders hunched over the ledgers opened in front of him.

"Good morning," Reginald said.

Hawthorne looked up with tired eyes. "There is nothing good about this morning. I have been up all night."

"Is there a particular reason why?"

"I was chasing down information that led me nowhere."

"I'm sorry to hear that."

Hawthorne yawned. "When I returned home, Father reminded me that I needed to review the accounts before I meet with my solicitor today."

"You look awful," Reginald said. "I suggest you go get some sleep before your meeting."

"I can sleep afterwards."

Reginald walked over to a chair that faced the desk and sat down. "What do you know about Mr. Wymond?"

Hawthorne closed the ledger. "I have only spoken to him on a few occasions, but he seems like a decent chap."

"I don't trust him."

Hawthorne gave him a bemused look. "Could it be that you don't trust him because he is interested in Evie?"

"That is most assuredly *not* the reason."

"Regardless, I do believe Mr. Wymond is harmless," Hawthorne said.

"That's what Evie said."

"Then I would take her word for it."

Reginald frowned. "Perhaps I should ask Talbot and Worsley to trail him, just to ensure he isn't up to no good."

"I daresay that would be a waste of time." Hawthorne leaned back in his chair. "Have you come to an understanding with Evie yet?"

"She scoffed at the idea of us being partners at first, but she has come around," Reginald replied.

"Any word on Rutledge?"

"One of Evie's informants told her that a man was abducted from a pub in the rookeries by a new weapons smuggler," Reginald shared.

"And you think that might have been Rutledge?"

"We are assuming it was until we have proof otherwise," Reginald responded. "I'm meeting with the smuggler tomorrow night anyway and hope to discover Rutledge's whereabouts."

Hawthorne shook his head. "Your lack of progress on the case will not impress Merritt."

"No, it most assuredly will not," Reginald agreed. "Will you be joining us at White's tomorrow for a drink?"

"I'm planning on it."

Dinah came into the room with a determined stride. "My sister might be in danger," she announced.

Reginald jumped up from his seat. "Where is she?"

"Right now, she is going to the bank to secure funds," Dinah replied. "She received a ransom note for Mr. Rutledge, along with his pocket watch, and she has decided to handle it herself."

Hawthorne came around his desk and approached his wife. "What did the note say?"

"It told Evie to bring a thousand pounds with her to Hyde Park at noon if she ever wants to see Rutledge alive again," Dinah informed them.

"Blazes," Hawthorne muttered under his breath.

Dinah placed a hand on his sleeve. "Aunt Nancy even suggested that Evie should bring you along, but she insisted there wasn't enough time."

Reginald ran a hand through his hair. "Hyde Park is vast. How does Evie know where to go?"

"The note told her to go to the south entrance and find an iron bench," Dinah replied.

Hawthorne fixed Reginald with a pointed look. "How does this person know that Evie and Rutledge are connected?"

"That's what I was wondering, as well," Reginald said. "We need to go help Evie before she gets herself abducted, or worse, killed."

Hawthorne leaned forward and kissed Dinah on the cheek. "Thank you, my dear," he said. "Send word to my solicitor to cancel my meeting. We will ensure that Evie remains safe."

"I fear her judgement is clouded right now," Dinah said, clearly concerned. "She could use some help."

As Reginald started walking towards the door, Dinah called after them, "The coach is out front and ready to take you to Hyde Park!"

Reginald didn't speak as he exited the lavish townhouse. He stepped into the awaiting coach and Hawthorne sat across from him. The coach jerked forward as it merged into traffic. Reginald kept his gaze on the window.

He was frustrated with Evie. They were supposed to be partners, and yet, she hadn't informed him about the ransom note. She'd made no effort to include him. Why had Merritt thought this was a good idea? Evie was a loose cannon, and she was going to get herself killed if she kept going on as she had.

Hawthorne's voice broke through his thoughts. "I know you're mad, but you need to set that aside until we ensure Evie is all right."

"Why does Evie have to be the most obstinate woman in all of England?" Reginald asked.

Hawthorne looked amused. "Do you truly want me to answer that, or is that a rhetorical question?"

"Evie and I are supposed to be partners, and she didn't even bother to notify me about the ransom note. I also caught her fishing for information at the market, also without informing me." His hands balled into tight fists. "How am I going to keep her safe if she continuously goes half-cocked around Town?"

"I think that might be some of the problem," Hawthorne remarked. "You're intent only on keeping Evie safe."

"I am, but that's because we are partners."

"No, you've always tried to protect Evie when she is just doing her job."

"I disagree. I'm only trying to help her."

Hawthorne lifted his brow. "Do you try to help me when I'm on an assignment?" he asked.

"It's different with Evie."

"Because she's a woman?" Hawthorne pressed.

Reginald didn't respond. How could he explain that he couldn't imagine a life without Evie, even if she didn't want him? He wanted—no, needed—her to be safe.

"Evie earned the right to be an agent," Hawthorne said as he adjusted the sleeves of his blue jacket, "and her accomplishment should not be diminished because of her gender."

"It has nothing to do with her gender," Reginald grumbled.

"Then what does it have to do with?"

Reginald hesitated. "I can't risk losing her." There. That was the truth.

Hawthorne gave him a look that could only be construed

as pity. "I know you care for Evie, but you will lose her if you don't learn to trust her."

"She is maddening."

"Most women are," Hawthorne joked. "But Evie has proven herself to be a capable agent. Merritt trusts her; why don't you?"

"I do trust her, but—"

"There should be no 'but'," Hawthorne asserted. "If it came down to it, do you believe that Evie would step in and save your life?"

"I do."

"Then what else matters?"

Reginald sighed. "I just wish I could keep Evie safe from all the evils in this world. Instead, she's been thrusted into a realm that she can't unsee."

"Evie knew what she signed up for."

"Yes, she did, but at what cost?" Reginald asked. "We both know the toll this has taken on us over the years."

"Yet we continue to work as agents to ensure England is protected from threats," Hawthorne said. "Evie is a great asset to the Home Office because no one would suspect she is a spy."

"I do not dispute that, but I wish there was another way."

The coach stopped near the south entrance to Hyde Park and Reginald opened the door, not bothering to wait for the footman to come around.

He stepped down and scanned the park. "Do you see her?"

Hawthorne stood beside him. "I do not, but there are many iron benches that are set off the path," he said. "I would imagine, for this type of meeting, that Evie would want to ensure some privacy."

Reginald started down the path, tipping his hat politely at the people he passed, slipping a mask of nonchalance over his features as he did so. Where in the blazes could Evie be? The sun was high in the sky, and there was not a cloud to be seen. The sun beat mercilessly down upon them, and he could feel sweat dripping down his back. This was not how he envisioned spending his day.

"We will find her," Hawthorne said, matching his stride.

"What if she doesn't want to be found?" Reginald asked.

"She wouldn't have hidden herself away; she's too smart for that," Hawthorne remarked. "She's here. Just be patient."

As Reginald's eyes swept over the trees, he finally saw Evie sitting on a bench set back from the main path. He felt profound relief at the mere sight of her. Their eyes met, and no words were necessary. Evie's glance told Reginald not to ruin the opportunity they'd been given, and he gave the smallest nod of acquiescence.

With a side glance at Hawthorne, he asked, "Did you see Evie?"

Hawthorne kept his gaze straight ahead. "I did," he replied. "What's our plan?"

"We keep walking until we find a bench that will allow us to keep a close watch on her," Reginald said.

Once they'd walked a short distance away, Reginald gestured towards a bench and went to sit down. Hawthorne claimed the seat next to him and adjusted his top hat.

"It is deucedly hot today," Hawthorne grumbled.

"That it is." Reginald tugged down on the sleeves of his emerald-green jacket as he tried to appear indifferent to his surroundings. He didn't want the park's many patrons to suspect what his true motives for being there were.

His eyes darted towards Evie. She appeared calm and collected, dressed in a pale green gown with her straw hat tilted slightly on her head. To anyone else, she appeared as if she was just enjoying the fresh air.

"Lord Haddington," a familiar voice greeted, drawing his attention. "Lord Hawthorne."

Lord Strathmore stopped in front of him, a pale-faced

young woman who appeared as if she was barely old enough to be out of the schoolroom on his arm.

This was a distraction Reginald couldn't afford at the moment, but it would be rude and out of character for him to dismiss Lord Strathmore. Rising, he greeted the man. "Lord Strathmore."

Strathmore gestured towards the girl. "Allow me the privilege of introducing you to my sister, Lady Susan," he said.

Reginald bowed. "It is a pleasure to meet such a beautiful young woman."

Lady Susan stared back at him with wide eyes. The poor thing looked afraid of him—of everything, really.

Strathmore cleared his throat. "What a kind compliment. Was it not, Susan?" he prompted curtly.

She bobbed her head and lowered her gaze to the ground.

Disapproval flashed across Strathmore's features. "Forgive my sister," he said. "She must be overly warm from our walk."

"I do not fault her for that. It is rather warm today," Reginald graciously replied.

"We'll not keep you; I only wanted you to meet my lovely sister," Strathmore said. "This is her first Season."

Reginald turned his attention towards Lady Susan. "Have you been enjoying it thus far?"

Lady Susan brought her gaze up and responded weakly, "Yes, my lord."

The frown lines around Strathmore's lips deepened. "We shall leave you to it," he said, nodding a goodbye and leading his sister away.

"That poor girl," Hawthorne muttered under his breath.

"My sentiments exactly," Reginald said.

Reginald turned towards the bench where he had last seen Evie and saw that it was empty. Where had she gone?

Chapter Six

Evie had barely identified the sound of footsteps behind her before the smooth metal of a pistol was pressed against the back of her neck. She tensed as she waited for direction.

Her attacker leaned close. In a low voice, he said, "I want you to walk away and leave the money on the bench."

"I will not," Evie responded.

"If you don't, I will kill you."

Playing on a hunch, she responded, "I don't believe you will. If that was your intent, you would have picked somewhere much more private."

The man paused. "What is it that you want?"

"I want answers."

The man removed the pistol from the back of her neck. "Walk into the woods," he ordered, "and I'll come to you."

Evie glanced over at Reginald and Nathaniel, who were conversing with Lord Strathmore and a girl who must be Lady Susan. She knew it was a risk to head into the woods with this man, but she had little choice. She was desperate for information about Rutledge.

She rose and tightened her hold on the bag that contained the ransom money. As she stepped into the trees, she reached through her pocket, retrieved the dagger that was strapped to her leg, and held it firmly in her hand. She didn't want to be caught unprepared if this man tried to kill her—which was looking more and more likely, judging by how far she'd already walked into the woodlands.

"That is far enough," the man ordered from behind a tree.

Evie stopped and waited for further instruction.

A short man with an unkempt beard stepped out from behind the tree. He held a pistol, and his beady eyes glanced back and forth between her and the bag. "Give me the money."

"How do I know Rutledge is still alive?"

The man smiled, revealing a rotting front tooth. "You'll have to trust me."

"But I don't trust you," she replied. "I want you to take me to him."

"I can't do that."

"Why not?"

The man's smile dimmed. "Where he is… you don't ever want to step foot there."

"How do I know you will release him if I pay you the money?"

The man took a commanding step towards her, but still left an ample amount of distance between them.

"You don't," he replied, "but I can guarantee that he is a dead man if you don't hand over that money right now."

Evie pretended to consider his words as she tried to formulate a plan. If she killed the man, then she might have just signed Rutledge's death warrant. Although, if she paid him the money, he might kill Rutledge anyway. She did not like her odds. No matter what she did, it was no guarantee that she would ever see Rutledge again.

The man heaved a heavy sigh. "I don't have all day, lady."

Coming to the only decision that made sense, Evie held the bag out. "Here's the money."

With a flick of his wrist, the man ordered, "Toss it over here."

She did his bidding, and the small bag landed by his feet. He leaned down and picked it up, all while keeping a close eye on her.

"Rutledge will be very happy to live another day," he said.

Evie gripped the dagger tighter in her hand, being mindful to keep it pressed up against her side so as not to make its presence known. "How did you know I would come and pay the ransom?"

"I didn't, but it was worth a chance," the man replied. "You should know that Rutledge spoke rather fondly of you."

Spoke In the past, Evie stilled as she hoped that this man had simply misspoken. Now she was forced to wonder if Rutledge was even alive.

"What did he say?" She needed to keep the man talking and get as much information as she could from him.

"He didn't say much, but he uttered your name when he was fading in and out of consciousness," the man replied.

"Did you torture him?"

The man sneered. "Of course," he said. "He was asking too many questions for my employer's liking."

"Who is your employer?"

"You've asked enough questions," the man growled, narrowing his eyes.

"I just want to know the name of the man I need to make pay for what's happened to Rutledge," Evie said.

The man chuckled. "He's not someone you want to cross."

"I'll take my chances."

The man looked unimpressed. "Let me give you a piece of advice," he said. "Go home and forget all about Rutledge. A proper lady like yourself shouldn't be mixed up with a man like him, anyways."

"I consider Rutledge a friend."

"Men like Rutledge don't have friends; they just use people

to achieve their purposes," the man said. "You were used, my dear."

Evie shrugged. "Perhaps I was, but that doesn't mean I wanted him dead."

The man visibly tensed. "Rutledge isn't dead," he said, though his voice lacked conviction.

"I think we both know that he is."

Bringing the pistol up, the man pointed it at her chest. "You better leave before you are unable to do so."

"Did you kill Rutledge?"

The man tightened his grip on the pistol. "Stop talking!" he shouted. "You weren't supposed to ask all of these questions!"

"Did you truly think I would just hand over the money without trying to find out all I could about him?" Evie asked.

"You were supposed to," he replied. "Why couldn't you follow instructions and just be done with it?"

"I'm not one to follow orders blindly."

Indecision crossed the man's face, and Evie saw his finger twitch on the trigger. As she brought her hand up with the dagger, a pistol discharged from behind her, the shot hitting the man squarely in his chest.

With a glance over her shoulder, she saw Reginald and Nathaniel rushing towards her with pistols in hand. She rushed over to the wounded man and crouched down next to him.

He was watching her with a bemused look on his face. "You are not who you seem, are you?" he asked as blood trickled out of his mouth.

Time was of the essence, and she didn't need to answer his question. Instead, she asked one of her own. "Is Rutledge dead?"

The man let out a raspy cough. "He will be by the time you get to him."

"Tell me where he is," she pressed.

"There's no point. You can't save him. No one can." The man closed his eyes and breathed his last.

As Evie stared at the man, she felt a hand grip her shoulder. "We need to get you out of here," Reginald said.

"Why did you have to kill him?" she demanded.

"Because he would have killed you if I hadn't interceded," Reginald replied.

Evie shrugged his hand off and rose. "You could have wounded him. Then we could have questioned him further."

Reginald huffed. "I saved your life," he declared. "One would think a little gratitude would be in order."

"But I'm not grateful. We are no closer to finding Rutledge than we were before," Evie stated.

"Perhaps if you had told me about the ransom note, we could have come up with a different plan," Reginald said as he stepped closer, "but instead, you tried to handle it on your own."

"I had it under control."

Reginald glanced down at the dead body. "I see that," he remarked dryly. "Pray tell, did you even have a plan?"

Evie pressed her lips together. "I was working on one," she reluctantly admitted, crossing her arms.

"You can't just make it up as you go along," Reginald said. "That's a good way to get yourself killed."

"I don't need a lecture from you."

"It would appear that you do."

Nathaniel glanced between them with a line between his brows. "It might be best if we continue this conversation elsewhere," he said. "It is only a matter of time before someone comes to investigate the gun shot."

"I concur." Reginald turned towards Evie. "Can we at least agree on that?"

"I suppose." Evie knew she was being unreasonable. Reginald had saved her life, but she was frustrated by their lack of progress in finding Rutledge. Would they find him in time to save him, or was he already dead?

Reginald crouched down next to the body and began searching through the pockets.

"What are you looking for?" Evie asked.

"I'm not sure, but whatever it is might give us a clue to the man's identity," he said as he pulled a torn piece of paper from the man's waistcoat pocket. He stuffed it into his jacket pocket and rose.

Nathaniel headed towards an overgrown path and disappeared into the trees. Reginald gestured after him, indicating Evie should go first. She retrieved the bag of ransom money before she hurried to catch up to Nathaniel, Reginald trailing close behind.

A short time later, they emerged from the trees. Evie scanned the park to see if anyone was paying them any heed, but no one cared or acknowledged them as they went on their way.

They stepped lightly onto a path, appearing as if they were out for a mid-day stroll. Reginald removed the piece of paper from his jacket pocket and examined it.

"I'm unsure of its importance," Reginald admitted as he extended it to Evie. "It appears to be a page out of a book that I am unfamiliar with."

"It's from *Robinson Crusoe*," she said after reading it, "but I am not sure what makes this page so special. Nothing of note truly happens. He spends most of his time lamenting about his situation."

"I must wonder if invisible ink was used to hide the real message," Nathaniel said. "It isn't uncommon for people to write with invisible ink in the blank spaces of books so as not to draw attention to it."

"That's true, but most men are smart enough to burn the message after they read them," Reginald remarked. "Why would he have kept it and possibly incriminated himself?"

Evie ran her finger over a triangular stamp. "Someone sent this as a letter through the Penny Post and paid the fee for it to be delivered. Why go through all that trouble to mail a page of a book if it wasn't important?"

Nathaniel nodded his head. "Generally, letters are sent by trusted couriers, not through the Penny Post."

Reginald held his hand out for the page. "With any luck, the real message will become visible when it is exposed to heat."

"And if that doesn't work?" Evie asked as she handed him the paper.

"Then we'll try acid," Reginald explained, tucking the paper into his pocket. He put his hand out again, this time gesturing for the small bag. "Allow me."

"Thank you," Evie said.

They walked in silence for a time. Evie couldn't help wondering what had become of Rutledge. She had failed him so far. But she wouldn't stop until she found him. If their roles were switched, he would do no less for her.

Reginald glanced over at her. "We will find him."

"I fear that it might be too late," Evie responded.

"Don't give up hope," Reginald encouraged. "I have the meeting with the smuggler tomorrow evening. Perhaps that will give us a lead."

"And if it doesn't?"

Reginald placed a hand on her sleeve and turned her to face him. "This isn't like you, Evie," he said. "You aren't one to be such a naysayer."

Evie felt tears prick at the back of her eyes, but she refused to cry in front of Reginald. He would think she was weak, and she couldn't abide that thought. "I'm just worried about Rutledge."

"As are we." Reginald's eyes shone with compassion. "Rutledge is a smart man. He will find a way to stay alive."

Evie forced a smile to her lips. "You're right."

Reginald leaned closer and whispered next to her ear, "You don't always have to act so brave around me, Evie." He stepped back and offered his arm. "I'm afraid we have a long walk back to our coaches."

Reginald felt the coach come to a jerking stop outside his home. The footman opened the door and he stepped out onto the pavement, briefly admiring his large townhouse with the portico over the main door.

The door opened and his butler greeted him with a slight bow. "Good evening, my lord," he said as he stepped back to allow Reginald to enter.

He removed his top hat and handed it to the butler. "Is my mother home?"

"Yes, and she has requested a moment of your time."

"Will you inform her that I will be in my study?"

The butler tipped his head. "As you wish, my lord."

Reginald was eager to discover if the paper he had discovered on the dead man had a coded message. This wasn't the first time he had encountered invisible ink. It was a common practice amongst spies, but one was usually smart enough to burn the message once it was received. No one wanted to risk having the message get into the wrong hands.

He removed the paper from his jacket pocket when he reached the study and held it up. It was inconceivable to him why someone would pay for a ripped-out page of a book to be delivered. It would have been more convenient if the address was still intact, but that had been blotted out.

Reginald set the paper on his desk and lit a candle. As he retrieved the paper, his mother stepped into the room with a look of frustration.

"There you are," his mother declared. "You have been gone all day."

"I had things I needed to see to."

His mother walked further into the room. "You need to go change, because Lady Calthorpe and her daughter, Agnes, are arriving soon," she announced. "They will be joining us for dinner."

"No, they will be joining *you*," he responded. "I already have plans for this evening."

His mother looked utterly aghast and horror-stricken at his words. "But what will I tell Lady Agnes?" she questioned.

Reginald shrugged. "I care not."

His mother frowned, "Surely, you can reschedule your plans," she attempted. "I am afraid that she would take this as a terrible slight."

"Frankly, I do not care how she perceives it."

"That is not how you should treat your betrothed."

It was Reginald's turn to frown. "I have made it abundantly clear that I have no intention of marrying Lady Agnes."

"But what of the marriage contract?"

"We both know that Father put a clause in the contract that I could terminate the engagement for a sum of ten thousand pounds paid to Lady Agnes."

"You truly intend to break the contract?" his mother asked, her words dripping disapproval.

"I do."

The lines around her face deepened. "If you do so, Lady Agnes will be ruined. Do you have no regard for her?"

Reginald walked around his desk and sat down. "I take no issue with her, but we would not suit. Besides, the money she'll receive will make her quite the catch."

His mother tossed her hands up in the air. "No couple in society suits! What one hopes for is mutual toleration. And squandering your inheritance in such a way is irresponsible."

"I have made my decision, and I ask you to respect it."

Walking over to a chair, his mother sat down and asked, "What did I do wrong with you? You used to be such an obedient child."

"Matrimony is not something I take lightly."

"Yet you have shown no interest in it," she said.

"My reasons are my own."

"Do you not wish to have an heir?"

"I do, but there is still time."

"Your father was a lot like you—stubborn to a fault," his mother said, smoothing her hair. "But even he recognized the importance of marrying well."

"I am not saying I won't marry, but it will be on my terms."

"Your terms?" his mother repeated back. "Pray tell, what terms are those?"

Reginald sighed. "Can we not do this now?"

"When would a good time be?" she asked. "I only ask because you are never home."

"I have many responsibilities that I must see to."

His mother rose. "I urge you to reconsider breaking the marriage contract with Lady Agnes. Her mother and I have been planning your union since you were born."

"That was your mistake, not mine."

"You are being impossible right now," his mother said, exasperated. "If you don't marry her, then she might end up being a spinster. Is that what you want?"

"No, Mother," he replied, "I wish no ill will towards her."

"And what will I tell Lady Calthorpe?"

"You could start with the truth."

His mother pursed her lips, then said, "The truth would be inconvenient at a time like this. One needs to be tactful when dealing with these types of delicate matters."

A knock came at the door before the butler stepped in.

"Lady Calthorpe and Lady Agnes have arrived," he informed them.

His mother turned back to Reginald, a pleading look in her eyes. "They will be so disappointed if you don't join us for dinner."

He was not fooled by her veiled attempt at manipulating him. It was a tactic she used regularly to try to sway the situation to her favor. "I am unable to do so, but send my regards."

She blinked, and her eyes now sparked with annoyance. "You may be the spitting image of your father, but he knew his duty, whereas I am unsure if you do."

Reginald watched his mother spin on her heel and exit his study with her head held high. He was all too aware that his mother was accustomed to getting her way, and it irked her when he didn't bend to her will.

The sound of the window being pushed open drew his attention. He glanced over and saw Evie on the other side.

"I didn't think your mother would ever leave," she said when he met her gaze.

"Whatever are you doing here?" He walked over to the door to shut and lock it, ensuring their conversation would remain private.

"I couldn't let you have all the fun of discovering the coded message," Evie said as she climbed through the window.

"We don't know if invisible ink was even used, and..." His voice stopped when he saw what Evie was wearing. She was dressed in trousers and an ivory shirt that was tied at the collar, her hair pulled back at the base of her neck. A worn brown cap hung low on her head.

Evie appeared unconcerned that he was perusing the length of her and removed her cap, tossing it onto the desk. "You can stop gawking at me. It is very unbecoming of you."

"How were you able to leave your townhouse dressed like that?"

"Very easily," she replied. "I left through the servant's entrance."

"Did they not question why you were dressed like that?"

"They have learned not to ask those questions," Evie said as she picked up the paper from his desk. "Did you put this up to heat yet?"

"I have not. I was distracted by my mother."

"I couldn't help eavesdropping. I heard what you said about Lady Agnes," Evie said, fingering the paper. "Are you truly going to call off the engagement?"

"I am," he replied. "It was never my intention to marry her."

A look came into Evie's eyes that he couldn't quite decipher. "That's good," she murmured.

Dare he hope that she was pleased by this?

"Is it?" he prodded.

Evie nodded slowly. "Marriage is not something you should take lightly."

"I agree, wholeheartedly," he responded. "My mother has tried to force my hand for far too long. I thought I had sufficiently made my thoughts known on the matter, but apparently she wasn't listening."

"I bet she was listening but thought she could sway you to her way of thinking."

"That does sound like my mother."

Evie gave him a curious look. "May I ask why you've waited so long to break the engagement if that was your plan all along?"

"My father asked me to not make a rash decision and made me promise that I would wait until my thirtieth birthday to enforce the clause," Reginald revealed.

"When was this?" Evie asked.

Reginald gave her a sad smile. "Right before he passed."

"Your father was a good man."

"That he was," Reginald agreed. "All that I am, or hope to

become, I owe to my father. He shaped me into the man I am today."

"I do miss his clever wit," Evie said. "He could always get me to smile, even when I was intent on staying angry."

"He was fond of you."

Evie laughed. "I doubt that," she said. "I do believe he *tolerated* me, considering you and I were constantly finding ourselves in misadventures."

"We were in a lot of scrapes when we were younger."

"That's putting it mildly."

Reginald grinned. "Poor Dinah tried to keep up with us, but she had no hope of doing so."

"She could hardly stand to get dirty."

"Yet, look at her now," Reginald said. "She even donned men's clothing and went into the rookeries to search for you."

"That she did, and she managed to land herself a husband," Evie joked.

Reginald stepped closer to Evie but was mindful to keep proper distance. "Dinah did very well for herself."

"I agree," Evie said. "I'm glad she didn't settle for anything less than a love match."

"As am I." He eyed her closely as he asked, "Is that what you want? A love match?"

With a stubborn tilt of her chin, she replied, "I believe I have already made my thoughts on matrimony known."

"You did, but I think it is rubbish."

Evie furrowed her brow. "I beg your pardon?"

Reginald took a step closer. "I believe you want a love match, but are too scared to go after it."

"You know not what you are speaking of."

"I think I do," Reginald said, "but what is holding you back?"

Evie held up the piece of paper in her hand. "I did not come to argue with you, but rather to discover if there was a coded message on this paper."

Reginald stifled a groan. Whenever a conversation grew too serious for Evie, she would change subjects. Knowing there was no point in pressing her for a response, he stood next to her and picked up the candle. "Go ahead, then," he said.

Evie brought the paper close to the flame, being careful to not light it on fire. Reginald knew he should focus on the paper, but let his eyes roam over Evie's face. She had a brushing of freckles along the bridge of her nose and cheeks that he found endearing. His eyes then landed on her lips, which were slightly puckered as she concentrated.

"Something is materializing," Evie said, her eyes growing wide with excitement.

Reginald turned his attention towards the paper, where words were indeed starting to form. He leaned closer and read, "35 Warring Road."

Evie turned towards him. "Are you familiar with that road?"

"Yes, it's by the docks," he replied. "It's not a place I frequent often."

"Do you suppose this is where they're keeping Rutledge?" Evie asked as she lowered the paper.

Reginald put the candle back onto the desk. "There is a chance, but—"

The door handle shook profusely, followed by his mother's voice.

"Reginald, dear," she called, "why is this door locked?"

He frowned as he glanced towards the door. "You need to hide," he urged.

Rather than argue with him, Evie walked around the desk and ducked under it, retrieving her cap in the process. Reginald approached the door and unlocked it before opening it up.

The moment it was open, his mother pushed past him and

said, "I thought you would like to give your regards to Lady Calthorpe and Lady Agnes yourself."

Reginald forced a smile to his lips when Lady Calthorpe and Lady Agnes followed his mother into the room.

"Ladies," he greeted with a bow. "It is a pleasure to see you again.

Lady Agnes gave him a shy smile. "Good evening, my lord," she said. "I was disappointed to hear that you won't be joining us for dinner."

"I'm afraid I have a previous commitment."

"That is a shame," Lady Calthorpe interjected.

Reginald glanced over at the desk and hoped that Evie wasn't too terribly uncomfortable. He brought his gaze back to the ladies. "I'm afraid I must get back to my work before I depart for the evening."

His mother gave him a pointed look. "Lady Calthorpe and Lady Agnes have graciously agreed to come for dinner in two days' time so you may join us."

"How wonderful," Reginald said through gritted teeth.

"Isn't it, though?" his mother asked as she walked to the door. "We shall leave you to it, then."

The last thing he wanted to do was dine with Lady Calthorpe and Lady Agnes, but he couldn't refuse in front of them—and his mother knew that.

Chapter Seven

Evie waited until the door closed before she emerged from under the desk.

"Your mother is relentless," she said with a shake of her head.

"That is a word for it," Reginald muttered as he turned to face her.

She came around the desk and asked in an eager voice, "Shall we depart?"

Reginald gave her a baffled look. "Where?"

Holding the paper up, she replied, "35 Warring Road." She walked over to the window. "If we leave now, we can arrive before it gets too late."

"That is not a good idea," Reginald said.

"Did you wish to go later?"

Reginald shook his head. "No, you misunderstood me. I don't wish for *you* to go at all."

Evie stiffened. "Pardon?"

Coming to stand in front of her, Reginald replied, "The docks are much too dangerous of a place for you."

"But not for you?" she asked, rearing back slightly.

"I didn't say that."

Evie crossed her arms over her chest. "Then what are you saying?"

Reginald ran a hand through his brown hair as he considered his next words carefully. "There are gangs that frequent the docks, and they don't care if you are a man or a woman. They will attack without the slightest hesitation."

"That is assuming they catch me."

"They lurk in the shadows, waiting for unsuspecting victims to emerge," he said. "I worry that I will not be able to adequately protect you."

"I can protect myself," she stated, annoyed by his presumptuousness.

"You seem to think that I want to protect you because you are weak, but that is the furthest from the truth." He took a step closer to her. "I want to protect you because I can't stand the thought of anything happening to you."

"Nothing will happen to me."

"You say that now, but you are far too reckless for your own good."

Evie tilted her chin stubbornly. "I may act impulsively at times, but it is always for a good reason."

"You've been lucky so far, but I would not continue to press your luck."

"Lucky?" Evie repeated back slowly. "Is that what you think I've been?"

"I do."

Evie's eyes narrowed. "I have earned my spot as an agent," she said. "I may not be as seasoned as you are, but I am not completely incompetent."

"I never implied that you were, but—"

She spoke over him. "Rutledge recruited me, just as he did you, and I don't think he made a mistake. Do you?"

"I do not."

"Then please stop patronizing me."

"That was never my intention," he said, exasperated. "Why do you insist on twisting my words?"

"Why do you keep saying things that are intolerably stupid?"

Reginald sighed. "You are the most vexing of females." He glanced over at the window. "It would be best if we waited until morning to scout out the location. It would be much safer."

"We need to go tonight," she asserted. "If there is even a chance that Rutledge is there, we need to go at once."

Indecision crossed Reginald's features, and Evie wasn't sure if he would accompany her. She had already made up her mind that she would go, with or without him.

"Is there any way I can talk you out of this?" he asked.

"None."

"Then we must hurry," Reginald said as he walked over to the door. "Go to the street corner and wait for me there."

She smiled broadly. "Thank you!" she gushed.

"Don't thank me yet," Reginald said. "We will be lucky to survive this night. And close that window!"

Evie hurried over to the window and crawled out, closing it behind her. She remained close to the wall, using the shadows to her advantage, until she reached the mews. She unlatched the gate and stepped onto the pavement. As she walked towards the corner, she felt some relief that Reginald would be accompanying her to the docks. She knew it was dangerous to go wandering through the rookeries at night, but she would do anything to find Rutledge.

What if Reginald was right? What if she was too reckless? Evie knew she had an unusual way of doing things, but there was always a rhyme or reason to it. She had found herself in some prickly situations since becoming an agent, but she always managed to survive the ordeal. Was she just running on luck? She truly hoped not.

Evie stopped at the street corner and tugged down on her

cap, tucking her hair fully beneath it as she did so. It was still early enough that people were milling about, and she didn't want to give any reason for someone to notice her.

A short time later a black coach halted in front of her. The door opened and Reginald ordered, "Get in."

Evie stepped up into the coach and sat across from him. As he closed the door, she removed her cap and put it on her lap.

Reginald eyed her closely as the coach jerked forward, merging into traffic. "Your disguise doesn't fool anyone."

"People see only what they want to see," Evie said. "Besides, most don't care enough to pay attention to what is right in front of them unless it affects them directly."

"That is a sad thought." His eyes shifted towards the window before asking, "Will your aunt not worry when you don't come down for dinner?"

Evie clasped her hands in her lap as she felt a twinge of guilt at that thought of her aunt. "I have no doubt that she will notice my absence and lecture me on it at her first opportunity."

"Where does she believe you have gone?"

"It depends," Evie replied. "As far as she is concerned, I spend an enormous amount of time at the orphanage with Lady Grenton."

"Your aunt doesn't take issue with you traveling to the rookeries?"

"She does, but I believe she has finally come to the realization that I am a grand disappointment to her."

Reginald eyed her curiously. "Why do you say that?"

"Dinah married an earl, and I disappear at all hours of the day," Evie said. "I care little about matrimony, and I've had nine Seasons."

"Has Nancy said you were a disappointment?"

Evie shook her head. "Heavens, no, but I can see it in her eyes," she replied. "When she looks at me, I can see all the pain the lies I am forced to tell her cause. I know she doesn't believe what I'm telling her, but I can't tell her the truth."

Reginald gave her a sad smile. "The life of a spy is a lonely one."

"I know, and Rutledge informed me of it, but I didn't believe it would be so hard to deceive the people I am closest to," Evie said.

"Does Dinah not know you are an agent?"

"I haven't told her that I work as an agent, but she knows I have assisted Nathaniel when the situation warranted it."

"Your sister is clever. I'm sure she has put the two together."

"Perhaps, but I do hope she isn't terribly disappointed in me," Evie said. "I don't think I could abide that."

Reginald gave her a puzzled look. "Your sister has always adored you. I don't see why that would change."

"I hope not." Evie turned her attention towards the window as she gathered the courage to ask the one question that had plagued her for months; but she didn't want Reginald to think she was weak and couldn't handle the demands of being a spy.

Reginald's voice broke through her musings. "What's wrong?"

"Why do you suppose something is wrong?" Evie asked, meeting his gaze.

"Because I know you, Evie," he replied with an amused look. "You may fake a smile, but you can't fake what you are feeling."

She should have known better than to try to hide from Reginald, but would he think less of her if she revealed what was troubling her? She decided to stop overthinking it and just ask the question. "Do you ever get the images out of your head?"

"What images?"

She shifted uncomfortably in her seat as she replied, "Of the men you were forced to kill?"

Reginald grew silent, and Evie suddenly felt very foolish. Why had she asked in the first place? He was a seasoned agent, and killing was occasionally part of the job.

"Forget I said anything," she said, waving dismissively.

"I still remember my first kill," Reginald started slowly, "as if it was yesterday. It was one of my first assignments. I was assigned to infiltrate a Luddite faction, but they discovered me almost immediately. I was able to escape into the woods, but a few of them followed me. I hid, but one of them stumbled across me. As he opened his mouth to give away our location, I stabbed him. I did a poor job of it, too. The poor man had to suffer further wounding before he succumbed.

"It was either him or me, but I will never forget the look on his face as he took his last breath," Reginald continued in a voice more somber than Evie could remember ever hearing from him. "I hid his body under some foliage before running deeper into the woods. I didn't stop until I happened upon a stream. I dropped down and I started washing the blood off my hands. It was only then that the realization of what I had done hit me."

Evie watched Reginald's eyes as he spoke. Although she wished he didn't have to live with that pain, she felt great relief that he understood what she was going through.

"Once I returned to London, I couldn't get the images out of my head, and I felt as if I needed to atone for what I had done," he said. "I made some inquiries and discovered that the man I'd killed was recently married, and his wife was increasing. It compelled me to act."

"What did you do?" Evie asked.

"I arranged for her to receive five thousand pounds—secretly, of course," Reginald said. "To this day, I still inquire about her wellbeing and that of her child."

"That was most generous of you," Evie acknowledged.

"It was the least I could do, since I killed her husband."

"Her husband was a criminal."

Reginald shrugged his shoulder. "That doesn't mean he deserved to die."

"He was trying to kill you."

"Aye, he was," Reginald said. "I tell myself those same things, but it doesn't seem to appease my conscience." He hesitated. "I have killed men since then, but it does not get any easier. Each kill slowly eats at your soul, until you wonder if you even had one to begin with."

Evie lowered her gaze to her lap. "I have only killed a few men, mind you, but their faces haunt me at night when I close my eyes."

Reginald gave her an understanding nod. "I wish I could tell you that it gets easier, but I won't lie to you. Those images will always remain with you, but you must not let them consume you. Sometimes it is easier to give in to the darkness than to fight for the light that is inherently inside of us."

The coach stopped, and a footman came around and opened the door. "We dare not go any further into the rook-eries, my lord," he said, indicating the soot-blackened buildings around them, some of them caved in on themselves.

"I understand," Reginald said as he exited the coach.

Evie donned her cap and followed him out of the coach. Her eyes roamed over the dilapidated buildings, wondering how anyone could live in them, and heard a baby wailing in the distance. A foul-smelling liquid flowed down the street toward the river, and a dead cat lay visible in a nearby alleyway.

"It isn't too late to turn back," Reginald said.

"You are welcome to head home, but I am going to the docks," Evie said, taking a resolute step forward.

Reginald chuckled from behind her. "You're going the wrong way."

Evie spun on her heel and ignored Reginald's amused look as she passed him.

Twenty-three.

That is how many threats Reginald saw lurking in the shadows as he walked with Evie down the narrow pavement. He had no doubt that many of the men that were eyeing them with interest assumed they were easy targets, but that was the farthest thing from the truth. He would defend Evie until his last breath—not that it would ever come to that. At least, not today. He could easily dispatch a ruffian or two. There would only be a problem if they joined forces to gang up on them.

Reginald glanced over at Evie and saw the determined gleam in her eye. Why was she so blasted stubborn? When she set her mind on something, nothing could deter her. It had always been that way. It aggravated him, but it was also something he admired about her.

"Are we almost there?" Evie asked, sidestepping some manure.

"We are," Reginald replied.

"It feels as if the people nearby see us as a public spectacle," Evie said, her eyes roaming the buildings.

Reginald nodded. "I daresay that we are too finely dressed for this stretch of town, despite changing into more common wear before coming. I have no doubt men are plotting to rob us as we speak."

"It would be foolish of them to do so," Evie said, unconcerned.

"My thoughts precisely."

Evie met his gaze. "Have I thanked you for coming along with me yet?"

"No," he replied with a teasing smile, "and I have thought you were being intolerably rude for not doing so."

"Well, thank you," Evie said.

"You don't need to thank me. We're partners."

"I feel as if I must. I am not used to relying on anyone, much less a partner." She paused. "I suppose it has not been as awful as I thought it would be."

Reginald could hear sincerity in her voice, and it warmed his heart to know that she was starting to see the advantages of having him as a partner.

A thin, young man with threadbare clothing stepped out from the shadows with a long shard of glass in his right hand. He held it up and demanded, "Give me yer money, or I'll cut you both."

Evie stopped and considered him for a moment, not appearing perturbed by the weapon in his hand. "How old are you?"

The youth puffed out his chest. "I'm thirteen."

"And you think a life of thieving is best?" Evie asked.

"Yer a woman," he replied, looking unsure.

"I am," Evie replied. "Does it make a difference?"

The young man slowly bobbed his head. "It does," he replied dejectedly as he lowered the shard of glass. "I don't rob women."

Evie took a step closer to him, and Reginald resisted the urge to tell her to keep her distance.

"You don't seem like the type to rob anyone," she said.

"I haven't eaten in three days," the young man admitted. "I saw ye walking and thought I should at least try."

Evie turned towards Reginald and exchanged a concerned look with him. It was evident what she wanted him to do. As he reached into his waistcoat pocket to remove a few coins, he asked, "Where is your family?"

"I got none," the young man replied.

Reginald extended him the coins. "This should feed you for a few weeks," he said.

The young man's eyes lit up at the sight of the coins. "Thank you, mister." He eagerly accepted the money and clasped it in his hand.

Evie spoke up. "Where do you sleep?"

He pointed towards the alley. "In there," he replied. "At least for now. I'll have to move on when the press gangs come looking for new recruits."

"Don't you get cold at night?" Evie asked.

"The cold don't bother me," he said. "It's better than dying at a workhouse."

"Have you ever lived at a workhouse before?" Evie inquired.

A pained expression crossed the young man's face. "The headmaster worked my mother 'til her last breath. I begged him to call a doctor, but he refused. He said he wasn't going to waste a penny on a worthless creature like her."

Evie's eyes held compassion. "I am so sorry to hear that."

"After she was tossed in a pauper's grave, I just ran," the young man revealed. "I never looked back, though I'm always starving."

"How do you survive?" Evie asked.

The young man shrugged. "I do odd jobs for people, but those are scarce. I don't get them too often."

Reginald glanced around and saw that they were garnering too much attention. They need to keep moving, and he thought this young man might prove useful.

"I might have a job for you," he said. "Are you familiar with 35 Warring Street?"

"I am," the young man replied.

"Will you take us to it?" Reginald asked.

The young man's brow shot up. "You don't want to go there, mister," he said. "Bad things happen there. People go in, and they never come out."

Reginald removed a farthing from his waistcoat pocket. "This is yours if you will lead us there without being detected."

The young man hesitated. "I'll take you there, but that's as far as I go. I never want to ever see it from the inside."

"I understand," Reginald said. "What's your name?"

"Paul."

Reginald handed him the coin. "Thank you, Paul."

"Don't thank me yet," Paul responded. "I wouldn't go anywhere near there if I were you. People cross the street just to avoid walking in front of it."

"You don't need to worry about us," Reginald said.

"Stay close," Paul urged, "and avoid the slick cobblestones. Someone just tossed a bucket out the window." He turned and hurried into the alley.

Reginald held his hand out to Evie, indicating that she should go first. He followed closely behind and saw that Paul was waiting for them at the end of the alley. They hurried to catch up to him, ignoring the pungent odors surrounding them.

They continued to follow Paul through a maze of alleys until he eventually stopped. He pointed towards a dilapidated brick building. No light came from within. "That's the place you seek."

"You've done good," Reginald said. "If you want an honest job, go to the Marquess of Haddington's townhouse in Mayfair and knock on the servant's entrance."

Paul's eyes grew wide. "D'you mean it?"

"I do, but it will be hard work," Reginald replied.

"I'm not afraid of working hard."

"Good," Reginald said. "The job will come with room and board, so you don't have to live on the street anymore."

"I'll go first thing tomorrow!" Paul gushed, his eyes bright.

"See that you do." Reginald retrieved his pistol and turned towards Evie. "I'll go first, and I want you to stay behind me."

Evie gave him a mock salute. "Yes, sir."

Reginald frowned. "Do avoid getting yourself killed."

With quick steps, he crossed the pavement and pressed himself up against the back of the building. There was no signage to identify the building's owners, which he assumed was intentional.

"There doesn't appear to be any movement from within," Evie said in a hushed voice.

"That doesn't mean it's empty," he remarked. "Just be prepared for the unexpected."

Reginald approached the back door and tried the latch. Locked. He reached into a pocket to retrieve his picks, but Evie crouched down next to him and started picking the lock. It was only a moment before he heard a distinctive click as it disengaged.

Evie rose and opened the door. To his dismay, she stepped in front of him and headed into the building first. He resisted the urge to groan as he followed behind her. It was sheer foolishness on her part, but he shouldn't be surprised.

They slowly walked down the hall and peered into each room on the first level. When that yielded no results, they headed up the stairs towards the second level. A black rat scurried down the side of the hall, its squeaking the only sound present.

Reginald matched Evie's stride as they walked down the hall, pistols in their hands. They turned a corner and saw a flickering light beneath a closed door. He pointed at it, and Evie nodded her understanding.

They stopped at the door and Reginald reached for the handle, raising the latch painstakingly slowly until it opened. With a glance at Evie, he tossed the door open wide and stepped into the room.

Two men were playing cards at a table, and they froze as they stared up at him and Evie in disbelief. Their own pistols were on the tabletop, but they made no move to retrieve them.

"No one has to die here today," Reginald said. "We're just looking for someone named Rutledge."

The dark-haired man spoke up. "As you can see, we are alone here." Reginald couldn't help but notice that the man didn't answer his question.

"This man may have been here previously," Evie said.

"If he ain't here, then he's dead," the other man said. "We aren't a boarding house, and keeping too many people around is bad for business."

Reginald took a step closer, keeping his pistol aimed at the men. "Were you here when Rutledge was?"

"I don't recall," the dark-haired man replied.

"But you know who Rutledge is?" Evie pressed.

"What? No!" he exclaimed. "This is the first I've heard of a Rutledge."

Reginald narrowed his eyes. "That is the wrong answer," he said. "You either help us or we will have no choice but to kill you."

"Listen, mister, I don't know who you think you are, but you can't just barge into this place and demand answers," the other man asserted.

Evie retrieved her dagger and held it up. "Do you know that people become more frightened by the sight of a dagger than a pistol?" she asked, stepping closer to the table.

The two men eyed the blade apprehensively.

"It's because people would rather be shot than stabbed," Evie continued. "After all, it is much more excruciating to be stabbed over and over again. Wouldn't you agree?"

The dark-haired man held up his hand. "Listen, lady, we don't want any trouble."

"Unfortunately, my friend Rutledge was abducted, and this place is somehow connected to his disappearance," Evie said. "Would you kindly explain why that is?"

"I don't know," the other man attempted. "It must be a coincidence."

Evie turned towards Reginald. "Did you hear that?" she asked. "He seems to think that we believe in coincidences."

"It's true," the other man pressed.

Reginald cocked his pistol. "We only need one of you alive," he said as he waved the barrel between them. "Which one will it be?" He stopped on the dark-haired man. "I think it is you."

The dark-haired man jumped up from his chair. "Rutledge was here earlier, but they came and took him away."

"Shut up," the other man growled.

"Let him speak," Evie commanded as she tucked the dagger into the waistband of her trousers. "Is he alive?"

"I don't know," the dark-haired man said. "He was in bad shape. They had to carry him out."

"Did you torture him?" Evie asked, a hard edge to her voice.

The dark-haired man swallowed. "I... uh... I did, but I wasn't the only one."

Evie pointed her pistol at the man and cocked it. Reginald repositioned to keep the other one in check.

"Who gave the order to abduct him?" Evie demanded.

"I don't know," the man said, holding up his hands. "I swear it."

"Then how did he come to a place like this?" Reginald asked.

"They're brought to us," the other man interjected, "and we extract as much information from them as possible before..."

"Before what?" Reginald pressed.

Lowering his gaze to the floor, the other man admitted, "Before we kill them."

"Is that what you did to Rutledge?" Reginald shouted.

"No! They came and took him away."

Evie stepped forward. "Who?"

"We don't know," the dark-haired man said, cowering before her. "They paid us and took Rutledge. I swear it."

Reginald met Evie's gaze. "I think we are done here."

Evie bobbed her head. "I agree."

"Please don't hurt us!" the other man cried. "We were just following orders, I swear it."

Reginald and Evie shared a glance. It seemed these so-called torturers were none too eager to get as good as they gave. They didn't speak as they bound and gagged the men. They'd send someone back for them later.

Once they were outside, Evie let out a frustrated sigh. "We arrived too late."

"We'll find him," Reginald said.

"I know we will," she said, "but will he still be alive when we do?"

"We mustn't give up hope."

"Hope?" Evie asked. "I think we are past hope now."

Chapter Eight

The golden sunlight of morning streamed into her bedchamber windows as Evie lay in bed. She wasn't quite ready to face the morning, so she stared up at the ceiling, wondering how she was going to find Rutledge.

Someone knew what happened to him. She just had to speak to the right person. Perhaps another visit to Mrs. Taylor was in order. Or she could wait to see if Reginald's meeting with the smuggler proved useful. It's what he would want, but she didn't have to follow his orders—she was his partner, not his subordinate.

The smallest of smiles came to her lips as she thought of Reginald. She'd felt a ridiculous amount of joy when he'd informed her that he was breaking off his engagement with Lady Agnes. It didn't affect her—she could never marry Reginald—but she was pleased that he would be able to find his own bride. He deserved that.

His mother had always disliked her. She criticized her at every opportunity, but would do it in such a way that it sounded like it was intended to be a compliment. Evie's own mother hadn't believed that Lady Haddington held animosity for her, but she knew. And Lady Haddington knew she knew.

That was part of the problem, because Evie refused to play along.

A lady always respects her elders. It's what her mother would always tell her; but what if the lady was a cunning, conniving woman who used people like pawns?

The door to her room swung open and her lady's maid stepped in with a worried look on her face.

"Mrs. Carter is coming," Abigail said in a hushed voice.

That was no surprise; Evie had expected it. Frankly, she wondered what had taken her aunt as long as she did.

Evie had just sat up in bed when her aunt stormed into the room and turned towards Abigail. "I wish to speak to my niece," she said curtly.

"Yes, Mrs. Carter," Abigail murmured as she hurried out of the room, closing the door behind her.

Her aunt pursed her lips and took a deep breath before she spoke. "Thank goodness you've managed to find your way home."

"Good morning, Aunt Nancy," Evie said cheerfully as she leaned her back against the wall. "I take it you slept well."

"Slept *well!*" her aunt exclaimed, tossing up her hands in the air. "How can I possibly sleep well when my niece is who knows where, doing who knows what?"

"I assure you that there is no reason to worry."

Her aunt blinked and folded her arms. "Well, if you say so. I suppose I'll stop pestering you with questions, then," she said dryly.

"I had something I needed to take care of." Evie hated keeping things from her aunt, but it was safer than revealing the truth. Her aunt would never be able to come to terms with her being an agent, and knowing it would cause her to worry even more than she already did.

"You aren't going to tell me, are you?" Aunt Nancy asked.

Evie shook her head. "I am not."

"I am so tired of all the secrets," her aunt sighed. "There was a time when you used to trust me."

"I do trust you."

Her aunt huffed. "You have a funny way of showing it." She walked over to the bed and sat down. "I missed you at dinner last night. The townhouse is lonely now that Dinah has moved in with Nathaniel."

"I am sorry about missing dinner, but I promise it couldn't be helped."

"What are you involved in, dear?"

Evie scooted her legs over the side of the bed and rose. "Nothing that I can't handle," she replied.

"Are you still looking for your friend, Mr. Rutledge?"

"I am."

Her aunt glanced at the trousers that hung over the back of the settee. "Have you been going into the rookeries to look for him?"

"I have," she replied, seeing no reason to deny it.

Disapproval crossed her aunt's face. "Do you not realize what would happen if anyone saw you?"

"I do."

"Yet you do not seem to be overly worried."

"I am."

Aunt Nancy frowned. "You could ruin this family," she chastised. "You may be an heiress, but you are not untouchable."

"I know," Evie said as she walked over to the dressing table and sat down. She removed the cap from her hair and reached for her brush. "Once I find Rutledge, it will be different."

"I do not believe that to be true," her aunt responded. "After you went missing, I daresay that a part of you never came home."

"That is foolishness."

"Is it?" her aunt asked. "You always had your secrets, but

they have only increased by tenfold now. And do not think I am unaware of how often you are wearing those trousers."

"My mother wore trousers," Evie said as she ran the brush through her hair.

"Your mother wore them at your country estate for riding only, and far away from prying eyes," her aunt corrected.

A knock came at the door, interrupting their conversation.

"Enter," her aunt ordered.

The door opened and Abigail stepped into the room. "Mr. Wymond has come to call on Miss Ashmore."

Her aunt brightened in response. "That is wonderful news!"

"Is it?" Evie asked as she put the brush down.

Her aunt looked at her like she was a simpleton. "Mr. Wymond would be a fine choice for a suitor."

"I'm not looking for a suitor," Evie said.

Rising, Aunt Nancy walked over to the wardrobe and removed a blue gown. "Regardless, it would be rude to refuse him," she said as she handed the dress to Abigail. "I will go down and entertain Mr. Wymond until you join us. Do try to hurry. It is impolite to make a gentleman wait for too long."

"Shall we dress you?" Abigail asked after she had left.

"I suppose so," Evie replied.

"Do you dislike Mr. Wymond?"

Evie shook her head. "Heavens, no," she said. "Mr. Wymond is tolerable."

"Tolerable?"

"Well, more than tolerable," Evie corrected. "I find him to be a pleasant enough man."

"Then what is the issue?"

Evie turned her attention towards the window. "I should be going out there and looking for Rutledge. Instead, I'll be entertaining a gentleman in the drawing room."

"You can't put your life on hold as you search for him,"

Abigail remarked. "You have accountability to your family, as well."

"I am well aware," she muttered.

Abigail held her gown up. "We should get you ready before you give Mrs. Carter another reason to be upset with you."

A short time later, Evie descended the stairs with her hair neatly coiffed and wearing the blue muslin gown. She knew she played the part of a lady well, but she tired of all the restrictions that came with the role.

She stepped into the drawing room. Mr. Wymond's back was to her as he sat on the settee, conversing with her aunt.

Aunt Nancy's eyes lit up when she walked into the room. "Evie," she said.

Mr. Wymond rose and turned to face her. His quick eyes took in her appearance, and he smiled openly.

"Miss Ashmore," he greeted with a slight bow. "Thank you for agreeing to see me."

She dropped into a curtsy. "Of course," she replied. "I rather enjoyed our previous conversation, and I look forward to our next one."

"As do I."

Evie walked over to an upholstered armchair and sat down, allowing Mr. Wymond to return to his seat.

Mr. Wymond met her gaze and gave her the briefest of smiles. "I do hope I didn't call upon you too early."

"You did no such thing," Aunt Nancy interjected. "Evie is usually an early riser, since she prefers to ride in the morning."

Evie resisted the urge to roll her eyes. Her aunt always tried so hard to play matchmaker, but sometimes she would prefer to speak for herself. She did have a working voice, after all.

Mr. Wymond bobbed his head in approval. "I prefer to ride in the mornings so I may avoid the crowds, especially in Hyde Park."

"Do people not just go to Hyde Park to be seen?" Evie asked.

"Some, perhaps, but not me," Mr. Wymond replied. "I detest crowds and all the pomp that accompanies the fashionable hour at the park."

Evie discovered she was smiling. "As do I, Mr. Wymond, but I fear that we are in the minority."

"That is a shame," Mr. Wymond said, returning her smile. "I hope I am not being too presumptuous, but would you care to go on a carriage ride tomorrow morning with me? Early enough to avoid the crowds, of course."

Evie heard Aunt Nancy suck in a breath as she waited for her reply. The thought wasn't entirely appalling. She found Mr. Wymond to be a pleasant man, and something about him intrigued her. He was typically solemn, and grief seemed to hang over him like a shadow. What had caused this man such pain?

"I would be honored," Evie said, tilting her chin.

Her aunt smiled broadly, but thankfully didn't say anything.

Barnes stepped into the drawing room and announced, "Lord Haddington has requested a moment of Miss Ashmore's time."

"Please send him in," Evie ordered.

Barnes tipped his head and stepped out of the room. It was only a moment later that Reginald walked in, wearing a ridiculous emerald-green jacket with a yellow waistcoat.

Reginald stopped in the center of the room and bowed. "Mrs. Carter," he said. "Miss Ashmore." He turned his attention towards Mr. Wymond and greeted him, as well, but there was a terseness to his words.

"Lord Haddington," Mr. Wymond responded, his words also sounding forced.

Reginald returned his gaze to Evie. "It is such a beautiful

day today that I was hoping you would accompany me on a carriage ride."

"I," Evie started, then darted a glance at Mr. Wymond, "I would be honored."

Reginald gestured towards the door. "Shall we depart?" he asked.

"Right now?" Evie questioned.

"Unless you take issue with it?" Reginald gave her an expectant look. What was he about? Evie couldn't imagine he'd truly want to take her on a leisurely carriage ride, so it must be about Rutledge.

It was rude of her to even consider leaving Mr. Wymond so abruptly, especially since he had come to call on her. But she didn't have time for idle conversation when Rutledge was still out there, hurt and alone.

While she debated on what excuse she could use that would be the least offensive to her guest, Mr. Wymond rose from his chair and said, "Thank you for the lovely visit. I shall see you tomorrow morning."

Rising, Evie replied, "I am looking forward to it."

Mr. Wymond said his goodbyes and departed. Aunt Nancy gave Reginald a chiding look.

"That was poorly done," she said. "You scared the poor man off."

"I did no such thing," Reginald responded. "Besides, if he was scared off so easily, then he is most assuredly not the man for Evie."

Evie approached Reginald and asked, "May I drive the carriage?"

"No," Reginald quickly replied. "I have no desire to die today."

Not taking offense, Evie took Reginald's arm when he offered it. He led her out to the entry hall before he leaned close and whispered, "Merritt wants to see us."

"Then we mustn't keep him waiting."

Reginald sat across from Evie in the carriage and tried to quell the growing irritation he felt for Mr. Wymond. That man was making quite the nuisance of himself. To make matters worse, Evie didn't appear to be put off from his presence, either. She almost seemed to enjoy his company.

No, this would not do. He had watched suitor after suitor fall over themselves to win Evie's favor, but she never gave them any heed. This time it was different. She had apparently accepted Mr. Wymond's offer to go on a carriage ride without even a hint of reluctance.

He refused to stand back and let Mr. Wymond win Evie's affection. Perhaps he should challenge the man to a duel and be done with it?

Evie eyed him curiously. "You seem upset," she commented.

"I'm not," he lied.

"You have hardly spoken one word to me since we left my townhouse," Evie pointed out.

Reginald gave a slight shrug of his shoulder. "I don't have much to say at the moment."

"But you always have something to say, to a fault, even," she said, amusement in her voice. "It is one of the reasons why you vex me so."

Tugging down on his yellow waistcoat, he asked, "Could it be that I vex you because I am so charming?"

"That is most assuredly not it." She perused his emerald-green jacket. "May I ask you a question?"

"You may."

"Why did you start dressing so flamboyantly?" she asked.

Reginald smiled flirtatiously. "I feel flattered that you have taken such an interest in what I am wearing."

Evie didn't appear amused. "Do be serious."

"I am," he replied. "But to answer your question, I have discovered that no one takes me seriously when I am dressed like a dandy. They assume I am something I'm not."

"Which is?"

"Someone who cares more about his appearance than anything else," Reginald replied, "a pompous man who seeks pleasure over serious contemplation."

"People see only what they want to see," Evie murmured.

"Precisely, and I use that to my favor," Reginald said. "I hide in plain sight, and no one is the wiser."

A line between Evie's brow appeared. "Do you ever tire of pretending to be something you aren't?"

"It is a necessary evil, I'm afraid." When the line between her brows persisted, he continued, "I must pose the same question to you."

"It's a game to me, really, but I wonder if I am winning or losing," Evie replied, lowering her gaze. "I'm not sure at this point."

Reginald didn't like hearing her so despondent. "You don't have to continue working as an agent."

Evie's eyes snapped up to meet his, and he realized that had been the wrong thing to say. "I never said that I can't handle the demands of being a spy."

"I never implied that you couldn't."

"I can do this job as well as any man," Evie asserted as she tilted her chin stubbornly.

Reginald held his hand up. "I never questioned that. But I do not believe Rutledge recruited you as an agent because you could think like a man." He held her gaze. "Embrace what makes you unique and shine in your own way."

Evie gave him a weak smile. "That is kind of you to say, but I suppose I have always struggled to find my place in this world. I've never quite fit in anywhere."

"You've managed to fool the *ton*."

Evie snorted. "That isn't saying much. Members of

Society are all the same. They want people to fall into line, to behave in a certain way to gain acceptance, and the rules are vastly different for men and women."

Reginald nodded. "That they are."

Evie smiled, but it didn't quite reach her eyes. "My father never once treated me differently. He used to tell me, 'If you aren't willing to risk being different, then you have no choice but to settle for the ordinary'."

"He was right."

"Father taught me how to throw daggers, climb walls, and fight," Evie shared. "I loved every moment he spent with me, and I hung on his every word. He was my hero."

"Your father was a good man."

"That he was, and I miss him every day. My mother, as well." Evie's eyes became moist, but she blinked back the tears. "Their deaths were wholly unnecessary, and left a void in my heart."

Reginald leaned forward and started to reach for her hand but stopped himself. It would be entirely too forward to hold her hand in public, and it was the fastest way to get the gossips' tongues wagging.

"There is no shame in grieving one's parents," he said. "There is not a day that goes by that I do not miss my father."

Evie clasped her hands in her lap. "What a pair we make!" she said lightly.

Reginald knew she was only trying to hide her heartache. She was always trying to be brave, but when would she realize that she didn't need to hide any part of herself from him?

The carriage came to a stop and a footman walked around to open the door. After Reginald stepped out, he assisted Evie onto the pavement. She withdrew her hand from his and smoothed down her gown.

He offered his arm and asked, "Shall we?"

Evie accepted his arm, and they strolled down the pavement with a maid trailing behind. He glanced over his shoulder and asked, "Is your maid to be trusted?"

"Yes, wholeheartedly. It took much effort on my part to convince her to come, but I assure you that she will keep our confidences."

"That is good."

Evie leaned closer and lowered her voice. "I bought Abigail at the market."

Fearing he'd misheard her, he asked, "I beg your pardon?"

"I bought Abigail at the market," Evie repeated. "Her husband put her up for sale, and I couldn't stand by and not do anything."

"So you bought her?" Reginald asked in disbelief.

"He had a rope around her neck as he led her around," Evie shared. "I couldn't very well leave her with that man."

"Did anyone else bid on her?"

Evie nodded. "There were a few men who offered ludicrous amounts, but I could see the lewd look in their eyes," she replied. "I stepped forward and shouted my bid."

"I take it that it was accepted."

"Not at first," Evie said. "Her husband didn't take me seriously until I offered ten pounds."

"Ten pounds? I'm afraid to ask what he was originally selling for."

Evie frowned. "The starting bid was a halfpence."

Reginald let out a low whistle. "That poor woman. I'm afraid to know what she had to endure at her husband's hand."

"Sadly, it is a plight that many women must endure."

They turned the corner and saw Talbot and Worsley leaning against the building. Reginald stopped in front of them and asked, "Where are the cats?"

Worsley straightened up from the wall as he addressed him. "It wasn't as lucrative as we thought it would be."

Evie spoke up. "That is a shame."

Worsley dropped into an exaggerated bow and said, "You are looking lovely, Miss Ashmore. Did you do something different with your hair?"

Talbot came to stand next to Worsley and elbowed him in the ribs. "You can't ask a lady if they did something with their hair." He bowed. "I do apologize for Worsley. He has no class, I'm afraid."

"There is no reason to apologize," Evie graciously replied.

Reginald glanced between them. "What is your next business venture?"

Talbot patted the brick wall. "We thought we would take this time to really invest in the thing that matters the most."

"The agency?" Reginald asked.

"No, us," Talbot replied. "We need to fully understand why Merritt assigned us to guard the building."

"Perhaps you were the only agents available," Reginald joked.

Worsley furrowed his brow. "You may joke, but there is more to life than fun and games. If it wasn't for us, the agency would cease to be."

Reginald opened his mouth to object when Evie spoke first. "I hope your path of discovery goes well, because we rely upon your skills to keep the agency safe."

Talbot smiled. "Thank you for you saying so." His smile went away as he shifted his gaze towards Reginald. "Not everyone is appreciative of our skills."

Reginald had had enough of these fools, so he led Evie towards the door. Evie greeted Mostyn with a smile as they stepped inside.

"Good morning," she said. "How is your wife faring today?"

Mostyn returned her smile as he stood behind a desk. "She is well right now. I do thank you for asking," he said. "Merritt has been waiting for both of you."

"Then we mustn't keep him waiting for a moment longer."

Evie turned towards her maid and ordered, "Wait here. We will be along shortly."

Once the maid was situated, Reginald escorted Evie towards Merritt's door and knocked.

"Enter."

Reginald opened the door and Evie stepped into the room. He followed her inside, closing the door behind him.

Merritt gave them both an expectant look. "Did you have fun gadding about?" he asked dryly.

Evie appeared unperturbed by Merritt's question and sat on an upholstered armchair. "We are here now."

"I expect my agents to be punctual, Agent A," Merritt said.

"The streets were terribly crowded," Reginald interjected, "and it took longer than expected to arrive."

"Next time, I recommend you leave earlier," Merritt advised as he looked at his pocket watch. "Have you discovered Rutledge's whereabouts yet?"

"Not yet," Reginald replied.

"Whyever not?" Merritt asked.

Reginald sat on the chair next to Evie. "We were able to ascertain that Rutledge was abducted and is being held hostage."

"That is very disconcerting," Merritt said. "Do you know where?"

"I'm afraid not."

Merritt leaned back in his seat. "Do you know at least who abducted him?"

"No, sir," Evie replied. "We were able to track him to a warehouse on Warring Street through a message written in invisible ink, but he was already gone by the time we arrived. The men we found there have been detained, though they seemed to know very little."

Glancing between them, Merritt said, "Find Rutledge and bring him back alive."

"We're trying," Evie responded.

"Try harder," Merritt shot back. "I don't accept failure from my agents." He rose from his seat. "I need to depart for a meeting. You are dismissed."

Rising, Reginald said, "I am meeting with the smuggler tonight."

"Let us hope it isn't a waste of your time," Merritt grunted.

"It won't be," Reginald responded. "We're hoping he's connected to Rutledge's disappearance."

Merritt came around his desk and said, "Finding Rutledge has become a top priority for this agency. Do not disappoint me." He opened the door. "Good day, agents."

Reginald and Evie didn't speak as they departed Merritt's office and headed out the building. It wasn't until they arrived at their carriage that Evie spoke.

"Have we been doing enough to find Rutledge?" Evie asked.

"I believe so. We're doing all we can."

Her brows puckered in a frown. "I'm just terribly worried about him. I fear that he is already dead."

"What did I say about not giving up hope?"

Pausing for a moment, Evie looked straight into his eyes, her own pools of worry. "But what if hope isn't enough?"

Reginald wished they weren't on the pavement so he could pull her into his arms and provide her with the comfort she so desperately seemed to need. Instead, he said, "Life is full of uncertainty, but that doesn't mean we allow our fears to cripple us."

"I suppose so," Evie muttered as she turned towards the carriage.

Reginald reached for her arm and stopped her. "I know that wasn't the answer you're seeking, but it is the truth. If you don't believe Rutledge is truly alive, what is the point of looking for him?"

Evie considered him for a moment before saying, "You're right, but where do we even start looking? We've exhausted all our leads."

"Not all of them," Reginald said. "Did you already forget that I am meeting with the smuggler tonight?"

"We don't even know if the two cases are actually connected."

Reginald realized that his hand was still on Evie's arm and dropped it. "Let's take it one day at a time."

"All right," Evie said. "I can agree to that."

Reginald smiled at this small victory. "Wonderful," he said as he held his hand out. "Allow me to assist you into the carriage."

Chapter Nine

Reginald sat in his usual corner of White's with a drink in his hand. He needed a clear head for this evening, so he wasn't indulging too much, but as much as he tried to focus on his upcoming meeting with the smuggler, he couldn't stop thinking about Evie.

She had been so open and honest with him, which was refreshing—and so unlike her. She normally viewed vulnerability as a sign of weakness, but he could see the walls she had built up around her were starting to crack. What would it take for her to truly let him in?

Evie would do whatever it took to find Rutledge, and Reginald was worried about what kind of toll that would take on her. The life of an agent was a lonely and difficult one, and it caused you to question everything. No one was safe from your scrutiny, even yourself.

He may play the part of a carefree dandy to members of Society, but Reginald was anything but. He had learned to watch, listen, and evaluate everyone he came in contact with, for he was certain that everyone had something to hide.

Bringing the glass up to his lips, Reginald took a sip of his drink and hoped that the meeting tonight would yield some clues as to where Rutledge was. He wasn't fully convinced that his case had anything to do with the missing agent, but he would explore every possibility. It was the least he could do for Rutledge, and he would do anything to bring a smile to Evie's face.

Gads! The more time he spent with her, the more he realized how much he loved her. In the naïveté of his youth, he'd always assumed that they would marry, have a horde of children, and grow old together. That thought had always appealed to him because he didn't want to imagine a life without his best friend.

Time had changed both of them, but his love for her had never gone away. She was in his thoughts unceasingly, haunting his dreams and invading his sanity. One way or another, he needed to convince Evie that he was the man for her.

A server approached his table and asked, "Would you care for another drink, my lord?"

"I would not," he replied.

The server acknowledged his words with a tip of his head before he moved on to another table.

Reginald pushed back his glass and sighed. Where were his blasted friends? They were late, and he couldn't wait much longer. Perhaps he should just leave and be done with it. He had no doubt they would speak of how blissfully happy they were now that they were married. It was aggravating, and he grew tired of them questioning him as to why he wasn't married.

He was about to rise when he saw Mr. Wymond walking towards the table with a solemn look on his face.

"Botheration," Reginald muttered under his breath.

Mr. Wymond stopped next to the table and greeted him politely. "Lord Haddington."

Reginald tipped his head. "Mr. Wymond."

"I was hoping for a moment of your time," Mr. Wymond said.

Reginald gestured towards a chair and attempted to keep his voice cordial. "Take a seat."

Mr. Wymond pulled out the chair and sat down. "I was hoping to speak to you about Miss Ashmore."

This was the last conversation he wanted to have with Mr. Wymond. "What is it you want?" Reginald asked, his words coming out much gruffer than intended.

Mr. Wymond didn't appear perturbed by his curt words and pressed forward. "What are your intentions towards her?"

"My intentions?" Reginald asked, leaning back in his chair. "Why do you ask?"

With a slight hesitation, Mr. Wymond replied, "I would like to court Miss Ashmore, but I do not want to do so if she is already spoken for."

Reginald considered Mr. Wymond for a moment. He could lie and say that he had an understanding with Evie, sending Mr. Wymond on his way, but for what purpose? There may be something between them, but that didn't mean he had a right to speak for her.

Finally, he decided to settle on the truth. "I have not spoken for Evie."

Mr. Wymond eyed him curiously. "May I ask why not?"

"No, you may not," Reginald replied sternly. "My business is my own."

"I understand, but I would be remiss to fail to notice the way you look at Miss Ashmore," Mr. Wymond said.

"Remember your place, Mr. Wymond," Reginald growled.

Mr. Wymond put his hand up. "I meant no disrespect, my lord, but I want to ensure you take no issue with me pursuing her."

"I do take issue," Reginald said. "Miss Ashmore is a dear family friend, and I desire her happiness above all else."

"That is an odd thing to say unless you secretly desire her for yourself."

Reginald leaned forward in his seat and lowered his voice. "You can try to win her affections, but you will fail. Just as every other suitor who has come before you has."

"I don't intend to fail."

"Then you will find yourself disappointed soon enough," Reginald said. "Miss Ashmore is unlike any woman you will ever meet, and I assure you that you are not worthy of her."

"And you are?"

"I never said that."

"You didn't need to," Mr. Wymond said. "Do you think she takes issue with me not having a title?"

Reginald scoffed. "She cares little about titles; or matrimony, for that matter."

"I hope to change her mind about the latter."

"I wish you luck, Mr. Wymond," Reginald said, leaning back in his seat, "because you are going to need it."

Mr. Wymond rose. "I was hoping we could remain civil about this, but I see that I was wrong."

"If you are asking me to step aside so you can court Miss Ashmore, you will be sorely disappointed," Reginald said, rising.

"At least I know who my opponent is." Mr. Wymond held his gaze for a long moment, challenging him, before he bowed. "Good day, Lord Haddington."

Reginald watched his retreating figure, and that is when he noticed Hawthorne was standing a short distance away, a bemused look on his face.

Hawthorne skirted the tables in the room and sat down across from him. "What did Mr. Wymond want with you?"

"He wanted to know if Evie had been spoken for," Reginald revealed as he sat down.

Hawthorne raised his brow. "What did you say?"

Reginald huffed. "I told him the truth."

"Which is?" Hawthorne pressed.

Reginald picked up his glass and finished what was left of it. Lowering the glass to the table, he replied, "I told him that I have not spoken for Evie."

"That was foolish on your part."

"I didn't want to lie to the man."

"Is it a lie, though?" Hawthorne asked. "After all, there is something between you and Evie; there always has been."

"That was long ago," Reginald said. "Nowadays, Evie wants nothing to do with me."

"Then convince her otherwise."

Reginald pushed the empty glass away from him. "How do you propose I do that when my very existence seems to insult her?"

Hawthorne gave him a knowing look. "You are a spy; think of something."

"I wish it was that simple, but Evie is a very complicated woman."

A server came and placed two drinks on the table and collected Reginald's empty glass. After he departed, Hawthorne reached for a glass and asked, "Have you made any progress with Rutledge?"

Reginald shook his head. "Nothing of note," he replied. "There was a note on that page, which sent us into the rookeries, but we got there too late. Rutledge was already gone."

"How is Evie handling it?"

"Not well," Reginald replied. "She's worried, and with good reason. We both know the longer he's missing, the less likely he will be alive."

"Do you require any assistance?"

"Not at this time," Reginald replied. "I'm meeting with the smuggler tonight and am hoping that will give us the direction we're waiting for."

"How are the cases connected?"

"I'm not sure, but an informant said that a smuggler

ordered the abduction of a man at the Odd Blokes pub on the night Rutledge went missing."

Hawthorne stared back at him. "That could have been anyone. How do you know it was Rutledge?"

"We don't."

Hawthorne opened his mouth to reply when Grenton spoke up from behind him. "I see that you have started drinking without me," he said in an overly cheerful tone. "I shall have to strive to catch up now."

Reginald turned his attention towards his friend. "You could have arrived earlier. I've been waiting for entirely too long."

"My apologies, but I was spending time with my wife," Grenton said. "I do not think I will ever tire of being in her presence."

"Saints above," Reginald grumbled. "Can we not speak of anything else besides your marital bliss?"

"What else would you care to discuss?" Grenton asked, amused.

"Mr. Wymond just paid Haddington a visit," Hawthorne interjected, "and asked for his permission to court Evie."

"He did not ask for my permission," Reginald muttered.

"No?" Hawthorne asked. "Then why else would he seek you out at White's? I doubt the reason was just to annoy you."

Grenton turned his attention towards Reginald. "Did you inform Mr. Wymond that Miss Ashmore was yours?"

"But she isn't mine," Reginald said. "Evie and I are only friends."

"You don't actually believe that, do you?" Grenton asked.

Reginald shrugged one shoulder. "It doesn't matter what I believe. Evie has given me no indication that she would welcome my advances."

"Then convince her otherwise," Grenton encouraged.

"It isn't that simple," Reginald asserted. Why did everyone keep saying that? "Evie has a mind of her own and a willful spirit. She isn't one to be swayed by flowery words."

"I don't pretend to know Miss Ashmore, but she helped save my life. She is a remarkable woman, and my wife is very fond of her," Grenton said, reaching forward and claiming the other drink. "You would be a fool not to fight for a woman like her."

Reginald frowned. "I daresay it might be a losing battle."

"Only if you give up." Grenton took a sip before saying, "To win someone's heart is no small feat."

"I liked you better when you were miserable," Reginald joked.

Grenton laughed. "Georgie showed me a happier life."

Reginald pushed back his chair and rose. "As enlightening as this conversation is, I'm afraid I have business I need to tend to."

"Will you be attending Mrs. Claverhouse's soirée this evening?" Grenton asked.

"Unfortunately, I have other plans," Reginald said as he pushed his chair back in. "I bid you good day."

Reginald hardly acknowledged their responses before he spun on his heel and headed towards the main door. He understood that his friends were blissfully happy with their respective partners, but that didn't mean he would be so fortunate. Maybe he was destined to be alone. If he couldn't have the object of his desires, what purpose was there for him to ever wed?

Evie stared out the window, ignoring the conversation going on behind her. She wasn't in a jovial mood. How could she pretend that all was well when she had failed her mentor?

She should be out there looking for him, but she had no

idea where to start. *Failure.* That is what she was. Why did she ever assume she could be an agent when she was unsuccessful at this task?

Nathanial sat across from her, a worried expression on his face. "How are you faring?"

Evie schooled her features. "I am well."

Nathaniel didn't look convinced. "Why don't you come and play cards with us?" he suggested. "It would be much more enjoyable than staring out the window."

"I'm afraid my mood is much too pensive for games."

"That's what I assumed, which is even more reason for you to do so."

Evie glanced over her shoulder at Dinah and her aunt, who were engaged in a lively conversation, before saying, "I'm worried about Rutledge."

"As am I," Nathaniel said, "but that doesn't mean we don't go on living. We are spies, and that means we must press forward, no matter what burdens we are forced to carry."

"Surely it can't be that simple."

"It can be."

"I should be out there looking for him," Evie said, scrunching her brows," not playing parlor games."

"Pray tell, where would you even start?" Nathaniel asked.

"I know not, and that's the frustrating part," Evie said. "I feel like an utter failure for not being able to find him."

Nathaniel leaned forward in his seat and lowered his voice. "You can't save everyone. Sometimes situations are out of our control."

"I refuse to give up on him."

"And I'm not saying you should, but you must prepare yourself. Rutledge might be dead before you find him."

Dread knotted in the pit of Evie's stomach. "I know, and that frightens me," she replied. "I'm not sure what I would do without him."

"You would go on living, taking one day at a time, until it doesn't hurt as bad as it did the day before."

She smiled weakly. "When did you get to be so wise?"

"I have always been wise, but you failed to notice until now." Nathaniel gave her an encouraging smile. "Haddington is meeting with the smuggler tonight. With any luck, he will get a clue about Rutledge."

"That might just be wishful thinking on our part."

"A wish can be a powerful thing."

Evie shook her head. "You aren't going to relent until I agree to play games, are you?"

"Am I so obvious?"

Before Evie could respond, Barnes stepped into the room with a large bouquet. He met her gaze and said, "These flowers just came for you."

"At this hour?" Evie asked as she glanced out the darkened window.

Barnes tipped his head. "Would you care to read the card?" he asked.

Rising, Evie approached him and opened the card.

Stop searching for Rutledge or there will be dire consequences.

Evie's gaze snapped up. "Who delivered these flowers?" she demanded.

"They were left on the doorstep," Barnes replied, looking confused.

Evie ran out of the drawing room and headed for the main door. She opened it and halted on the top step. Her eyes roamed over the street, not knowing what she was looking for, but she was sure she would know it when she found it.

Her eyes landed on a man leaning his shoulder against a metal post. His dark hair was shoved under a brown cap and his jacket was tattered. He smirked when their eyes met, then spun on his heel and hurried into an alleyway.

Not fully thinking through the repercussions of her actions, Evie hurried down the steps and crossed the street. She kept her gaze set firmly on the alley the man disappeared into. She stepped into it, but there was no sign of him.

Evie reached into the folds of her gown and retrieved her muff pistol. She held it to her side as she slowly walked further into the alley, being mindful of the shadows. She hadn't truly thought this through, but she needed to know why this man had been loitering outside her townhouse.

As she inched further into the alley, the man stepped out from the shadows of a doorway. He had a pistol aimed at her and a sneer on his face.

"I thought you were supposed to be clever," the man said.

Evie tightened her hold on her muff pistol. "Who told you that?" she asked.

"It doesn't matter now, but I'll be rewarded handsomely for finishing you." The man cocked his gun. "Frankly, I thought you'd be harder to kill."

Evie tried to distract the man with a question. "Who wants me dead?"

"The boss does."

"That's not very specific," Evie said. "If you are going to kill me, I should at least know the name of the person who wants me dead."

The man gave her an amused look. "Why should I tell you?" he asked. "You will be dead soon enough, and then it doesn't matter what you know."

Evie watched as the man's finger twitched on the trigger and rushed to bring her pistol up. A gunshot echoed throughout the alleyway, and she braced herself for the inevitable pain. To her surprise, her attacker crumbled to the ground, his pistol dropping onto the cobblestones.

She looked up and saw Nathaniel approaching her with a smoking gun in his hand. "Are you all right?" he asked.

"I am," she replied. "Thanks for saving my life."

"You would've done the same for me," Nathaniel asserted as he stepped over the man. "We need to get you back to the townhouse before anyone sees you."

"I won't argue with that," Evie said with a final glance at the dead man.

Nathaniel placed his hand on her sleeve and led her out of the alleyway. "What were you thinking chasing after that man?" he asked in a hushed voice. "You could have been killed."

"But I wasn't," she replied.

"Fortunately, I had the good sense to go around the other side of the alleyway," Nathaniel said. "If not, we wouldn't be having this conversation."

Evie allowed Nathaniel to lead her back towards the townhouse. Frankly, she wasn't in a mood to argue with him. She found that she was rather shaken from the whole ordeal. She'd never been so close to death before.

Right before they stepped inside, Nathaniel tucked his weapon under his jacket and whispered, "You should put your pistol away."

Evie slipped the muff pistol into the folds of her gown as they walked through the open door. Once they were in the entry hall, her aunt hurried over to her and embraced her. "Oh, thank heavens!" she cried. "We were so worried when we heard the gun shot!"

"I'm fine," Evie rushed to assure her.

Her aunt released her and stepped back. "You should have never left the townhouse unescorted."

"I had little choice in the matter," Evie said. "The man took off the moment he saw me, and I needed answers."

"Answers to what?" Aunt Nancy asked.

Not wanting to bring her aunt into her confidences, she replied, "It matters not."

"It does matter," her aunt stated. "Who was that man?"

Evie shrugged. "I don't know."

"Then why did you chase after him?" her aunt pressed.

Dinah stood next to Nathaniel and interjected, "It might be best if we don't bog Evie down with questions right now."

Her aunt placed a hand on her hip. "At least assure me that you had nothing to do with the pistol discharging."

Nathaniel cleared his throat. "I'm afraid that was me."

Aunt Nancy spun towards Nathaniel. "Did you scare the man off?" she asked.

"I can confirm with great confidence that he will never be bothering us again."

"You make it sound so ominous," her aunt said. "You didn't hurt him, did you?"

"I only did what needed to be done." Nathaniel turned his attention towards Evie. "May I speak to you for a moment?"

"You may," Evie replied before she walked towards the drawing room. After she stepped inside, she turned and saw Nathaniel and Dinah step into the room.

Nathaniel placed a hand on his wife's shoulder. "It might be best if you entertain your aunt while I speak to Evie."

Dinah pressed her lips together. "If you think you're going to get rid of me, then you are sorely mistaken."

"I just think—"

Dinah cut him off. "I am not a simpleton. I'm a part of this, whether you choose to admit it or not."

Nathaniel removed his hand from her shoulder and held it up in surrender. "You may stay, but you must let me ask the questions."

"I can agree to that," Dinah said.

Shifting his gaze towards Evie, Nathaniel asked, "Why did you rush outside?"

Evie realized that she was still clutching the card in her hand and held it out to Nathaniel. "Read it for yourself."

Nathaniel accepted the paper and read it. "Why do you suppose someone went to such great lengths to threaten you?"

"I don't rightly know, but I have little doubt that man was sent to kill me," Evie said.

Dinah gasped. "Who would want to kill you?" she asked.

"That's what I'd like to know."

"Did the man say anything to you before I shot him?" Nathaniel asked.

"He made a comment about how he thought I would be harder to kill." Evie walked over to the window and saw people running towards the alleyway where the man had been shot. Some people delighted in seeing a dead body, but she never would understand that kind of morbid fascination.

Nathaniel's voice broke through her musings. "You and Nancy will reside at my townhouse for the foreseeable future."

Evie spun around. "I think not."

"Be reasonable," he said. "Whoever wants you dead knows where you live."

"I'm not scared," Evie said, tilting her chin.

Nathaniel took a step closer to her. "You should be!" he exclaimed. "Someone just lured you outside and tried to kill you."

"And they failed."

"Only because I was there," Nathaniel pointed out.

Dinah approached and placed a hand on Evie's sleeve. "Nathaniel has a point," she said. "You aren't safe here."

"Aunt Nancy can go with you, but I am not running," Evie said. "This is my home. Besides, it's not as if our relation to you is a secret. They'd definitely come there next."

Nathaniel stared at her for a long moment before letting out a heavy sigh. "Fine, but I will assign guards to watch over you."

Evie opened her mouth to object, but Nathaniel spoke first. "I'm not going to argue with you on this."

She reluctantly nodded. "I am amenable to that." It wouldn't be a problem, because it wasn't the first time she'd had guards assigned to watch over her. She knew she could outsmart them if she needed to.

"Good," Nathaniel said. "I know just the two men."

Dinah removed her hand from Evie's sleeve and asked, "What are you going to tell Aunt Nancy? After all, I doubt she is going to drop the matter."

Evie winced slightly. "I'll need to think of something."

"Do try to make it believable," Dinah said.

"I will."

Chapter Ten

Reginald walked alongside the River Thames as he made his way to the old wharf near Tooly Street. The moon reflected off the water, but it did little to distract from the pungent odor emanating from it.

His bright, finely-made clothes had been replaced with tattered dull ones, and the holes in the soles of his boots allowed him to feel every worn cobblestone beneath him. He looked, and played, the part of a man down on his luck very well. He knew that if his mask slipped, it could mean the difference between life or death for him.

An image of Evie came to his mind, but he banished it just as quickly as it had come. He didn't have the luxury of dwelling on her now, even for a moment. He needed to be fully present if he didn't want to get himself killed.

Up ahead, he saw the old wharf and a burly man standing guard by the main door. His eyes drifted over the dilapidated building, which was in desperate need of a good coat of paint, among other badly needed repairs.

The burly man put his hand up, causing his steps to falter. "What business do ye have here?" he asked in a loud, booming voice.

"I was told there's work."

"Ye were told wrong," the man huffed as he crossed his arms.

The door opened and a tall man stepped out, wearing a blue jacket and buff trousers. "You will have to excuse Boothe here," the newcomer said as he gestured to the burly man, "but he forgets his manners at times." He held the door open. "Would you care to step inside?"

Reginald was not fooled by this man's carefree demeanor, noting the outline of a pistol under his waistcoat. If he had to guess, this man was attempting to size him up, just as he was doing to him.

As Reginald took a step forward, Boothe placed a hand on his chest, stilling him. "Do ye have a weapon on ye?"

"I do."

Boothe put his hand out. "Give it here."

"I think not," Reginald said. "Pistols are expensive, and I'm not about to give you mine."

The other man spoke up. "May I ask how you were able to afford a pistol?"

He smirked. "I got it off a man I mugged," he lied with mock pride. "It was pretty easy, since he was a dandy."

The man nodded approvingly. "Follow me, then," he ordered. "Just don't brandish the gun, and we won't have an issue."

Reginald walked past Boothe, ignoring the heated glare being sent his way. It was evident that Boothe took his job very seriously, and he didn't fault him for that. Work was hard to find in the rookeries.

The door was closed behind him, leaving him alone with the other man.

The man smiled. "My name is Towle." He held his hands up. "I am in charge of this operation here."

Reginald glanced around at the large crates stacked orderly throughout the space. "What kind of work is this?"

"Patience, my good man," Towle replied. "You will find out soon enough, but it would be best if you joined the others."

Towle didn't wait for his response before walking down a path between crates. Reginald easily caught up to him, but his eyes roamed over the crates as they walked, looking for any sign of what he was dealing with.

Towle stopped in front of a door. "Wait in there," he ordered. "I'll be along shortly."

Reginald opened the door and stepped inside. It was a square room with two broken windows along the back wall. Men leaned against the worn papered walls as they conversed with one another. He counted ten men in the room.

Reginald spotted his friends seated at the lone table in the middle. He approached and asked, "Do you know what we got ourselves into?"

Mellor shrugged. "I care not, assuming I get paid."

Boden nodded in agreement. "Who cares what we have to do to get paid?" he asked. "I'm tired of going hungry."

Reginald pulled out a chair and sat down. "I just don't want to do anything that'll get me killed or transported."

"You worry too much," Mellor said as he leaned back in his chair. "I was told this is an easy job."

"There's no such thing as an easy job in the rookeries." Reginald turned towards Smith, who was being unusually quiet. "Are you having qualms about it?"

Mellor chuckled. "No, Smith is just licking his wounds," he said. "His wife just had another useless daughter."

Smith glared at Mellor. "Don't remind me. Now I have two daughters and no sons. What am I supposed to do with them?"

"You could love them," Reginald suggested.

Smith scoffed. "Do be serious. I can barely feed two mouths, let alone four," he said. "That's why I'm here."

Reginald glanced around the room and noticed that all the

men wore ill-fitting, tattered clothing. They needed a good score, and he knew they wouldn't shy away from disreputable work.

The door opened and a few more men drifted in, their eyes weary. Once they found a place to stand, Towle stepped inside with papers in his hand.

"Good evening," Towle said, his eyes roaming the small room. "Before we begin, would anyone care to leave?"

When no one moved, Towle nodded approvingly. "I do believe you have all made the right choice." He glanced down at the papers in his hand. "The job is simple; you will deliver crates to the address listed on your paper."

A man in the back asked, "What's in the crates?"

Towle brought his gaze up. "Does it matter?" he asked.

"It does to me," the man pressed.

Gesturing towards the door, Towle said, "If you are uncomfortable with this job, you are free to leave. We are asking for your discretion, not your input."

The man put his hands up. "I can be discreet. I just didn't want to go in blindly."

"We are paying you to deliver the crates—nothing more, nothing less. No questions." Towle's eyes grew steely. "If we discover that you tampered with the locks on the crates, you will be killed."

Reginald took a moment to size Towle up. His clothing and speech marked him as a gentleman, but his eyes were troublesome. They were hard, unyielding, and he would be wise not to underestimate him.

Towle held the papers up. "Here are the addresses you will be delivering to," he said. "I'll give each group an address right before you depart. Be sure to memorize it. If you fail on this, it will be the last mistake you ever make. Do I make myself clear?"

The men in the room bobbed their heads.

"Good," Towle acknowledged. "You will report back here

in two days' time to deliver the crates. Once they have been delivered, you will receive what is coming to you."

Towle lowered the papers to his side and continued. "Once you have secured a partner, you are free to leave," he said. "I must stress the urgency of not discussing this job with anyone. It is for their safety as much as for your own."

Reginald watched Towle depart from the room before he turned towards his friends. He didn't want to partner with anyone, but he was left with little choice. If he wanted to discover what was in those crates, he would need to give the impression that he planned to fulfill the assignment.

Smith met his gaze from across the table. "Will you be my blasted partner so I can leave?" he asked gruffly.

Mellor elbowed Smith in the side. "Are ye anxious to return home to help with the little one?"

"Not at all," Smith replied, "I plan on hitting the pub and getting roaring drunk before I go home."

"What a lovely sentiment," Boden teased.

Smith frowned. "Talk to me after you have children," he grumbled.

"I have no intention of ever doing so," Boden replied. "Children are nuisances."

Mellor shifted in his seat to face Reginald. "You're being awfully quiet. What is yer take on it?"

Reginald chuckled. "A child brings forth a whole host of problems."

"That they do," Mellor agreed.

"But I'm not against them, assuming I find the right woman," Reginald said.

Boden smirked. "Is there such a thing?" he asked. "After all, I think the right woman is the one that I'm currently with."

"I can't believe any woman would waste her time with ye," Mellor joked. "You stink."

"I do not." Boden leaned down and took a whiff of his

dirty shirt. "It might be time that I wash this shirt," he amended.

"You should have done that weeks ago," Smith remarked. "That's precisely why ye need a wife."

"I do say that she would be more preoccupied with other wifely duties," Boden joked cockily.

Smith pushed back his chair and rose. "It has been decided," he said, breaking up the conversation. "Daventry and I will partner up for the job."

Mellor rose. "I believe I shall join ye at the pub."

"You're more than welcome," Smith encouraged. "Anyone else care to join us?"

Boden shook his head. "I have things I need to see to."

"As do I," Reginald said.

"Your loss." Smith walked over to the door and opened it. "With any luck, I won't remember tonight."

"Your wife is a lucky woman," Mellor mocked as he followed Smith out of the room.

Boden turned towards Reginald and lowered his voice. "I do have some reservations about this."

Reginald didn't want to admit that he had a lot of reservations about the job. It seemed too easy, which was never a good sign. "Why is that?"

With a glance over his shoulder, Boden asked, "What do ye think are in those crates?"

"I don't know," he replied. "Some weapons, I suppose."

"Yet we are supposed to just trust Towle?"

"What choice do we have?" Reginald asked. "It's a paying job."

Boden didn't look convinced. "Towle mentioned nothing about an insurrection coming or who his boss is."

"Perhaps he's just a middleman."

"You might be right." Boden rose. "Forget I said anything."

Rising, Reginald kept his voice low. "I would trust your gut," he encouraged. "There will be other jobs."

"Not for men like us."

Reginald knew Boden was correct in his assumption. Jobs were few and far between for men like him.

They didn't speak much as they left the building, which was fine by him. He was looking for any sign of what was in those crates. He assumed it was weapons, because they were dealing with a weapons smuggler, but there were a myriad of things it could be.

One thing was certain—he would be back in two days' time.

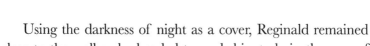

Using the darkness of night as a cover, Reginald remained close to the wall as he headed towards his study in the rear of the townhouse. He'd learned long ago that it was easier to come and go through an unlocked window rather than the main door. It helped curtail questions that he in no way could answer. The less his staff knew about his peculiar hours, the better.

Reginald arrived at the window, opened it, and climbed through. Once he'd straightened, he removed the tattered jacket and draped it over the back of the chair. He had moved towards the drink cart when he came to an abrupt stop. He wasn't alone. A lone figure sat on the chair, his whole person clouded in darkness.

As he reached for his pistol, a familiar voice reached his ears. "Good evening."

Reginald's hand dropped and he breathed a sigh of relief. "Hawthorne, that's a good way to get oneself killed."

"I've seen you shoot. I'll take my chances," Hawthorne joked.

"I am an excellent shot."

"So you say." Hawthorne rose with a drink in his hand. "I do apologize for remaining in the shadows, but I didn't dare light a candle. It would alert your servants to my presence."

"Then I must assume you came through the window."

"That I did," Hawthorne said before he took a sip of his drink.

Reginald walked over to his desk and took a moment to light the candle. "Not that I'm complaining, but what brings you by this evening?"

"We need to talk."

Hawthorne's demeanor gave him pause. What was so important that his friend needed to talk to him late at night?

"Is Evie all right?" he demanded, panic rising inside him.

Hawthorne nodded. "She is, but someone tried to kill her tonight."

Reginald felt like someone had punched him in the gut. It took a moment before his breathing steadied. "What happened?"

"It might be best if I start at the beginning." Hawthorne reached into his jacket pocket and removed a piece of paper. "Flowers were delivered to her this evening, along with this card."

Reginald approached his friend and accepted the paper, which he unfolded and read. It was an obvious threat, but it gave no hints on who could have written the note. "Who delivered the flowers?"

"They were left on the doorstep."

"Of course they were," Reginald mumbled.

"After the flowers were delivered, Evie discovered a man loitering outside and followed him into an alleyway," Hawthorne shared.

Reginald shook his head. "That's not wise."

"No, it wasn't," Hawthorne agreed. "I went around back and entered the alley from the other side, only to see the man was pointing a pistol at Evie. I had no choice but to shoot him."

"I'm glad you did."

"As am I, because I do believe he was sent to kill Evie."

Reginald ran a hand through his dark hair. "Were there any witnesses?" he asked, knowing Evie's reputation could be at risk if anyone saw her enter the alleyway.

"Thankfully not," Hawthorne replied. "I promptly led her back to her townhouse and questioned her about what the man said before he was shot."

"Did he give anything away?"

"I'm afraid not."

Reginald walked over to the settee and dropped down. The thought that someone tried to hurt Evie weighed heavily on him. He wished he had been there to help her, but he had been busy chasing a clue across town. What would've happened if Evie had been hurt? Would he have ever forgiven himself? He should have been there! He should have protected her.

Hawthorne sat across from him. "I know that look."

"What look?"

"You're trying to blame yourself for what happened to Evie."

Reginald gave him a wry smile. "Is it so obvious?"

"Only to me." Hawthorne leaned forward and set his drink down. "I tried to convince Evie to stay at my townhouse for the foreseeable future, but she adamantly refused."

"That doesn't surprise me in the least."

"I was hoping she would be reasonable."

Reginald chuckled. "Then you don't know Evie very well. She's as stubborn as she is beautiful."

"Regardless, I'm assigning Talbot and Worsley to guard her," Hawthorne said.

"Those two imbeciles? Do you think they can handle

her?" Reginald asked. "She tends to come and go as she pleases."

"I'll warn them."

"How did Evie respond when you told her that guards would be watching over her?"

"She agreed."

Reginald leaned back in his seat. If Evie agreed to guards, she must have been more shaken up than she cared to admit.

"We do have a problem," Hawthorne said.

"Another one?"

A smile came to Hawthorne's lips. "After I escorted Dinah home, I visited the magistrate and asked nicely if I could examine the body of the man I shot."

"You asked nicely?"

"Yes, with ten pounds," Hawthorne said as he reached into his jacket pocket and removed a piece of paper. "I discovered this."

Reginald leaned forward and accepted the paper. It was another page that had been ripped out of a book, and in the far corner it had the triangular stamp from the Penny Post. "Was there a hidden message?"

"There was," Hawthorne confirmed. "It was the address to Evie's townhouse, confirming my suspicions that he was there to kill her."

"Blazes," Reginald muttered as he handed the paper back to his friend. For once, he was at a loss for words. How could he keep Evie safe when he didn't even know where the threat was coming from?

"Do you still have the note you found on the man in Hyde Park?" Hawthorne asked.

"I do," Reginald asked. "Why do you ask?"

Hawthorne pointed towards the triangular stamp at the top of the paper. "Besides the words "Penny Post Paid", it gives the initials of the sorting office in the center," he explained. "Perhaps they were sent from the same sorting office."

Reginald jumped up and hurried over to his desk. He unlocked the top drawer and pulled out the paper, which he extended to Hawthorne.

Hawthorne glanced between the two papers and nodded. "They match," he said. "That's too much of a coincidence to ignore."

"I agree," Reginald said as Hawthorne returned the paper to him. "We'll need to search the sorting office at once." He walked over to the door and opened it. "Shall we?"

Hawthorne put his hand up. "It would be best if we waited until tomorrow and go speak to the workers first."

"Why wait?"

"I know you are eager for answers, but breaking into a sorting center is not something that we should do lightly."

"We have broken into places for less," Reginald pressed.

Hawthorne rose and picked up his glass. "Come have a drink with me," he encouraged as he walked over to the drink cart.

Reginald reluctantly closed the door. "Why am I assuming you're trying to pacify me?"

"Because I am." Hawthorne put his glass down on the drink tray and picked up the decanter. "If we break into the sorting office and our presence is noticed, we might lose the only lead we have on finding Rutledge. We need to be discreet."

"What do you propose?"

"I think I will write Dinah a letter that needs to be posted from that sorting office," Hawthorne said, pouring drinks for both of them. "We'll look for anything that might arouse suspicion. Then, we can discuss breaking into the sorting office if it's necessary."

Hawthorne set the decanter down and picked up the two

glasses. He held one of them up, and Reginald crossed the room to accept it.

After he took a sip, Reginald asked, "Why does someone want Evie dead?"

"I've been asking myself the same question, and I cannot seem to find an answer that satisfies me."

Reginald also had more questions than answers. "I don't like this, not one bit," he grumbled.

Hawthorne walked over to the settee and sat down. "How did your meeting go tonight?" he asked. "Did you find any information about Rutledge?"

"No," Reginald said with a sigh, sitting across from his friend. "I've been hired to deliver crates across Town."

"What's in the crates?"

"I wasn't able to determine that, but I assume it's weapons of some sort," Reginald said.

Hawthorne swirled the drink in his hand. "Any mention of an insurrection?"

"Unfortunately, nothing was mentioned in that regard," Reginald replied. "I believe I was hired just to be a delivery boy."

"You need to get a look at what's inside those crates."

Reginald bobbed his head. "Agreed. We were warned that if we tamper with the lock we will be killed."

Hawthorne gave him a knowing look. "I assume that won't stop you from doing so."

"You are correct." Reginald tossed back his drink and placed the empty glass on the table. "I do have a problem."

"Which is?"

"I was forced to take a partner to help deliver the crates with me," Reginald said. "It'll complicate the situation some, but it won't make it impossible."

Hawthorne took a sip of his drink, then fixed him with a look. "Do avoid getting killed on this assignment."

"I have every intention of remaining alive," Reginald said. "Why the sudden concern?"

"I cannot help fearing that you are distracted by Evie and the threat on her life," Hawthorne replied, leaning forward.

Reginald frowned. "You don't need to concern yourself with me."

"I know that Evie is important to you, but—"

"Do you truly intend to lecture me on how to be a spy?" Reginald asked incredulously. "I have survived much worse things than this."

"It's different when someone we love is threatened."

"I never said I loved Evie."

"You never had to." Hawthorne put his glass down on the table. "We only have one life to give to king and country, so you better make sure it isn't wasted."

"I thank you for your concern, but it is unwarranted," Reginald said. "Yes, I am worried about Evie, but I know that she can take care of herself."

"Do you?" Hawthorne questioned. "I know that you would move heaven and earth to keep her safe."

"That I would, without a doubt."

The long clock in the corner chimed the hour, and Hawthorne glanced over at it. "It is time I go home to my wife."

Reginald felt a twinge of envy at his friend's words. "You are most fortunate in that regard."

Hawthorne smiled. "I am lucky that I found the one person who speaks to my soul."

"That you are."

Hawthorne met his gaze. "Love is always worth fighting for."

"Unless you are the only one fighting for it," Reginald countered. "How can I expect to ever win Evie's heart when she keeps it locked up so tightly?"

"You will just need to find the right key to open it."

"That is easier said than done, my friend."

Hawthorne nodded. "If you recall, Dinah and I did not have a smooth path to true love," he said. "I lied to her, used her, and yet she still found it in her heart to forgive me."

"As you said, you were lucky."

"There is some luck involved." Hawthorne walked over to the window. "I shall see you tomorrow."

After Hawthorne exited, Reginald leaned back and rested his head against the back of his seat. What would it be like to secure Evie's affections? A smile came to his lips at that thought. If he was able to accomplish that feat, he could accomplish anything.

Chapter Eleven

Evie stared up at the canopy of her bed. The morning sun peeked through the closed drapes, but she was in no hurry to get up. She'd had little sleep as she tried to deduce who was trying to kill her. But, for once, she was at a loss about what she should do. She wasn't about to stop looking for Rutledge, even if her life was threatened for it.

She knew precisely what he would advise her to do. He would tell her to stop looking for him. He'd always been fiercely protective of her. It was her turn to help him. She just had to find him first—which was proving to be quite difficult.

She'd been lucky last night. If Nathaniel hadn't shot that man, she had no doubt that he would have killed her, even if she managed to shoot him in return. She had never come so close to death and, truth be told, it frightened her a little. She had always felt like she was invincible, but that was not the case. Her perspective had changed in the blink of an eye.

Reginald came to her mind, and rather than pushing the thought aside, she allowed herself to dwell on him. Would he miss her if she was gone? She hoped so. He may try to dictate her life, but she knew it came from good intentions. He thought her reckless, and she didn't disagree. She couldn't. She was well aware that she took far too many chances, but that was the only way she truly felt something. Her heart had grown numb long ago. Frankly, this was the only way she'd learned of to cope with it.

The door to her bedchamber swung open and Abigail stepped into the room. "Mrs. Carter is on her way to see you," she informed her.

Evie sat up in bed. "I did put her off last night."

"Do you want me to tell her that you are unavailable?"

"That won't be necessary."

Aunt Nancy's voice came from the doorway. "Well, I should be grateful that you're willing to see me."

"I am always willing to see you."

"Just not willing to confide in me," her aunt accused as she walked further into the room.

"I have my reasons." Evie picked up her pillow and positioned it between her back and the wall.

Her aunt glanced at Abigail. "You are dismissed."

Abigail crossed her arms over her chest. "No offense, but I do not answer to you," she said. "I take my orders from Miss Ashmore." She turned towards her. "Would you care for me to leave?"

Evie nodded. "Yes, thank you, Abigail."

Abigail departed from the room, closing the door behind her.

"I don't know why you insisted on hiring Abigail," Aunt Nancy remarked. "She is uncouth, and the other servants say that she is terribly aloof with them."

"Abigail had a very rough life before joining us here."

"Clearly, but she has no right to be a lady's maid," her aunt said. "Did you even check her references?"

"She didn't have any references."

Her aunt pursed her lips together. "Dear heavens, have I taught you nothing?" she asked. "You can't hire every vagrant off the street."

"Abigail is not a vagrant."

Taking a step forward, her aunt lowered her voice and asked, "What if she tries to kill us in our sleep?"

Evie laughed. "Perhaps you'll learn to sleep with a pistol under your pillow, like I have suggested on multiple occasions."

"Ladies do not sleep with pistols under their pillows."

"Some do." Evie reached over to the pillow next to her and lifted it, revealing a pistol. "I have for quite some time now."

Her aunt sat beside her on the bed. "Why do you need to sleep with a pistol under your pillow?"

"It's just a precaution."

"For what?" Aunt Nancy asked. "You are safe here."

Evie lowered the pillow. "I prefer to be cautious."

"I'm worried about you, Evie."

"There is no need to be."

"But there is," her aunt pressed. "I fear that you got into something and are in over your head."

"I'm not—"

"Why don't we return to the countryside for the remainder of the Season?" Aunt Nancy interrupted. "I even promise that I won't complain when you don a pair of trousers and ride astride."

Evie smiled. "Is that even possible?"

Her aunt returned her smile. "It would be extremely difficult, but I am willing to give it my best effort."

"That is kind of you, but it is imperative that I don't leave London right now."

Her aunt's smile dimmed. "Because of Mr. Rutledge?"

"Yes," Evie replied. "I need to find him."

"But why does it have to be *you*?" her aunt asked.

"I can't stand by and do nothing."

"I don't understand what is going on with you," Aunt

Nancy said, rising, "and, quite frankly, I am at a loss for what to do."

"Once I find Rutledge, everything will go back to normal."

Her aunt tossed her hands up in the air. "What is 'normal' anymore?" she asked. "I'm afraid we are too far past that to ever go back."

She had a point. Evie had changed these past few months, and she would never go back to the way she was before. She knew too much to ever do so. Being an agent of the Crown was exhilarating, and it gave her the adventure she so desperately craved.

Aunt Nancy's face softened. "I know I have been hard on you as of late, but I don't know what I would do if anything happened to you."

"Nothing will happen to me," Evie rushed to assure her.

A knock came at the door and it opened, revealing a maid. "Pardon me, but Mr. Wymond has come to call," she said. "Are you available to receive him?"

"I am," Evie replied, tossing back her covers. "Inform him that I will be down in a moment, and do seek out Abigail for me."

"Yes, miss," she said before she departed from the room.

Evie put her feet over the side of the bed and rose, then walked over to the wardrobe and removed a pale yellow gown.

Her aunt followed her with her eyes. "I sense you have no reluctance in seeing Mr. Wymond."

"Why would I?" Evie asked. "He is Marielle's brother, and I find his company to be more than tolerable."

"Dare I hope that you would accept his offer of courtship, assuming he asks?"

Evie shook her head. "Mr. Wymond is a friend, nothing more. Do not read more into this than is intended."

"Does Mr. Wymond know that you only consider him a friend?"

"Mr. Wymond knows that I have no intention of marrying," Evie said. "I said as much when he first asked if he could call. We've decided to simply be friends."

Her aunt eyed her curiously. "What if he believes that he has the power to change your mind?"

"Then he is sorely mistaken." Evie turned towards the door when Abigail walked through it. "We must hurry if we don't want Mr. Wymond to wait for too long."

Abigail walked over to the dressing table chair and patted the back. "Let's begin with your hair," she said.

"I will go down and keep Mr. Wymond company until you arrive," Aunt Nancy stated.

"That might be for the best," Evie agreed, "Thank you."

Her aunt walked over to the door and laid her hand on the latch. "I think you would be very happy as Mrs. Wymond."

Evie shot an annoyed glance in the mirror at her aunt. "You must promise me that you will not conspire with Mr. Wymond."

Aunt Nancy put a hand to her chest. "Why would I do such a thing?" she asked too innocently before she departed from the room.

Abagail spoke up. "Do you truly believe Mrs. Carter would conspire against you with Mr. Wymond?"

"I'm not entirely sure," Evie responded. Her aunt wanted her to marry above all else, no matter how opposed she was. Why couldn't she accept that was never going to happen?

A relatively short time later, Evie hurried down the steps with her hair neatly coiffed. She could hear Mr. Wymond's pleasant laugh as it drifted into the entry hall. He wasn't awful; quite the contrary. She enjoyed spending time with him, but as she'd told Aunt Nancy, friendship was all that was between them.

Mr. Wymond rose from his chair and bowed when she stepped into the drawing room.

"Miss Ashmore," he greeted. "You look a vision of perfection."

Evie dropped into a curtsy. "Thank you, sir." She walked over to her aunt and sat beside her. "I do apologize for taking so long."

Mr. Wymond put his hand up. "Nonsense. I apologize for calling at such an early hour, but I was hoping you'd still care to join me on a carriage ride," he said. "If I recall correctly, we both dread the fashionable hour at Hyde Park, so I thought an earlier ride would be much more enjoyable."

Evie found herself smiling. "I think a carriage ride sounds lovely."

Mr. Wymond looked pleased. "Shall we depart before it grows too crowded?"

"That we should," Evie agreed as she rose.

Mr. Wymond stepped forward and offered his arm. "I hope you don't mind, but I brought my dog along."

Evie's eyes widened. "You have a dog?"

"I do," Mr. Wymond said as he led her out of the drawing room. "He's a puppy and does not like to be separated from me, even for a moment."

"I adore dogs," Evie gushed.

"Wonderful! But you must prepare yourself for being licked," Mr. Wymond said. "I've been working on training him, but it turns out that I am terrible at it."

"I can't imagine that to be true."

Mr. Wymond chuckled. "I can command a shipful of men, but I can't train a puppy."

They had just stepped out of the main door when the sound of barking reached them from the carriage. As they approached the vehicle, a footman opened the door, and a brown puppy wiggled in excitement at the sight of Mr. Wymond.

Mr. Wymond reached for the puppy. He held it at arm's

length, but the little thing kept lunging forward, trying to lick his face.

Evie watched the scene with a smile. There was something oddly charming about a man holding a puppy.

"What's his name?" she asked.

"I haven't decided yet," Mr. Wymond replied. "Perhaps you could help me pick one out."

"I'd be happy to."

A footman held his hand out to assist her into the carriage. Once she was situated on the bench, Mr. Wymond sat across from her, the puppy still wriggling in his hands.

"He is a feisty one," Evie said.

"That he is," Mr. Wymond replied, "I had no intention of getting one, but I saw two men selling cats and dogs from a cart."

Evie resisted the urge to laugh. She had a sneaking suspicion of who those men were.

Mr. Wymond put the puppy on the floor. "They charged me an outrageous sum, but I saw something in this dog that I couldn't refuse."

"Which was?"

A pained look came to Mr. Wymond's eyes. "I had a cabin boy who bought a dog similar to this one when we were in port. He tried to keep the animal hidden from the officers, but we all knew he had it. It wasn't long before everyone cared for the animal."

Mr. Wymond was silent as his eyes grew moist. "The day our ship went down, I lost a lot of good men, including my cabin boy and his dog."

"My condolences," Evie said, knowing her words were hardly sufficient for what he had revealed.

"Thank you," Mr. Wymond murmured.

The carriage jerked forward, and Evie watched Mr. Wymond blink back his tears.

"May I ask what the dog's name was?"

"Bandit," Mr. Wymond replied. "Johnny named it Bandit."

Evie glanced down at the rambunctious puppy. "What about calling him Bandit, in honor of Johnny?" she asked.

His lips curved into a smile. "I think that is a fine idea." He turned his attention towards the dog. "Your name will be Bandit now."

The puppy barked and wagged his tail in response.

Mr. Wymond brought his gaze back up to meet hers. "I believe that name will suit him nicely. Thank you."

"You are most kindly welcome—"

Bandit jumped onto her lap and attempted to lick her face, preventing further speech as she caught hold of him.

"Bandit!" Mr. Wymond exclaimed as he leaned forward. "No!"

Evie laughed. "It's all right," she said as she petted the animal, keeping him firmly in her lap. "Bandit is just being a dog."

"I promise that I will train him soon enough."

"I know you will, but until then, just love him."

Mr. Wymond leaned back in his seat. "I assure you that won't be a problem."

"Botheration!" Reginald exclaimed as he stared through his spyglass.

Hawthorne glanced over at him. "What's wrong?"

Reginald lowered the spyglass. "Mr. Wymond brought a puppy to woo Evie with."

"You take issue with that?"

"Everyone knows that women find puppies irresistible," Reginald said.

Hawthorne gave him an amused look. "I do not think that is a written rule."

"It may as well be."

"Now that we've determined that Evie is safe, it would be best if we let her enjoy her carriage ride with Mr. Wymond," Hawthorne suggested.

Reginald shook his head. "I don't think that is wise."

"And why is that?"

"Evie hates carriage rides through Hyde Park," Reginald said. "She doesn't like to feel like she is on display."

"But it isn't the fashionable hour," Hawthorne pointed out.

"Maybe Mr. Wymond asked her to go on a carriage ride in such a way that she was unable to refuse."

"I doubt that. Evie is not one to be swayed so easily. Her excuses are legendary."

"Regardless, someone is trying to kill her, and we need to ensure that she remains unharmed," Reginald said. "Evie may not care about her safety, but I do."

Hawthorne glanced skyward and sighed. "And you think lurking in the woodlands nearby will keep her safe?"

"I do." There were better ways to protect Evie, but Reginald didn't want to make his presence known. Not yet. He had just shown up at her townhouse to speak to her when Mr. Wymond's carriage merged into traffic. He'd followed her to Hyde Park, not fully thinking through the repercussions of his actions. Now they were in the woods, and he was beginning to think this wasn't his finest idea.

Mr. Wymond's coach came to a stop a short distance away under the shade of the trees. If Reginald listened carefully, he could hear Evie's laughter drifting on the wind. He tightened his hold on his spyglass until his knuckles grew white. He wanted to be the one to make her laugh.

"Perhaps we should go," Hawthorne suggested.

"No!" Reginald exclaimed. "Evie should have never put herself in danger by going on a carriage ride."

"I agree, but there is nothing that can be done about it."

"Yes, there is," Reginald said as he took a step forward.

Hawthorne moved quickly and stepped in front of him, blocking his path. "I would advise you to stop and think about what you are about to do."

"I know precisely what I am doing."

"Do you? Because it almost appears as if you are a jealous suitor."

"I am no such thing. I am Evie's partner, and I'm trying to keep her safe."

Hawthorne lifted his brow. "Stay in the shadows and guard her, but don't approach her," he said. "I promise you that it will not end well for you if you do otherwise."

"You don't know that for certain."

"I don't need a crystal ball to decipher it."

Reginald shifted in his stance. Hawthorne was right. If he approached Evie, it wouldn't end well. But he couldn't just stand here and do nothing. Her life was in peril!

Coming to a decision, he stepped aside to go around Hawthorne when he saw Evie approaching them through the cluster of trees. A frown marred her features, and she stopped a short distance away.

"May I ask what you two are doing here?" Evie asked, placing a hand on her hip.

Hawthorne gave Reginald an expectant look as he took a step back.

Reginald cleared his throat. "We're here to guard you."

"By lurking in the woodlands?" Evie asked. "That seems highly unlikely."

Reginald took a step closer to her. "What in the blazes were you thinking going on a carriage ride with Mr. Wymond?" he demanded.

Evie blinked. "What I was thinking was that it sounded like an enjoyable excursion."

"Do you not care a whit for your safety?" he asked, taking another step. "Someone is trying to kill you, and you are traipsing around Hyde Park as if you don't have a care in the world!"

"I am not traipsing," Evie said.

"No?" Reginald asked. "I suppose you were too busy flirting with Mr. Wymond to even recognize the danger that you are in."

"First of all, I was not flirting with Mr. Wymond…"

Reginald huffed.

"Secondly, I have a dagger and a muff pistol on my person."

"Do you think that will be truly sufficient against an attacker?"

Evie tilted her chin. "You need not concern yourself about me. I can protect myself."

"Like you did last night?"

"That's not fair of you to say."

"It makes it no less true."

Evie dropped her hand from her hip and gave him an exasperated look. "Go home, Reginald," she said. "Your presence is not required here."

"Do you even want to find Rutledge?"

Reginald knew he had gone too far when he saw Evie's cheeks flush, despite the rest of her becoming perfectly still.

"Every thought I have of late is about Rutledge. I am risking my life to find him," Evie asserted.

Reginald felt like a jackanapes. He had no right to say what he did.

"I'm sorry," he said. "I was out of line."

"Yes, you were." Evie glanced down at the tube in his hand. "Was a spyglass truly necessary?"

"It served its purpose," Reginald said.

Evie turned her attention towards Hawthorne. "And you went along with this?"

Hawthorne put his hands up. "It was not our finest moment."

"No, it wasn't," Evie responded. "Why are you both here? And I would prefer the truth."

Reginald spoke, drawing her attention. "I was worried about you, especially after what transpired last night."

"It was unfortunate—"

Reginald cut her off. "You could have been killed."

"But I wasn't," Evie shot back. "Nathaniel saved me, and we were able to return to the townhouse before anyone discovered our involvement."

"I read the note, and I think you should stop looking for Rutledge," Reginald said.

Evie's brows shot up. "Absolutely not!"

"It would be for the best. It's the only way to keep you safe."

"There's another way," Evie said, shaking her head.

"Which is?"

"We find Rutledge and the person who abducted him," Evie said. "Only then will I be truly safe."

"That is proving to be a very difficult task."

Evie eyed him curiously. "Did you discover anything about Rutledge at your meeting with the smuggler?"

"I did not," Reginald replied. "I was hired to transport crates from the wharf to another location."

"What's in the crates?"

Reginald shrugged. "I'm unsure at this point, but I intend to find out before I deliver them."

Evie opened her mouth to respond but promptly closed it when Mr. Wymond appeared by her side.

Mr. Wymond tipped his head. "Lord Haddington," he acknowledged before shifting his gaze towards Hawthorne. "Lord Hawthorne."

Reginald forced a smile to his lips. "Mr. Wymond."

"I am sorry for interrupting, but I came to ensure that Miss Ashmore was all right," Mr. Wymond said.

"As you can see for yourself, she is well," Reginald responded harshly. What was it about Mr. Wymond that he found to be so aggravating?

Mr. Wymond turned towards Evie, and his face softened. "I apologize. I will be in the carriage anxiously waiting for your return."

"I will be along shortly," Evie promised.

Mr. Wymond stared at her a moment longer than Reginald considered proper before he started walking back to the carriage.

Evie watched his retreating figure until he'd stepped out from the trees, then turned back towards Reginald.

"That was poorly done on your part," she remarked.

"What did I do?" Reginald asked.

"You could have been nicer," Evie replied.

"For what purpose?"

Evie rolled her eyes. "You're being impossible right now."

"Out of curiosity, how did you know we were here?" Reginald asked.

"I saw the light reflecting off the spyglass and came to investigate," Evie said. "That's when I heard you two arguing."

"Do you not have any regard for your safety, woman?" Reginald growled. "What if someone was trying to lure you into the woods to kill you?"

"Then I would have dealt with the attacker," Evie replied calmly. "I am not completely incapable of protecting myself."

Hawthorne stepped forward, putting himself between Reginald and Evie. "It's time for us to depart, and for you to return to Mr. Wymond. We shall retrieve you this afternoon so we may report our findings to Merritt."

"I look forward to it," Evie said as she lifted her chin and turned to leave.

Reginald kept an eye on Evie until she arrived safely at the carriage. Mr. Wymond offered his hand and assisted her into the vehicle, his hand lingering on hers too long for his liking.

Hawthorne's voice came from behind him. "The role of a jealous suitor is not a good look for you."

"I am not a jealous suitor," he grumbled.

"No?" Hawthorne asked. "Then what are you?"

"I already told you—I am her partner."

"Ah. Looks can be deceiving," Hawthorne said.

Reginald turned around and glared at him. "Why am I friends with you again?"

"That's easy," Hawthorne replied with a smirk. "I daresay that I am the only one who can tolerate you and your foolish behavior."

Reginald grunted as he brushed past him. He hated to admit it, but Hawthorne was right. He wasn't going to win Evie's affections by insulting her or acting jealous. But he refused to sit back and let Mr. Wymond swoop in and claim her heart. He would find a way to turn Evie's heart towards him.

Chapter Twelve

The carriage jostled back and forth, but the puppy didn't seem to mind as he lay on Evie's lap. She stroked his brown fur as she retreated to her own thoughts. She couldn't believe that Reginald had shown up at Hyde Park to spy on her! Of all the outlandish things he had done over the years, this one beat them all.

Mr. Wymond met her gaze and offered her a smile. "You are quiet," he said. "I do hope the reason is not me."

"Of course not," Evie rushed to assure him. "I was just thinking about Reginald and…" She stopped, not knowing what else to say about it. "It matters not. He is gone, and that is all that matters."

Mr. Wymond shifted uncomfortably in his seat. "I must pose the question—do you have an understanding with Lord Haddington?"

"No," she said firmly. "We are just friends."

"Yet he showed up at Hyde Park and spied on us from the woodlands?"

"He can be… eccentric."

Mr. Wymond didn't look convinced. "It's evident that he has feelings for you."

"You are mistaken," Evie said with a shake of her head. "Lord Haddington does not have feelings for me."

"I disagree."

"We've been friends since we were little, and we are comfortable around each other," she said. "That's all. Well, besides some terrible protective antics."

The puppy let out a whimper as it slept, causing her to lower her gaze.

Mr. Wymond adjusted the lapels of his jacket. "I care for you, Evie. I hope you know that."

Evie brought her gaze up and blinked. "I thank you for your honesty, but my position has not changed. I have no desire to marry."

"I am willing to wait until you change your mind."

"You would be sorely disappointed," she said. "Marriage is an institution that oppresses women."

"Not if you marry the right person," he argued. "I take it your parents did not have a loving union."

"On the contrary. They had a wonderful marriage, but it was taken away when they died in a carriage accident."

"I am sorry to hear that."

Tears pricked the back of Evie's eyes, but she blinked them away. No good would come from crying, especially not in front of Mr. Wymond.

Mr. Wymond leaned forward and offered his handkerchief. "I do not mean to dredge up bad memories."

"I only have fond memories of my parents, especially my father," Evie said as she wiped her eyes with the handkerchief. "He taught me the most unusual skills."

"Such as?"

"I can throw daggers, climb brick walls, and shoot a rifle," Evie replied.

"Those are odd pastimes for a genteel woman."

Evie nodded. "That's true, I'll admit. I adored every

moment my father spent with me, and I wanted to grow up to be just like him."

"Not like your mother?"

"My mother was much more reserved than my father," Evie said. "She radiated grace in every step, and had a smile that could break through anyone's defenses."

"She sounds like a wonderful woman."

Evie smiled. "She was," she replied. "I was lucky to have her."

Mr. Wymond grew reflective. "My mother was a good woman, as well. I know it took a great toll on my father when she passed on. It was as if a part of him died the same day she did."

"We both were fortunate to have parents who cherished one another," Evie said. "That is a rarity amongst the *ton*."

"I do not belong in the *ton*."

Evie laughed. "Neither do I, but here we are!"

Mr. Wymond sat back in his seat. "There is nothing more beautiful than the sound of your laugh."

"Flattery, Mr. Wymond?" Evie joked. "I did not think you would resort to such a thing."

"It is merely the truth."

Evie shook her head. "You don't want to court me, Mr. Wymond."

"And why is that?"

"I am not like most girls of the *ton*."

"Perhaps that is what I find most fascinating about you."

Evie tightened her hold on the handkerchief. "You want a proper wife, one who will be content with her role in your home and within Society."

"How do you know what I want?"

"It's what every man wants."

"You will find that I am not like most gentlemen," he said with a smirk, using her words against her. "Besides, I had no intention of looking for a wife until I met you."

Before she could reply, the carriage slowed to a stop in front of her townhouse. How had she not noticed they were so close to home? The puppy's head sprung up, and he started barking at the people on the pavement.

"Bandit!" Mr. Wymond exclaimed. "Stop barking!"

Evie extended Bandit to him and accepted the hand of the footman. Once she was on the pavement, she looked up at Mr. Wymond and said, "Thank you for a wonderful carriage ride."

He was moving to exit the coach. "Allow me to escort you to your townhouse."

"There is no need," she said, backing up unceremoniously. "Good day, Mr. Wymond."

Evie turned and approached the door, which Barnes promptly opened. As she stepped inside, she let out a sigh of relief. She didn't think she could have remained in Mr. Wymond's presence a moment longer. He was a charming man, but she could never give him what he desired of her, and trying to convince him of it had put her nerves on edge. Perhaps her heart would have been turned if she had never known Reginald.

She glanced down at the handkerchief she still held in her hand. She would need to wash it and return it to Mr. Wymond. To keep it might give him the wrong impression.

Her sister's laugh drifted out of the drawing room as she slipped the handkerchief into her pocket through the folds of her gown. She eagerly walked towards the room to find out what was so amusing. There, she found Aunt Nancy, Dinah, and Lady Grenton sitting in jovial conversation.

"Pray tell, what is so amusing?" Evie asked as she joined her sister on the settee.

Dinah shifted to face her. "Georgie was just telling us the most amusing story about Mrs. Hughes," she replied. "Apparently, she has been downright cordial to her since she arrived home from her wedding tour."

"It's true," Georgie said with a nod. "She even made me biscuits one afternoon."

"Were the biscuits poisoned?" Evie asked.

"That's what I first assumed, but I decided to eat them anyway," Georgie replied, "and I didn't die."

"That is a relief," Aunt Nancy said with a smile.

Georgie laughed. "I don't know what Evie said to Mrs. Hughes, but it's changed the way she treats me."

Evie's lips twitched. "I may have told her that you were considering firing her if she didn't change her ways."

"Well, it worked," Georgie said. "Thank you."

"It was my pleasure. I found Mrs. Hughes to be a delight," Evie responded.

Georgie gave her a look of disbelief. "A delight?"

"While I was tending the orphanage in your absence, Mrs. Hughes may have walked in on me sharpening my dagger," Evie confessed.

"So you didn't threaten her?" Dinah asked.

Evie shook her head. "Heavens, no!"

Her aunt leaned forward and retrieved her tea cup. "Poor Mrs. Hughes," she said. "She is no match for the two of you."

"I wouldn't feel too badly for her, because she was awful to me when I first became headmistress," Georgie stated.

"That she was," Evie agreed as she reached for her sister's cup of tea and took a sip.

Dinah gave her a chiding look. "Would you care for your own cup?"

"I just wanted a sip," Evie replied, returning the cup to the saucer.

"How did your carriage ride with Mr. Wymond go?" Aunt Nancy interjected.

"It went well," Evie said, not wanting to reveal too much. She didn't dare admit that Reginald and Nathaniel had shown up to spy on her.

"Should we start planning the wedding?" her aunt asked as she brought her teacup to her lips.

Evie should have assumed her aunt would have jumped straight to matrimony. "Mr. Wymond is a charming enough man, but I am not interested in marrying him—or anyone, for that matter."

"But you find Mr. Wymond charming?" Dinah pressed.

"I do," Evie admitted, seeing no reason to deny it.

Dinah smiled. "That is interesting."

"There is nothing interesting about it," Evie said. "I can think a man is charming without falling prey to the parson's mousetrap."

"I just don't believe I have ever heard you refer to a man as charming before," Dinah pointed out.

"I'm sure I have."

Dinah turned to Georgie. "What say you?" she asked.

Georgie put one of her gloved hands up. "I do not have an opinion on the matter."

"Thank you," Evie said. "At least one of you is being reasonable."

"But, if I did, I would ask what Lord Haddington thought about all of this," Georgie remarked.

Evie pressed her lips together, then asked, "Why should it matter what Lord Haddington thinks?"

Georgie gave a slight shrug. "I couldn't help but notice that you two appear rather close."

"That's because we've known each other since we were small," Evie asserted. "I assure you, there is nothing more to it."

"I believe you," Georgie said flippantly.

There was a lull in the conversation, and Evie reached for Dinah's teacup again. Her sister waved her hand off.

"Allow me to pour you your own cup," Dinah said, reaching for the teapot.

"Thank you," Evie murmured as she took a sip after her sister handed her a fresh cup.

"How is the orphanage?" Aunt Nancy asked Georgie.

"It is thriving," Georgie replied, her hands growing animated. "We are still looking for a new headmistress, but I thoroughly enjoy spending time with the girls."

"Do you have any trouble traveling to the rookeries?" her aunt asked.

"I do not, especially since William ensures I am well protected when I go there," Georgie shared. "He doesn't take any chances with my safety."

"I should say not," Dinah said.

Georgie shifted her gaze to Evie. "You haven't visited in a few days. The girls have been asking about you."

"I'm afraid I have been busy as of late, but I promise I will visit as soon as I am able to," Evie said.

"Wonderful," Georgie responded. "The girls are quite fond of you. Although I do wish you hadn't shown them how to climb the walls."

"You never should have left me in charge, then," Evie countered.

Georgie laughed, as she'd intended. "That was one of the best decisions I have ever made."

Reginald stayed in the coach and waited for Hawthorne to collect Evie so they could report their findings to Merritt. He'd spent the remainder of his day engrossed in the ledgers for his country estate. It was a tedious task, but he didn't mind it. The estate had been in his family for generations, and it was his duty to maintain it.

The townhouse door opened and Hawthorne escorted Evie down the steps. She was now wearing an alluring blue gown with a square neckline, and her hair was pulled back into a simple chignon. Evie's beauty always shone brightly, no matter what she wore.

A footman opened the coach door, and Evie sat across from Reginald, who slid over on the bench so Hawthorne could claim the seat next to him.

Once the door was closed, it was only a moment before the coach merged into traffic. Reginald noticed that Evie's back was rigid as she stared out the window with her hands clasped in her lap. This did not bode well for him. She was most likely still upset with him for following her to Hyde Park earlier.

Reginald decided that the silence had gone on long enough and said, "Good afternoon, Evie."

"Good afternoon," she replied, barely sparing him a glance.

"May I ask what occupied your time today?"

"My sister and Lady Grenton came to call," she informed him. "They only left a short time ago, and then I adjourned to the library."

Evie had answered his question cordially enough, but there was an underlying curtness to her words that he did not like.

Hawthorne spoke up. "What did you end up telling your aunt about last night?"

Evie's eyes dimmed, and Reginald could see the toll of her lies was great. "I didn't tell her much, and I know she's terribly disappointed in me."

Hawthorne gave her a compassionate look. "It's best that she doesn't know the truth."

"I agree, but it's hard to continuously lie to her," Evie said.

"It will get easier," Hawthorne encouraged.

Evie glanced down at her hands. "That's a sad thought."

They all seemed to retreat to their own thoughts after that. A short time later, the coach came to a creaking halt.

Hawthorne put his hand out through the window and opened the door, not bothering to wait for the footman. Reginald followed Hawthorne out onto the pavement before he turned back to assist Evie out of the coach.

"Allow me to escort you inside," Reginald said, offering his arm.

She looked hesitant, but placed her hand on his sleeve with a murmured, "Thank you."

As they started walking down the narrow pavement, he said, "Again, I must ask for your forgiveness for my behavior this morning."

Evie's gaze remained straight ahead. "You did what you thought was necessary to keep me safe."

"Yes, but I said some rather distasteful things."

"That you did," Evie agreed.

Reginald wished they weren't surrounded by people so he could have a frank conversation with her, rather than speaking vaguely with one another.

They turned the corner and Evie dropped her hand at the sight of Worsley and Talbot holding squirming puppies.

Evie hurried over to them. "What adorable puppies!" she gushed.

Talbot extended one towards her. "Would you care for one?" he asked.

"I would, but my aunt is not fond of them," Evie replied as she tenderly fondled the animal.

"You look like a gentleman that could benefit from a dog," Talbot said, turning to Reginald. "Would you care to purchase one for ten pounds?"

"Ten pounds?" Reginald repeated back. "That is an outlandish amount for a puppy!"

"We've already sold one," Worsley interjected.

"That man was a fool, then," Reginald stated.

"Perhaps, but he was a satisfied customer," Worsley responded.

Hawthorne glanced at the dog in Evie's arms. "Where did you get them?"

"Someone abandoned them in the alleyway, and we thought selling puppies would be more lucrative than selling stray cats," Talbot said.

Worsley nodded. "Cats have a mind of their own, which proved problematic."

"Did you sell any?" Reginald asked.

"Not one," Talbot replied, "but we have high hopes for our puppy business."

Hawthorne stepped forward and lowered his voice. "Your puppy business will have to wait. I have a job for you."

Talbot and Worsley sobered immediately.

"I need someone to guard Miss Ashmore for the next few days, and I thought you two could handle the assignment," Hawthorne said.

Worsley shifted the puppy in his hands and gave him a mock salute. "Consider it done."

"Don't lose her," Hawthorne warned.

Evie extended the puppy she held to Talbot, who accepted it. "Just for the record, I don't think I require anyone to guard me."

Hawthorne met her gaze. "We will continue this conversation inside." He walked over to the door and opened it.

Reginald followed Evie through the doorway. Mostyn was on guard, his hand behind the desk. He relaxed when he recognized them.

Evie smiled at the aged agent. "Good afternoon, Mostyn."

He returned her smile. "Good afternoon."

"Did your wife receive the flowers I sent?" she asked.

"She did, and it brightened her day," Mostyn said.

"That was the hope," Evie responded. "I do hope she is feeling better."

"I'm afraid the cough isn't getting much better," Mostyn

shared hesitantly, "and the apothecary is at a loss as to what we should do."

"Then I shall have to send over my doctor to examine her," Evie said.

"I do not wish to be a bother—" Mostyn started.

"It is no bother at all," Evie pressed.

Mostyn shifted. "This is the part where I swallow my pride and be grateful for your generous offer."

Evie laughed. "It would save us a considerable amount of time."

"Then I accept," Mostyn said.

"Wonderful," Evie responded. "I'll send the doctor over tomorrow."

"You are truly a godsend," Mostyn acknowledged appreciatively.

Evie tipped her head before she walked to the hall door. Reginald rushed over to open it and stood to the side as she entered the main hall. They skirted desks as they made their way back towards Merritt's office.

Hawthorne knocked on the door.

"Enter," Merritt ordered.

Hawthorne opened the door and allowed Evie to walk through first. Reginald was the last to enter and was mindful to close the door behind him.

Merritt's body was hunched over the desk as he reviewed the documents laid in front of him.

"Give me a moment," he growled.

Evie didn't appear perturbed by Merritt's gruff voice and sat on an upholstered chair that faced the desk.

Merritt finally looked up. "I hope you are here to tell me that you found Rutledge."

"We have not," Evie said.

"Pray tell, what have you been doing these past few days?" Merritt asked.

Evie tilted her chin. "We've been busy chasing down information."

"And does chasing down information mean taking leisurely carriage rides through Hyde Park with your suitor?" Merritt asked.

"Mr. Wymond is not my suitor," Evie said.

"My apologies," Merritt mocked, "but I am not paying you to enjoy the trappings of the Season."

Taking pity on Evie, Reginald spoke up. "We found where Rutledge was tortured, but he was gone before we arrived."

"You should have arrived sooner," Merritt muttered.

Hawthorne stepped forward. "Evie received a threat telling her to stop searching for Rutledge or be killed. When she confronted a man loitering outside her townhouse, he tried to shoot her."

Merritt's eyes shot to Evie. "Why did you confront the man?"

"I had little choice in the matter," Evie asked.

"Did you learn anything from him before you shot him?" Merritt asked.

Evie shook her head. "I was unable to do so, but Hawthorne was the one who shot him."

Merritt shifted his gaze to Hawthorne. "Please tell me that you did something that will aid in this assignment."

"I did," Hawthorne replied. "I paid off the magistrate to see the body and discovered a torn page from a book with a hidden message on it."

"What did it say?" Merritt asked.

"It just gave the address to Evie's townhouse, but that wasn't the interesting part," Hawthorne said. "We compared it to the first note and discovered that it was sent from the same sorting center."

"That is quite the coincidence," Merritt acknowledged.

"It is, and we feel that it's worth pursuing," Hawthorne stated.

"I concur." Merritt turned his attention towards Reginald. "How did your meeting go with the smuggler?"

"It went well, but I've found no connection between him and Rutledge's disappearance," Reginald revealed. "They're hiring a group of men from the rookeries to transport crates."

"I propose we turn that over to the magistrate and be done with it," Merritt said.

"I think that would be a mistake," Reginald responded.

Merritt lifted his brow. "Why is that, agent?"

"I believe I only dealt with a middleman," Reginald replied. "If constables are sent in, the person leading the whole business will be able to escape."

"We are not in the business of tracking down smugglers."

"I know, but I think something bigger is going on. I just need time to discover what is in those crates."

Merritt considered him for a moment. "Fair enough, but do not disappoint me." He gestured over the contents on his desk. "Every day, we have more threats against the Crown. We don't have time to dawdle with something a magistrate can handle."

"I understand," Reginald said.

Leaning back in his seat, Merritt shifted his gaze towards Evie. "What am I going to do with you, Agent A?" he asked. "I fear your cover has been blown and that you are in grave danger."

"This is nothing that I can't handle," Evie asserted.

Merritt didn't look convinced. "I think it might be best if you sit the rest of this assignment out."

"I think not!" Evie exclaimed. "I am more than capable of finding Rutledge. I just need more time."

"Time might not be something you have if someone is trying to kill you," Merritt said.

Evie rose from her seat. "I've had people want to kill me before, and that didn't distract me from my purpose."

Merritt made a clucking noise with his tongue. "I will give

you two more days to find Rutledge, but do not make me regret this, agent."

"I won't," Evie stated with relief in her voice.

"If you are anything like your father, as I suspect you are, you would have worked the assignment with or without my permission," Merritt said.

Hawthorne interrupted, "I did assign Worsley and Talbot to guard Evie for the next few days."

Merritt bobbed his head approvingly. "Very good. With any luck, that will end their pet selling business."

"It's better than some of the other ruses they've come up with for loitering outside this building," Hawthorne said.

"Agreed." Merritt picked up a piece of paper from a pile. "You are dismissed."

After they departed and were walking back towards their coach, Evie asked, "May I accompany you when you go to the sorting center for the Penny Post?"

Hawthorne smiled. "We assumed you would want to join us."

Chapter Thirteen

Evie exited the coach and stared up at the post office, a brown brick building on a corner next to a bakery.

Reginald offered his hand. "May I escort you inside?"

"You may," Evie replied as she placed her hand on his.

They walked inside of the building and waited in line until it was their turn to speak to the postmaster. Evie noted two men sorting through the mail along the back wall. A tall, rounded man stood behind a counter.

"How may I help you?"

His words were polite, but his tone was anything but. There were hard lines at the sides of his mouth, and his eyes were cold.

Nathaniel stepped forward and presented a letter. "I would like to post this."

"That'll be three pence," the postmaster said as he briefly glanced down at the letter.

As Nathaniel reached into his waistcoat pocket for the coins, he asked, "Is it possible for the letter to be delivered today?"

"Not if you send it by Penny Post," the postmaster

informed him. "I can guarantee it'll be delivered today for two pounds."

"Two pounds?" Nathaniel repeated. "That seems rather steep."

"Not for it to be personally delivered," the postmaster said. "I guess you'll have to decide how important this letter is."

Nathaniel extended him the coins. "I suppose the Penny Post will do."

The postmaster accepted the coins and deposited them into a metal box, then picked up a triangular stamp and marked the top of the letter. "Will that be all?" he asked as he put the letter in a bin behind him.

Reginald spoke up. "You must have seen some odd things being shipped here."

"I have," the postmaster said, eyeing him curiously. "Why do you ask?"

Reginald retrieved the torn-out book page from his pocket and showed it to the postmaster. "This was delivered to me, but I don't know who it was from."

"I'm afraid I can't help you with that," the postmaster said. "We just deliver the post."

"Is it every day that someone mails a torn-out page from a book?" Reginald pressed.

The postmaster put his hands up. "I don't care, nor do I ask," he replied. "What people want to mail is their business."

Reginald reached into his pocket and removed a guinea, which he slid across the counter. "Perhaps this might entice you to remember."

The postmaster snatched the money and tucked it into his jacket pocket. "What I can tell you is that I haven't seen that paper before."

"Could someone else have stamped it?" Reginald asked.

"No," the postmaster replied. "I am responsible for the stamp, and I take my position very seriously."

"What if you are unavailable for work?"

The postmaster scoffed. "If the sun is up, I am at work." He glanced over their shoulders. "You have taken enough of my time."

"One more question——" Reginald started.

"Next!" the postmaster exclaimed, cutting him off.

The person behind them cleared their throat loudly.

Evie had just taken a step back when she noticed a dark-haired young woman watching her from behind the counter. When their eyes met, the woman's eyes widened and she spun on her heel, disappearing through an opening along the back wall.

Reginald leaned close and asked, "What's troubling you?"

"I don't know," Evie replied. "Did you notice the woman's odd reaction when she saw me?"

"I did not."

"I need to get into the back room," Evie said.

Reginald gave her a look of disbelief. "Why?"

"I need to speak to that woman," Evie replied.

"For what purpose?"

Evie winced. "I can't say."

Reginald offered his arm. "Let us continue this conversation outside."

Once they were outside, Evie glanced towards the alley that ran adjacent to the building.

"I can sneak into the back room from the alley," she said.

Nathaniel followed her gaze. "What if you get caught?"

"You need not worry about that," Evie said, attempting to reassure him. "I have broken into buildings before."

"At night," Nathaniel pointed out. "You now intend to break in during broad daylight."

"Trust me," Evie said.

"What if the woman doesn't want to talk to you?" Nathaniel asked.

"Then no harm done," Evie replied as she started walking backwards towards the alley.

"You have ten minutes," Reginald said, "and then we'll come in after you."

"That should be enough time."

Evie glanced both ways before she stepped into the alley. She continued until she found the door that led into the post office. She removed some pins from her hair and crouched down. As she slid the pins into the locking mechanism, the door opened, and she fell to the ground.

The dark-haired woman gasped. "I am truly sorry," she said as she helped her up. "I heard a noise and came outside to investigate."

Evie accepted her hand and rose, then dusted off her gown. "I'm glad you did, because I was hoping to speak to you."

The woman's face became guarded. "What would you wish to speak to me about?"

"I couldn't help but notice your reaction when you saw me."

A relieved smile came to the woman's face. "That's easy enough to explain," she said. "I used to work at a milliner shop that you frequented, and I was surprised to see you in the post office."

"Why did you leave the milliner shop?"

The smile on her face dimmed. "My father thought it wasn't a good fit for me and asked me to help out here."

"Forgive me, but you don't seem pleased by that."

"I'm not." The woman held up her hands, showing blackened fingertips. "I'm tired of trying to scrub ink off my fingers every night."

Evie took a moment to study the woman. They were of similar age, but the young woman had dark brown hair, almost black. She had a small, fading bruise on her cheek, which she'd tried to cover with rouge.

"If you are so miserable, why do you not go back to the milliner shop?" Evie pressed.

The young woman blew out a puff of air. "I wish, but no one dares tell my father no."

"Is that how you got the bruise?"

Her hand flew up to her cheek. "He was drunk, and I should have never bothered him. I knew better."

"No man should ever hit a woman."

"That's wishful thinking," the young woman murmured as she lowered her hand.

Evie glanced at the entrance to the alley. Her time was short, and she still had questions.

"May I ask you something?" Evie asked.

The young woman looked at her blankly. "What would you like to know?"

"Have you noticed anyone disreputable coming into the post office as of late?"

"No, I haven't," the young woman replied with a shake of her head.

"What about letters that have been sorted here, have any of them seemed odd to you?"

"Odd, how?"

Evie debated how much she should reveal. She wasn't entirely sure she could trust this woman, so she decided to ask another question. "Does your father carry the postage paid stamp around with him everywhere he goes?"

"Oh, yes," the young woman said. "He would be in big trouble if he ever lost it."

"What if someone borrowed it?"

The woman furrowed her brow. "Why would he allow anyone to borrow it?" she asked. "He would be fired if he did such a thing."

"I suppose you're right," Evie said. "I'm sorry to waste your time."

"Freya!" someone shouted from within the post office.

The woman tensed. "I better go," she said, fear evident in her voice. "Father doesn't like to be kept waiting."

"Thank you, Freya."

She gave Evie the briefest of smiles. "I'm afraid I wasn't much help to you."

"But I thank you for your time, nonetheless."

The door slammed open, and the postmaster narrowed his eyes when he saw Evie.

"What are you doing here?" He glanced between them. "And why are you talking to my daughter?"

Evie opened her mouth to explain, but Freya spoke first. "She recognized me from my previous employment and asked about me designing a hat for her."

The postmaster waved his hand dismissively at Evie. "Be off with you," he said. "My daughter doesn't cater to you folk anymore."

Freya gave Evie an apologetic look. "I wish you luck finding someone to design that hat for you."

Evie took a step back. "I didn't mean to cause any problems."

The postmaster huffed. "You're all the same," he said. "You just assume that everyone will drop everything for you and your whims."

"Father," Freya said. "You said your peace, and now you should let her leave."

"You need to mind your tongue, girl."

Reginald's voice came from the end of the alley. "Is there a problem here?" he asked as he stepped further into the alley.

"Yes, your lady is bothering my daughter," the postmaster growled. "I want her gone, and I never want to see either of you at my sorting center again."

Reginald placed a hand on Evie's sleeve. "Come along, my dear," he encouraged. "Let us seek out friendlier sky."

Evie allowed Reginald to escort her out of the alley,

keeping a wary eye on the postmaster. They didn't speak until they joined Nathaniel in the coach.

"I didn't like the postmaster," Evie commented.

Reginald nodded in agreement. "Neither did I, but that doesn't mean he's behind the messages we found on the dead men," he said. "Were you able to get his daughter to reveal anything?"

"Unfortunately, no," Evie replied, "but it's evident that she is afraid of him."

Nathaniel opened the drapes to let air circulate around the coach. "It might be best if we have an agent follow the postmaster to see if he is associating with any disreputable people."

"I agree," Reginald said.

Evie sat back against the bench, feeling slightly defeated. "We didn't find anything that would help us discover Rutledge's whereabouts."

"We will," Nathaniel encouraged. "We just haven't asked the right question yet."

Evie turned towards the window and released a sigh. When were they going to get the break in the case they so desperately needed?

The moon hung low in the sky as Reginald exited his coach and approached the main door of his townhouse. The door opened, and his butler stood to the side to allow him entry. Once he stepped into the entry hall, he removed his black top hat and extended it to the butler.

He realized that he had made a tactical error by coming through the main door when he heard Lady Calthorpe's voice drifting out of the drawing room. He wanted to be far away, but before he could take his first step, his mother stepped out of the drawing room.

"You missed dinner with Lady Calthorpe and Lady Agnes," she said as she approached him, keeping her voice low.

"I assure you that it couldn't be helped."

"I do hope Lady Agnes does not take offense to your objectionable behavior."

"I do not see why, since we have no understanding between us."

"You are impossible, son," his mother said. "A marriage between you and Lady Agnes would be most advantageous. You would be the envy of the *ton*."

That was the last thing Reginald wanted to be. He played the role of a dandy to remain disregarded in the eyes of the *ton*. He didn't want to be scrutinized on every outing or conversation.

Reginald leaned in and kissed his mother's cheek. "I have work I need to see to."

"Will you not at least come say hello to Lady Agnes?"

"For what purpose?" he asked.

"To be the polite, courteous man I raised you to be."

He stifled a groan. He didn't want to spend his evening with Lady Agnes, pretending they had something in common.

"I will come say hello," Reginald said with a pointed look, "but then I must adjourn to my study for the evening."

A victorious smile spread across his mother's lips. "Wonderful."

As they walked the short distance to the drawing room, Reginald knew that he had yet again been outplayed by his mother. He'd always had a soft spot for her, but he refused to marry the woman of her choosing.

There was only one woman he would ever consider marrying. He'd given her his heart a long time ago—and had never gotten it back.

Reginald stepped into the drawing room and forced a smile.

"Lord Haddington," Lady Agnes greeted with a sheepish smile, "I hadn't expected to see you this evening."

"I do apologize for missing dinner, but I'm afraid it couldn't be helped," he responded. "I do hope you enjoyed it."

"Oh, yes," Lady Agnes said.

"You are fortunate to have such a divine cook," Lady Calthorpe added.

"That we are," Reginald agreed.

His mother sat across from Lady Calthorpe and her daughter. "I was able to steal him right from under Lord Wentworth's nose," she said.

"That is terrible of you," Lady Calthorpe chided lightly.

"Life is far too short to have a mediocre cook."

Lady Calthorpe bobbed her head, drawing Reginald's attention to the loose skin under her chin. "I wholeheartedly agree, which is why we employ a French cook," she said. "Monsieur Andre has even been gracious enough to teach Agnes how to make a few dishes."

Reginald couldn't help but notice that a blush colored Agnes's cheeks at the mention of Monsieur Andre. How interesting.

Lady Calthorpe continued. "Furthermore, it gives Agnes an opportunity to practice her French. They spend hours in the gardens each day, cultivating the language and learning from one another."

Agnes's blush deepened. "We don't spend hours in the gardens, Mother," she said.

"Perhaps I exaggerate, but I think it is a fine thing you have taken such an interest in the French language," Lady Calthorpe said. "You hardly spoke a word before Monsieur Andre arrived."

Reginald found it fascinating that people tended to see

what they wanted to see. It was evident that Agnes held affection for Monsieur Andre, and he knew that wouldn't end well for anyone involved.

He glanced at his mother to see if she had come to the same conclusion he had, but she gave no outward sign that she did. Instead, she was smiling fondly at Agnes.

Reginald clasped his hands together and announced, "I do apologize, but I have work that I must see to."

His mother shifted towards him. "Before you go, would you mind showing Lady Agnes the garden?" she asked. "It is perfectly enchanting in the evening."

He opened his mouth to object when Lady Agnes spoke first. "I would love to see the garden, my lord."

Reginald had been backed into a corner. If he refused, he would look petty and rude.

"It would be my honor," he said, tripping over his words.

Lady Agnes rose and approached him. Reginald offered his arm and led her towards the rear of the townhouse. A footman opened the door and then followed them outside.

They left the veranda and started walking down one of the paths. Reginald attempted to think of something to say, but he was at a loss for words. He hardly knew Agnes, and what he did know, he wasn't exactly fond of.

Agnes dropped her arm and moved to create more distance between them. "I know you do not wish to marry me, my lord."

"I'm sorry—"

"You misunderstand me," she rushed out. "I don't wish to marry you, either."

"No?" Reginald asked, wondering if this was a ploy to try to win his heart.

Agnes kept her gaze straight ahead of her. "My mother told me from a young age that I was to marry you, and I always accepted that. I knew what was expected of me."

"May I ask what changed your opinion?"

"Not what, but whom," Agnes said.

Reginald gave her a knowing look. "I must assume you are speaking of Monsieur Andre."

Agnes's mouth dropped, but she quickly recovered. "Was it so obvious?"

"Only to someone intuitive," Reginald replied. "But you do realize the scandal that would erupt if the *ton* received word that you have fallen for a French cook?"

"I do hope for your discretion on the matter."

"You need not worry in that regard," Reginald said. "Your secret is safe with me."

Agnes glanced at him with a furrowed brow.

"Why did you object to marrying me?" she asked. "Did I say or do something that offended you?"

"You did nothing wrong," Reginald said, shaking his head. "Like you, someone else has my heart."

"Does she know that she holds something so precious?"

"I'm afraid not," he replied.

Agnes stopped on the path and turned to face him. "You need to tell her."

"It isn't that simple."

"It can be."

Reginald ran a hand through his hair. "It's rather complicated."

A smile came to her lips. "More complicated than the daughter of an earl falling in love with a French cook?"

"When you put it that way…"

"I am not an expert on love, mind you, but I do believe this life is too short to not be with the person you love."

"Even if it causes a scandal?"

"Yes, even then," Agnes replied. "I know what I am willing to give up to follow my heart, but do you?"

Reginald grew silent. He would give up everything he possessed if it meant he could win Evie's affections. But would that be enough for her?

Agnes glanced back at the townhouse. "We should head back, or else our mothers might start planning our wedding."

He chuckled. "Mine started planning years ago."

"Then I suppose that is something they have in common," Agnes said.

"How do you think your parents will take the news about you and Monsieur Andre?" Reginald asked as they started walking back.

"Oh, they'll be furious," Agnes replied. "I have no doubt they'll disown me, but that means very little to me."

"Truly?"

"I know you must think me heartless, but I hardly see my parents," Agnes revealed. "My father is always with his mistress, and my mother hides away in her room, feigning headaches."

"I'm sorry to hear that."

"Don't feel sorry for me. My plight is no different than most children of peers."

Agnes had a point. "What will you live on?" he asked.

"I intend to use the funds that you will pay me when you break the betrothal contract," Agnes said. "That should be more than enough money to help establish us."

They arrived back at the veranda and the footman opened the door. After they entered the townhouse, Agnes lowered her voice.

"I thought you should know that our mothers devised a plan for me to compromise you in the gardens."

Reginald's steps faltered and he turned to face her.

"I beg your pardon?" he asked harshly.

Agnes stopped next to him.

"Don't worry, I never intended to go along with it," she said. "They just assumed I would be weak-minded enough to do so."

"I cannot believe my mother would do something so underhanded."

"You may not, but I do," Agnes replied. "Quite frankly, your mother frightens me at times."

"I admit that she can be rather intimidating."

Agnes laughed—snorted, really, which he found rather amusing.

"Your mother has this look that I am confident would turn someone into stone."

"She has perfected the art of the hardened glare."

"That she has."

Reginald offered his arm. "Shall I escort you back to the drawing room, where I have no doubt we will find two very disappointed mothers?"

Agnes accepted his arm. "You may, my lord."

They walked down the polished marble floor until they arrived at the drawing room. As they stepped into the room, Lady Calthorpe and Reginald's mother perked up.

Lady Calthorpe looked expectantly at her daughter. "How did the tour of the gardens go?"

"Very well," Agnes replied, removing her arm from Reginald's. "We both are in agreement that we should end the betrothal."

Lady Calthorpe let out an unladylike groan. "But what about our plans?"

Reginald's mother jumped up from her seat.

"Let's not be too hasty," she said. "You two just need to spend more time together."

"I think not, Mother," Reginald responded. "We have both come to the same conclusion: that we do not suit."

"No one suits in this madcap world!" his mother exclaimed, tossing her hand up.

Reginald frowned. "May I ask why this marriage is so important to you?"

She returned to her seat. "Marjorie and I have been planning your wedding since we were little girls," she said. "It was our hope that we would unite our families through marriage."

"It was a valiant effort, but it was in vain," Reginald responded.

Agnes caught his eye before saying, "Lord Haddington and I decided it would be best if we parted ways as friends."

Lady Calthorpe rose and approached her daughter.

"Come along, you inane girl," she said. "We will discuss this travesty with your father."

After they had departed from the study, Reginald turned his attention towards his mother and asked, "Did you truly ask Lady Agnes to entrap me?"

A flurry of emotions crossed her face, until her features settled on a guilty expression. "I did, but I did it for your benefit."

"My benefit?" he asked in disbelief.

"She would make a fine bride for you, but you are too closeminded to see that."

Reginald sat beside his mother on the settee. "I saw her in a whole new light this evening, but that doesn't mean we would suit."

His mother leaned back. "Pray tell, what did you take issue with?" she asked. "Is her dowry not large enough? Is she not beautiful enough?"

"None of those things," Reginald replied. "Any man would be lucky to have Lady Agnes as a bride—other than me."

His mother grew silent for a long moment.

"This is about Evie, isn't it?" she asked curtly.

"It is."

"She would make a terrible marchioness."

"I disagree."

"You have made me develop a headache, and I need to go lay down," his mother said, rising and putting a hand to her forehead.

Reginald stood as well. "Would you care for me to escort you to your room?"

"No, you have done enough for me this evening."

His mother walked over to the door and stopped. "Why Evie, son?"

"Because it has always been her."

His mother gave him a scathing look. "You are a fool, much like your father was," she said before she departed.

Reginald dropped down onto the settee and sighed. This is not how he planned his evening would go.

Chapter Fourteen

Evie watched out the drawing room window as Talbot and Worsley guarded her townhouse. They had set up a table and were performing card tricks for the people passing by. She knew they were competent agents, even though they had some questionable tactics when they performed their jobs. But that didn't mean she was going to sit around as they stood sentry. No; she needed to find Rutledge, and she was done waiting for someone to tell them where he was.

Her aunt stepped into the drawing room and joined her at the window. "Are those two still out there?"

"They are."

"I'm surprised the magistrate hasn't removed them from the pavement yet."

"They're doing no harm," Evie defended.

"It's unseemly for them to be in this section of Town," Aunt Nancy said with a shake of her head. "It's evident they do not belong here."

"I don't mind them."

"Regardless, it is only a matter of time before they are told to move along," her aunt said, pushing the drape to the side.

"Most likely," Evie agreed. "Until then, they will continue to delight our neighbors with their card tricks."

Her aunt walked over to the settee and sat down. "Dare I ask what you have planned for the day?"

"I do not have any plans at the moment," Evie replied.

"That doesn't sound like you," her aunt said. "Are you well?"

"I am."

A maid stepped into the room with a tea tray, which she set on a table next to her aunt.

"Would you care for me to pour, Mrs. Carter?" the maid asked.

"That won't be necessary," her aunt replied.

The maid dropped into a curtsy and departed.

Aunt Nancy leaned forward and picked up the teapot. "Would you care for a cup of tea?"

"No, thank you," Evie replied.

Her aunt poured herself some tea, then settled back on the settee with her cup. "I did receive something that will be of interest to you."

Evie left the window and sat across from her aunt. "What would that be?"

"Your cousin sent word that Lord Strathmore visited him and asked for his permission to offer for you."

"What did he say?" Evie asked.

"He granted permission, of course, and is hoping you will accept," Aunt Nancy revealed. "He feels that this would be an auspicious marriage for you."

"I have no intention of ever marrying Lord Strathmore."

"I assumed you would say that, but you must be careful not to offend Lord Gladstone. After all, we are living off his good graces by remaining at his townhouse."

"This is my home."

"No, it became your cousin's home after your father died,"

her aunt corrected. "He is just allowing us to live here during the Season."

"That's because he would rather live with his mistress across Town."

"It doesn't matter the reason," her aunt said. "We don't want to give Lord Gladstone any reason to suddenly take note of us."

"I shall buy my own townhouse."

"You certainly have the funds to do so, but it's expensive to maintain a household," her aunt said before taking a sip.

Evie frowned. "You don't think I should accept Lord Strathmore's proposal, do you?"

"Heavens, no!" her aunt answered. "That would be a terrible union."

She breathed a sigh of relief. "I am happy that we are in agreement, then."

Aunt Nancy leaned forward and put her teacup down. "Now, if only there was an eligible lord that you could marry…" her voice trailed off as Barnes stepped into the room.

"Lord Strathmore has come to call for Miss Ashmore," he announced. "Are you available for callers?"

"No," Evie said. "Please send him on his way."

"Wait," Aunt Nancy ordered. "Send him in."

As Barnes went to do so, Evie muttered, "Speak of the devil and he shall appear."

Her aunt shot her a look. "You will behave," she said firmly.

There was no use in arguing, especially now the man was approaching. It was too late to do anything about it. Luckily, Evie always had a pistol concealed in the folds of her gown. That might come in handy if Lord Strathmore dared to become too familiar.

Lord Strathmore stepped into the room and his eyes lit up when he saw Evie. "Miss Ashmore," he greeted.

Evie tipped her head. "Lord Strathmore."

Lord Strathmore turned towards her aunt. "Mrs. Carter."

Her aunt smiled. "Would you care for some tea?"

"I would love some."

Evie pursed her lips together. Drat. That meant Lord Strathmore intended to stay for a time.

As her aunt poured a cup for their guest, Lord Strathmore sat on an upholstered armchair near Evie. A tangy lemon scent filled the room, and she wondered if he had bathed in it to achieve that kind of saturation.

Lord Strathmore accepted the cup from her aunt and leaned back in his chair. "I do not mean to be crass, but I am hoping your rash has abated."

"Unfortunately not," Evie replied, feigning disappointment. "The doctor believes I will have episodes for the rest of my life."

Lord Strathmore gave her a puzzled look. "Did you not contract it when you came in contact with baneberry?"

"I did, but the infection has since spread internally and attached itself to the bone."

"Is that even possible?"

Evie pouted. "The doctor said I might lose one of my arms, possibly both."

Lord Strathmore's brow shot up. "You might lose your arms?"

"Sadly, yes," she replied. "But at least I will still have use of my legs."

His eyes darted to her arms. "Pardon me for saying so, but I do not see a rash."

"That's because it comes and goes," Evie said. "One day it's red and oozing, and the next it's gone."

"I'm not sure that's how rashes work," Lord Strathmore remarked.

Aunt Nancy cast her eyes heavenward. "You must excuse my niece, but she is just having some fun at your expense."

Lord Strathmore glanced between them before he let out a bark of laugher. "How amusing," he said. "I should have known you were teasing me."

Evie put a smile on her face. "I hope you did not take offense, my lord."

"Of course not," Lord Strathmore responded. "I find you to be a delight, and I know that my children will feel the same."

"How old are your children?" Aunt Nancy asked.

Lord Strathmore scrunched his brow together as if he were sorting out a puzzle. "My son is two months old, but my daughter is…" He paused. "I do believe she is three."

"Three is a fine age," her aunt remarked.

"I suppose it is," Lord Strathmore said.

Evie worked hard to keep the smile on her face. She was not impressed by the man's difficulty recalling his daughter's age.

Lord Strathmore leaned forward and put his cup down. "I'm glad you are interested in my children, Mrs. Carter, because they are in desperate need of a mother," he said. "As you both know, my wife died two months ago during childbirth."

"You have my condolences," her aunt murmured.

"Thank you," Lord Strathmore said. "It was a tough blow when Phoebe died, but I have decided that I have grieved her enough. It is time that I move forward."

Evie's smile faltered. She hadn't thought it was possible to have a lower opinion of Lord Strathmore than she already did, but he'd proved her wrong. How could he be so indifferent about the mother of his children?

Lord Strathmore reached into his pocket and removed a gold band. He held it up and met Evie's gaze. "I was hoping you would do me the grand honor of becoming my wife."

Evie was at a loss for words, even though she had expected

his offer. She hadn't imagined he would propose marriage while having tea with her aunt.

Lord Strathmore mistook her silence as permission to press forward with his suit. "You have had nine seasons, so I know you are not naïve enough to believe this would be a love match. What say you?"

"No." It was the only thing she could say.

Lord Strathmore gave her a baffled look. "You reject my offer?"

"I do," Evie replied.

He stared at her for a moment before asking, "You would rather remain a spinster than marry me?"

Evie opened her mouth to respond but Lord Strathmore spoke first. "If you are hoping for a loftier title, than I daresay you will be disappointed."

"I do not care about a title—"

Lord Strathmore huffed. "You would be most fortunate to marry me, because I am willing to overlook your eccentric behavior."

"Lord Strathmore—"

He abruptly rose. "You are beautiful, there is no denying that, but I do not want a foolish woman as my wife."

Reginald's commanding voice came from the doorway. "I think it is time for you to leave," he ordered.

Lord Strathmore's eyes remained on Evie. "I agree. There is no reason for me to tarry here." He bowed. "Good day."

Evie watched as he walked towards the door and brushed past Reginald. The main door opened and slammed shut before she breathed a sigh of relief. He was gone! With any luck, she would never have to see Lord Strathmore again.

Reginald stepped further into the room. "I do apologize for not letting my presence be known earlier, but I thought it wouldn't be prudent, given the circumstance."

Aunt Nancy nodded. "You would be correct."

"Ignore what Lord Strathmore said," Reginald told Evie. "He was wrong to take his anger out on you."

"He wasn't entirely wrong," Evie said. "I would rather remain a spinster than marry him."

Reginald sat down next to her. "I think that is wise. Lord Strathmore wasn't truly looking for a wife. He was looking for a mother for his children."

"I know." Evie didn't want to spend another moment thinking about that odious man, so she said, "May I ask what brings you by today?"

"Nothing but the pleasure of your company," Reginald responded with a boyish grin.

Evie's heart raced, but she kept her expression flat. "I think not."

"I was hoping to speak to you privately for a few moments," he said, glancing at her aunt.

Aunt Nancy rose. "I will allow it, but choose your words wisely. I will return in a few moments."

After she'd left the drawing room, Reginald lowered his voice. "I want to ask a favor."

Now he had her full attention. "Anything."

"You don't know what I'm going to ask."

"I assume it will be dangerous."

Reginald nodded. "You assume correctly."

"Then I am more than happy to help."

Reginald attempted to ignore the cold wind coming off the River Thames as he walked towards the wharf. His threadbare clothing did little to keep out the elements.

Boothe was standing guard by the door. As Reginald approached, he gave him a scathing look. "Oh good, you've returned," he mocked.

Unperturbed by his lackluster greeting, Reginald said, "I have." He wasn't quite sure what he'd done to earn the guard's ire, but he found it rather humorous.

Boothe moved to open the door. "Just get inside before anyone sees you," he ordered.

Reginald stepped inside and saw other men standing near six wagons loaded with crates. Smith was standing to one side, bearing dark circles under eyes that didn't seem to want to stay open.

When Reginald approached, he grumbled, "Do be wise and never have children."

"I can see that it doesn't agree with you."

"My wife was up all night with the babe, and it wouldn't stop crying," Smith revealed with a yawn. "I tried to sleep with a pillow over my head to mask the noise, but it did no good."

Towle approached them all with papers in his hand. He came to a stop and let his eyes roam over the ragged group.

"Good evening, men," Towle greeted. "Your assignment is easy enough. Deliver the crates, and you will be rewarded. If you fail at this simple task, then you will be killed." He paused. "Do we understand one another?"

The group of men all murmured their understanding.

"Good." Towle held up the papers. "Each pair will be given an address. I want you to engrave it into your brain, because any misstep will be your last."

Towle continued. "Once you arrive at your assigned location, you will leave the wagon and walk away, never to speak of this assignment again."

"Or it could be your last," Smith muttered under his breath.

Towle's eyes narrowed. "Do you think this is a game?" he growled.

Smith shook his head. "No, sir."

Towle walked closer to Smith and said, "If you do not

understand the seriousness of this job, then you are welcome to step aside."

"My apologies," Smith said as he lowered his gaze.

Towle stood there for a moment before he turned back towards the group. "Someone will be waiting for you to make your delivery. This person will also make sure you get what is owed to you." He gestured towards one of the crates. "Each crate is locked. If you try to tamper with the lock, we will know."

A man stepped forward and asked, "What kind of weapons are we transporting?"

"You do not need to concern yourself with the contents of the crates," Towle replied dismissively.

"I do if I don't want to get transported," the man pressed.

Towle pulled a pistol out of the waistband of his trousers and brandished it. "I would be more concerned about leaving this wharf alive," he said. "I'm afraid it is too late to withdraw from this job and keep your life."

Fear flashed in the man's eyes, and he tipped his head. "Understood, sir."

"Are there any other reservations that I should know of?" Towle asked, scanning the group. When no one said anything, he pressed forward. "Good. Now, on to your assignments."

Towle glanced down at the papers in his hand and shouted, "Daventry."

Reginald put his hand up. "Here, sir."

Towle came closer and asked, "Who is your partner?"

"Smith," Reginald replied as he gestured towards his friend.

"Ah, the jokester," Towle said, unimpressed. "Well, let's see if you can complete this assignment without getting yourselves killed."

"We'll do our best," Reginald responded.

Towle leaned closer and said in a hushed voice, "You will

report to the alleyway near 26 Garrett Road. A man will meet you there."

"Does this man have a name?" Reginald asked.

"He does, but you don't need to know it." Towle motioned towards a wagon. "Take that one and go."

Reginald stepped up on the wagon and reached for the leads. Smith sat next to him on the bench, and he flicked the reins, directing the team out of the building.

Once they were on the road, Smith turned towards him and asked, "Do you know where 26 Garrett Road is?"

"I do," Reginald replied. "It shouldn't take too long to arrive, but I dread visiting it at night."

"Why is that?"

"It's a lawless part of town."

Smith smirked. "You just described the rookeries."

"It's different," Reginald said. "I hope yer carrying a pistol."

"I am."

"Good, we might need it." Reginald extended Smith the reins. "I need you to drive while I check something out."

Smith accepted the reins and gave him a quizzical look. "What are you about?"

"I want to see what's in those crates."

"Are you mad?"

Reginald gave him a pointed look. "Do you honestly think we should deliver these crates without knowing what we got ourselves involved in?"

"But Towle said they'll know if we tamper with the lock."

"Don't fear," Reginald said as he crawled into the back. "I promise no one will ever know."

Reginald crouched down next to one of the crates and grasped the metal lock on it. He removed lock picks from the pocket of his jacket and slipped them into the mechanism, twisting one until he heard a distinctive click.

He tugged down on the lock and smiled when it opened.

He returned the picks to his pocket and removed the lock, then opened the crate.

Smith glanced over his shoulder. "What's in the crate?"

"Pikes," Reginald replied.

"What do you think they are for?" Smith asked.

Reginald put the lid back down. "Whatever it is, it can't be good," he said as he slipped the lock back into place.

"Is your curiosity quelled now?" Smith asked as he returned to his seat.

"It is, but I have a sneaking suspicion we need to be on our guard when we deliver this."

"You worry too much," Smith said. "We just deliver the crate and get paid. Then I can go drink away my woes."

Reginald gestured towards the street. "Turn here," he advised, "and do not slow down."

As they rolled down the road, Reginald's eyes roamed over the darkened buildings. Rough-looking men loitered outside, appearing much too eager to start a fight.

They passed 26 Garrett Road, and Smith turned into the alleyway adjacent to it. He pulled back on the reins and asked, "What now?"

"We wait," Reginald replied.

"For what?"

Reginald stepped down from the wagon and pulled his pistol from his waistband. He wasn't sure what to expect, but he wasn't about to be unprepared.

Some time later a door creaked open, letting out a triangle of light from within, and a stocky, blond man stepped into the alleyway. He wordlessly walked up to the wagon and hopped in the back. He tugged on the locks, seeming satisfied when they didn't budge.

The man jumped down from the wagon. "You did good," he said.

Smith climbed down as well. "Do we get paid now?"

"You definitely deserve what's coming to you." The man

approached Smith as he reached into his pocket. Before Reginald could even raise his pistol, the man pulled out a dagger and stabbed Smith in the side. Reginald watched helplessly as he fell to the ground.

"Why did you kill him?" he asked as he raised his weapon.

The man appeared unconcerned at having a gun pointed at him. "No one can be a witness to what is about to happen."

"Which is?"

"You must think me foolish if you think I am willing to reveal our plans."

The man whistled. A door opened promptly and another man stepped into the alleyway; only, this man was bigger in stature than the first, and a scar ran down the length of his right cheek. He pointed a pistol at Reginald.

The blond man smirked. "It appears you've lost." He held his hand out for Reginald's pistol. "I'll take that."

"I still have one shot."

"But there are two of us," the blond man said, "and my friend is an excellent shot."

Reginald needed to keep them talking, or else he would lose out on this rare opportunity to garner more information. "Since you're going to kill me anyways, you may as well tell me what the weapons are for."

The blond man hesitated, then shrugged and said, "We're going to start an insurrection."

"For what purpose?"

"Where do I begin?" the man asked. "The monarchy doesn't care about us. We have no jobs, no food, and are living in squalor. It's time the people rise up and get what's rightfully ours."

"Which is?"

"Freedom from oppression. Our king is mad, and the Prince Regent is no better than his father. We're stuck in the same vicious cycle, and there is only one way to end it—fight."

"You and what army?" Reginald asked.

The blond man put his hand on the wagon. "You don't need to worry about it, 'cause you'll be dead."

The other man spoke up. "Lower your pistol."

"I think not," Reginald said. "This pistol is the only thing keeping me alive right now."

A gunshot rang through the alleyway, and the man with the scar dropped, his pistol clattering onto the cobblestones. Reginald glanced up and saw Evie step further into the alleyway.

The blond man shouted as he charged towards Reginald, dagger raised. Reginald pulled the trigger, and the man stopped, dropping to his knees with a surprised look on his face.

Reginald lowered his smoking pistol and asked, "When is this insurrection supposed to happen?"

The blond man grinned. "You can't stop it; no one can," he said before he toppled onto the ground.

Evie stopped next to Reginald. "I waited as long as I could," she said as her eyes drifted towards the man with the scar.

"I know." Reginald crouched by the blond man. He searched through his pockets, but found nothing of worth in them.

Reginald reached for Evie's hand. "Come; we need to get out of here before people come to investigate the shootings."

Reginald helped Evie onto the wagon before sitting next to her. He reached for the reins and urged the horses forward. They didn't speak until they had driven a few blocks and he was sure no one was following them.

"Thank you for what you did back there," Reginald said.

"It was only fair; you've saved my life on more than one occasion."

"That has always been my pleasure."

Evie glanced over her shoulder. "What's in the crates?"

"Pikes," Reginald replied. "Someone intends to use them to start an insurrection."

"Do you know who?"

"I don't," Reginald replied. "That man wasn't exactly forthcoming with his information."

"What do you know?"

Reginald let out a frustrated sigh. "I'm afraid very little."

Evie placed a hand on his sleeve. "We can figure this out together—assuming you will continue to allow me to help you."

"I don't know if that's such a good idea," Reginald said. "It might be dangerous."

"I hope it is."

Reginald frowned. "Be serious, Evie," he said.

"I am," she replied. "When will you see that I'm capable of so much more than you give me credit for?"

"I know what you're capable of, but..." His voice trailed off. How did he tell her that he couldn't risk the chance of losing her? He wouldn't be able to live with himself if something happened to her.

"But, what?" she prodded.

Reginald turned his attention towards the street. "We need to get you home before your absence is noticed."

"I'm not concerned," Evie said with a wave of her hand. "Everyone was asleep before I snuck out."

"Out of curiosity, how did you sneak past Talbot and Worsley?"

Evie smiled. "I didn't," she replied, pointing into the shadows. "They did a good job of following me."

"Perhaps they aren't as incompetent as they appear."

"No, they most assuredly are not."

Chapter Fifteen

Merritt paced in his small office, setting Evie's nerves on edge. How long would she have to watch him walk back and forth before he finally said something?

She glanced over at Reginald and gave him a weak smile. He gave her a reassuring look before turning back to watch Merritt. She marveled at how, with a word, a glance, he could calm her soul, making her feel like everything would be made all right in the world.

Merritt stopped pacing and gripped the back of his chair. As he leaned in, he said, "Perhaps I made a mistake in partnering you two together."

"Pardon?" Evie asked. She hadn't expected that.

Merritt sighed. "I fear you two might be too distracted with one another to be working the case as diligently as I would expect of my agents."

"Sir, if I may," Reginald said. "We have not shirked our responsibility."

"No?" Merritt asked. "Then why haven't you found Rutledge yet?"

"We're trying!" Evie exclaimed.

"Not hard enough," Merritt muttered.

"That isn't fair of you to say," Evie said.

Merritt pushed off the chair. "I expect the unattainable from my agents, and you don't have time for messing about."

Evie opened her mouth to argue, but Reginald spoke first. "We will find Rutledge," he asserted.

"Every day you waste is another day that Rutledge could end up dead," Merritt said, "and that's assuming he isn't already."

"We don't believe he is," Reginald said. "My informants have been combing London, looking for any sign of him, dead or alive."

Merritt yanked his chair back and sat down. "What of your spectacular failure last night?"

"I was able to secure crates full of pikes," Reginald replied.

"What about the numerous crates that were delivered by other messengers?" Merritt asked with a lifted brow.

Reginald winced. "We'll track those down," he said.

"First, you must figure out when this insurrection is supposed to happen," Merritt responded. "If they intend to target the Prince Regent, we must know at once so we can squash it."

"I asked Hawthorne to trail Towle after I left with the wagon. With any luck, he discovered his whereabouts, and we can end this once and for all."

"I don't care how you get it done, just find a way," Merritt said. "I do not have time to coddle you."

Reginald rose from his seat. "I assure you that there is no need for coddling."

Merritt didn't look convinced. "Do try to avoid getting yourself killed," he said. "I have enough paperwork to deal with at the moment."

Reginald walked over to Evie and offered his hand. She slipped hers into his and allowed him to assist her in rising. She withdrew her hand and approached the desk. "I'm sorry."

"Agents do not apologize," Merritt said, meeting her gaze. "You would be wise to remember that."

Evie tipped her head before she turned and walked out of the office. Reginald followed her, and they didn't speak as they left the building.

Once they'd stepped outside, Reginald touched her arm and asked, "What was that about in there?"

"It was nothing," she said.

"It was something," Reginald argued. "I daresay that I can't remember the last time you apologized for anything."

"I am perfectly capable of apologizing when I am in the wrong."

"Then you must not be wrong very often." Reginald smiled, trying to lighten her mood.

Evie felt her shoulders slump a little. "It's been days, and we've come no closer to finding Rutledge than before."

"We'll find him," Reginald encouraged.

"How?" she asked. "We have no clues. We have nothing."

"You mustn't give up hope."

Evie scoffed. "Hope?" she asked, her voice rising. "Where has that gotten us?"

Reginald gently placed his hand on her sleeve and walked her over to an alley. "What's gotten into you?"

"I'm tired of pretending all is well," she replied.

"That's the job of a spy."

Evie crossed her arms over her chest. "I want to be out there looking for Rutledge and not sitting in my drawing room, waiting for information to drop into our laps."

"You must be patient."

"I'm tired of being patient!" she declared. "Rutledge is out there somewhere, and I have failed him!"

"You have not failed Rutledge."

"I have," she said, tears pricking the back of her eyes as she avoided Reginald's kind expression.

He put a finger under her chin and lifted it until she met

his gaze. "You are many things, but a failure is not one of them."

"I haven't found Rutledge yet."

"*We* haven't found him yet," Reginald said, dropping his hand, "but that doesn't mean we won't. We just need more time."

A tear escaped her eye, and Evie reached up to brush it away. "You're right," she attempted, pleased her voice was steady. "I'm just being foolish."

Reginald held her gaze, as if gauging her sincerity. "What's truly bothering you?" he asked.

"What do you mean?"

"I know when you're keeping something from me, Evie," Reginald pressed.

Evie lowered her gaze to the lapels of his jacket. "It doesn't matter."

"It does to me."

"Why?" she asked, her eyes snapping up. "Why does it matter so much to you?"

"Because," he said, stepping forward, "you matter to me."

Evie couldn't think right when Reginald was this close to her. It wasn't fair. How was she supposed to form coherent thoughts around someone so ridiculously handsome? He was even wearing that silly yellow waistcoat.

Reginald gave her an expectant look. "Pray tell, what are you keeping from me?"

Evie thought about continuing to lie to Reginald, but she was unable to do so convincingly with him looking at her like that. So she took a deep breath and revealed, "I really am a failure."

"Why would you think that about yourself?"

"I've tried so hard to be something I am not, but I have failed time and time again," she said as the tears flooded her eyes, refusing to be held at bay any longer.

She'd barely said the words when she found herself in

Reginald's comforting embrace. He pulled her close and kissed the top of her head. She relaxed against him, allowing herself to savor being encircled in his arms.

Reginald tightened his hold on her. "You can do anything you put your mind to. That's something I have always admired about you."

"I'm afraid it isn't true."

He leaned back and looked her in the eye. "I wish that you could see yourself how I see you," he said softly.

"How is that?"

"To me, you are perfect."

Evie shook her head. "I am far from perfect," she said. "I will never be good enough."

"Where did you get that ridiculous notion from?" Reginald asked.

The memory of Lady Haddington and the harsh words she had spoken to her on that fateful day after Reginald left for Eton came to mind. Evie had carried the weight of those words for so long. Perhaps it was time to let them go and be the person she so desperately wanted to be.

Reginald's eyes bore into hers. "You are, and always will be, good enough, Evie," he said. "Don't let anyone convince you otherwise."

The sincerity in his voice brought more tears to her eyes. "Do you truly think I'm good enough?"

"I do, wholeheartedly," Reginald replied.

Evie smiled despite her tears. She couldn't adequately express how much it meant to her that he believed in her so deeply.

She watched as Reginald's eyes dropped to her lips. "I can't resist you," he said quietly. "You know that, don't you? And I'm tired of pretending I can."

Barely daring to breathe, Evie watched as Reginald slowly leaned forward, his breath mingling with hers. She knew she should refuse him—it was the proper thing to do—but she'd never been good at simply doing what was proper. She had waited so long for this moment, fearing that it would never happen.

As their lips brushed against each other's, Nathaniel appeared next to them as if summoned. "There are better places to kiss than an alleyway."

Reginald released her and moved to create distance between them. Evie silently cursed.

Nathaniel leaned his shoulder against the wall and addressed Reginald. "I should challenge you to a duel for what I just witnessed."

Evie turned towards her brother-in-law. "You will do no such thing."

"You can't go around kissing in public," Nathaniel said, "unless you are prepared for the consequences of your actions."

"No one witnessed what just happened," Evie responded.

Nathaniel motioned up the street, where Talbot and Worsley watched with amused looks. They waved back at her.

"You've made your point," Evie said.

"Good, because we have more important things to discuss," Nathaniel remarked as he straightened from the wall.

"Such as?" Reginald asked.

"I followed Towle to a building on Grimstead Road," Nathaniel replied. "He went inside for a few hours before he went home to his boarding house."

"Did you have a chance to look inside this building?" Reginald asked.

Nathaniel shook his head. "No. It's well guarded."

"When has that stopped you before?" Reginald inquired.

"I thought it would be best if we went together," Nathaniel suggested.

Evie bobbed her head. "I think that is a grand idea."

Nathaniel gestured towards Worsley and Talbot. "We

might need their help, especially since we don't know how many people we are up against."

Reginald moved to offer his arm to Evie but stopped when Nathaniel stepped forward. "If you don't mind, *I* will escort Evie to the coach."

Evie placed her hand on her brother-in-law's sleeve. "Thank you," she murmured before she snuck a glance at Reginald. He smiled when she caught his eye, and she felt her cheeks flame.

Reginald had so many things that he wanted to say to Evie, but it was not the time or place to do so. He wanted her to understand how much she truly meant to him. He had always loved her, and he would continue to do so forever.

Hawthorne shifted beside him. "We're almost to Grim-stead Road."

Evie adjusted the sleeves of her blue gown. "How many guards did you see?"

"Three," Hawthorne replied. "Two in the front and back of the building and one on the roof."

"That should be easy enough," Evie remarked.

"We need to proceed cautiously so we don't give away our advantage," Reginald said. "They don't know we're coming, and that will work in our favor."

The coach stopped and the door was promptly opened by a footman.

Worsley and Talbot joined them on the pavement.

Talbot ran a hand through his tousled hair. "It is far more pleasant to ride inside the coach than outside," he complained. "I think I ate a bug on our ride over here."

Worsley bobbed his head. "I agree; and your hair is in

such a state. I have come to expect the nicer things in life now that we are businessmen."

Reginald shook his head. "Where is this heavily guarded building?"

Hawthorne motioned towards the street. "A few blocks over," he replied. "Shall we?"

As they proceeded up the pavement, Reginald made sure that he was walking next to Evie. He reveled in being so close to her and hoped that she felt the same. He glanced over at her and saw her face was expressionless. She seemed to be mentally preparing herself for whatever they might encounter.

Hawthorne ducked into an alley, and they followed him. Once they were huddled around him, he said, "It's across the street. Three levels, brown brick building."

Reginald decided to take charge; this was his assignment, after all. "I'll deal with the guard in front, and Hawthorne will take care of the one in back."

"What about the one on the roof?" Evie asked.

"We'll deal with him later," Reginald said.

"I can do it."

Reginald frowned. "I don't think that's a good idea."

"I can climb the wall and make sure he is dealt with," Evie pressed.

"Can you even climb in a gown?"

"That won't be an issue."

He wanted to refuse her, but he knew that she was the best person to deal with the guard on the roof. He had never met someone who could climb walls as precisely as she could, and she was scarily proficient with her weapons.

Reginald knew he had to make a choice. He could trust her and her abilities, or he could continue trying to smother her under the guise of keeping her safe. It was time that he let her prove what she was truly capable of.

He met her gaze. "You deal with the guard on the roof, but do not go inside until we deem it safe."

The briefest of smiles crossed Evie's lips. "Yes, sir."

Reginald turned towards Worsley. "You will follow behind us and take out anything else that moves," he ordered.

"What would you have me do?" Talbot asked.

"You have a very important job," Reginald replied. "If anything goes awry, I want you to go inform Merritt of our location and ask for immediate assistance."

Talbot gave him a mock salute. "Consider it done."

Reginald reached behind him and retrieved his pistol. "We have one shot at this. We need to get into that building and see what's worth protecting. Any questions?"

Worsley raised his hand

"Yes, Worsley?" Reginald sighed.

"It isn't a question so much as a comment," Worsley said. "It is an honor to be working with this team again, and I was thinking we should come up with a name for us."

"A name?" Reginald asked.

"Yes, like the Vindicators," Worsley replied.

"That's a brilliant idea," Talbot interjected.

Reginald cast his eyes heavenward. "We do not need a name to define us."

"It doesn't have to be the Vindicators," Worsley continued, "it could be the Liberators, or the Sentinels."

"Do be serious," Reginald said.

"No, he's right," Hawthorne remarked. "I think we do need a team name."

"Why are you encouraging them?" Reginald asked before he turned towards Evie and saw that she was nowhere to be found. Blasted woman! "We'd best hurry before Evie is discovered."

Reginald returned his pistol behind him before he exited the alley and crossed the street. The guard in front was leaning up against the wall, but he straightened when he approached.

The guard rested his hand on the pistol tucked into the waistband of his trousers. "Move along," he ordered.

"I'm afraid I'm lost. I'm trying to find Mulgrove Street," Reginald said.

"It ain't here," the guard replied.

Reginald stopped a few feet from the guard and glanced up the street. "Do you think it's that way?" he asked, pointing.

"I don't know, mister," the guard said.

"Or maybe that way?" Reginald inquired, turning his gaze towards the other side of the street.

The guard narrowed his eyes. "Just move along."

"Perhaps I should ask the people in the building," Reginald suggested, taking a step forward. "They might know."

Another voice materialized behind the guard. "Is there a problem, John?" The guard from the back of the house seemed to have heard their conversation.

John jerked his hand towards Reginald. "This man won't leave."

"I think we should give him incentive to," the newcomer said, coming to stand next to John.

Reginald put his hands up in front of him. "I'm just asking for some directions to Mulgrove Street. I'm not looking for any trouble."

"I'm afraid you found it," John said as he clenched his hands into fists.

"I found Mulgrove Street? But you said you didn't know where it was," Reginald joked.

John took a step forward and then crumpled to the ground. Reginald closed the distance and punched the other man, rendering him unconscious.

"It's about time you showed up," Reginald said as he leaned down to pick up the guard he had downed.

Hawthorne secured his pistol before he went to retrieve John. "I was waiting for the perfect opportunity to strike."

They dragged the two men to an alley and leaned them up

against the wall, stripping them of their weapons before returning to the front.

Reginald glanced up at the roof. Evie waved at them.

"I don't know why you doubted her," Hawthorne said.

"It's not so much that I doubt her, but I would prefer if she stayed out of harm's way completely," Reginald said.

"Then you fell for the wrong girl." Hawthorne walked to one of the side windows and peered in. "It looks empty."

"It can't be empty," Reginald said as he went to stand next to Hawthorne. Why would someone guard an empty building?

Hawthorne opened the window. "Shall we go inside and take a look around?"

Reginald couldn't believe their luck that the window had been left unlocked. "After you," he replied.

After they crawled through the window, they looked around the room, which had tables spread evenly throughout. The tables were stacked high with pikes and carpentry tools, and wood shavings were piled high on the ground. It was evident that this was where the pikes were made.

Reginald walked over and picked up a pike. "Where is everyone?"

"Perhaps they sent everyone home once they'd made enough pikes," Hawthorne suggested.

Together, they walked through the hall and into the next room. To his surprise, he saw Evie standing next to a desk, a book in her hand.

Evie held the book up, showing them the title. "This is the book they tore the pages out of." She dropped it onto the desk. "Where is everyone?"

"I was asking myself the same thing," Reginald said.

Evie walked towards a table pushed up against the wall. She picked up a vial of liquid and sniffed it. She reared back and made a face. "This must be what they used to make the invisible ink."

"There are many ways to make invisible ink," Hawthorne said. "It's easier than one would think."

Reginald walked up to a blueprint secured to another wall. It showed the layout of Carlton House in great detail.

Hawthorne stood next to him. "You don't think they are going to try to infiltrate Carlton House, do you?"

"It would appear so," Reginald said.

"We should alert the Prince Regent of the potential threat to his residence," Hawthorne asserted. "His guards need to be on high alert."

Evie's voice broke up their conversation. "We have another problem," she said as she held up a large piece of paper. "I think they are going after Princess Charlotte, as well."

"Why is that?" Reginald asked as he crossed the room.

"Here's the layout for Windsor," Evie revealed. "It's common knowledge that the princess resides there when she isn't in Town."

"Why would they go after Princess Charlotte?" Reginald asked. "She is beloved by the people."

"Not everyone loves her," Hawthorne corrected. "Many associate her with the lavishness of her father."

"But Windsor is miles outside of London," Reginald pointed out.

Evie put the schematics down and picked up a newssheet. "This paper is about her upcoming engagement to the Prince of Orange."

"If it happens," Hawthorne remarked. "It's been reported that she has voiced concerns about a betrothal to Earl Grey."

A door slammed somewhere in the house, and they all reached for their pistols.

"It would appear that we aren't alone after all," Reginald murmured, walking over to the door. "I'll go first, but be prepared for the unexpected."

Reginald stepped into the hall and walked in the direction

the noise had come from. It was quiet now, and the only noise he could hear was his own soft footsteps. A door was open, revealing a flight of steps that led to the level below.

He turned and saw Evie and Hawthorne silently approaching him. Reginald gestured towards the stairs before he started to descend them. He had just reached the last step when he heard a groan coming from a nearby room.

Reginald took a moment to let his eyes adjust to the darkness on the lower level. There were small, square windows along the side walls, but they did not provide adequate light.

He cautiously walked down the hall until it opened up, revealing a large cell crudely built into the corner. A person lay on the ground in the rear of the cell, facing away from him.

As Reginald stepped closer to the iron bars, the man shifted towards him, casting light on his face—Rutledge.

"Haddington? Is that you?" Rutledge asked weakly.

"It's me," Reginald confirmed as he quickly searched the walls for a key. "We're going to get you out of here."

Footsteps came from behind him, but he didn't realize they didn't sound like Evie's or Hawthorne's until it was too late.

Chapter Sixteen

Evie watched as Reginald descended the stairs to the lower level and continued on to the other staircase. She pointed her pistol towards the top of the stairs and didn't see any threat. She motioned towards Hawthorne, indicating that she was going to go up to the next level.

With light steps, she walked up the stairs and started down the hall. She started opening the doors, searching each room, but found no one lurking upstairs. It wasn't until she pushed the last door open that she found Freya, tied to a chair with a gag in her mouth.

Freya's eyes lit up when she saw her, and she started wriggling in the chair. Evie's eyes roamed the room to ensure they were alone before she lowered her pistol. She rushed over to Freya and crouched down next to her.

"What are you doing here?" Evie asked as she removed the gag.

"My father went mad after you visited the post office," Freya informed her. "He accused me of turning against him, and has held me hostage here since then."

Evie pulled out her dagger and cut the rope. "We have to get you out of here," she urged.

Freya rubbed her red wrists as she rose. "I have no objections, but there's someone else you have to save first."

"Who's that?" Evie asked.

"I believe his name is Rutledge. Father has been keeping him here for over a week."

Evie could scarcely believe her good fortune. "Where is he?"

"In the basement," Freya replied.

She didn't need to be told twice. Evie spun on her heel and headed towards the door, Freya following behind. They continued down the hall and descended the stairs.

At the top of the stairs leading to the basement, Evie removed her spare pistol from her reticule and extended it towards Freya. "You must leave this place," she encouraged.

Freya stared at the weapon, not moving to accept it. "What do you want me to do with that?" she asked in disbelief.

"Do you know how to shoot?"

"I've done it on occasion, but I don't think I could kill anyone."

Evie forced the pistol into her hand. "There are a hundred ways to shoot someone without killing them," she said.

"Can I come with you?" Freya asked, her voice betraying her fear.

Evie hesitated. It would be better if Freya left and fled to safety, but what if there were new guards outside? She didn't think Freya would be able to fend them off.

"Follow me and stay close," Evie said before she started down the stairs.

She arrived at the bottom and scanned the darkness, but there was no sign of Rutledge. She kept her pistol in front of her as she started walking down a narrow hall.

Evie stopped in surprise when the hall opened into a room where Reginald was behind the iron bars of a cell.

"Reginald," she said in a hushed voice, closing the distance between them, "what are you doing in there?"

"I was taken by surprise, but I'm fine." He paused, then amended, "We're fine."

"Is Rutledge in there with you?" Evie asked.

Reginald shifted aside to show Rutledge lying on the ground, his face battered and bruised. "He's alive, but not for much longer if we don't get him help."

"Did you try to pick the lock?"

"It was the first thing I did when I woke up, but my attempts have proven unsuccessful," Reginald said. "Do you see a key?"

"Get away from her!" Rutledge shouted.

Evie jumped, stunned by the sudden harshness of his words. "It's me, Rutledge," she said, attempting to reassure him.

Rutledge awkwardly rose and waved his hand in front of him. "You will not hurt her!"

Someone laughed behind Evie. "You need not concern yourself with that, old man."

Evie turned around and saw Freya was pointing a pistol at her—*her* pistol.

"You seem surprised," Freya said. "By the expression on your face, you didn't expect this at all."

Freya turned towards Rutledge. "Where did you find this one?" she asked. "She seems much too naïve to be working with you."

Rutledge staggered towards the iron bars and gripped them. "You don't need her—"

"But I do," Freya said. "So, this was my replacement?" Her eyes perused the length of Evie. "She's a thin little thing. I do believe she could stand to eat a biscuit or two."

Evie tightened her hold on her pistol as she waited for a chance to take Freya by surprise. But Freya lifted her free hand

and snapped her fingers. Four guards stepped out of the shadows and aimed their guns at her.

Freya put her hand out. "I'll take that pistol."

Evie reluctantly stepped forward and handed her the weapon.

"That's a good girl," Freya said as she handed it to one of the guards. She removed a chain from around her neck and produced a key.

Evie decided the best course of action would be to keep Freya talking until she could think of a way to get out of this mess. "Was your father even a part of this?"

Freya shook her head. "He's a fool. He only cares about the General Post Office and wouldn't do anything that might tarnish its legacy."

"But you don't feel the same?"

"Working at the post office was the perfect way to set up my operation," Freya said. "No one suspected someone would send hidden notes through the Penny Post."

"How did you get the stamp off your father?"

Freya gave her an amused look. "My father leaves the stamp on his desk every night when he goes to bed. It was easy to obtain, and my father was none the wiser." She walked over to the cell, unlocked it, and opened it. "Get in."

Evie walked over to the cell and stepped inside. Freya slammed the door shut behind her.

"You won't get away with this," Evie said.

Freya laughed. "Who's going to stop me?" she asked. "You? Rutledge?"

"You're mad," Rutledge interjected.

Freya's humor was immediately replaced with rage as she turned her attention to Rutledge. "If I am, it is entirely your fault!"

"No, I didn't do this," Rutledge said. "You've turned your back on us."

Freya stepped closer. "You abandoned me, leaving me to fend for myself. You ruined my life!"

"I did no such thing."

"You promised me so many things, but you lied!" Freya seethed. "Just look at you now. You are nothing."

A commotion came from behind Freya, and two men appeared in the hall dragging an unconscious man by the arms. Freya unlocked the cell door, and they tossed the man inside.

Evie ran to him. "Nathaniel," she said, "are you all right?"

Nathaniel groaned in response and reached for his head.

"We'll get out of here," Evie said, rising and turning to Freya, "and you will pay for what you've done."

Freya raised her pistol and pointed it at her. "Perhaps I should just kill you now and be done with it."

"No!" Reginald shouted, jumping in front of her.

"Aw, how sweet," Freya said with a wry smile. "You have a protector, and he's willing to risk his life to save you." She lowered her pistol. "I don't have time for this. I have an insurrection to start."

Worsley stepped into the room, his hands up in the air, and followed by a guard. "This is the last one," the guard informed Freya.

Freya opened the cell and Worsley hurried inside.

Once the door was closed, Freya pointed at two men. "Stay here and guard them," she ordered. "If they try to escape, shoot them."

Freya gave them a final glance before she departed from the room, taking the rest of the men with her.

Worsley looped his arms through the bars. "I've never been on this side of a prison cell before," he said. "I don't care for it, but at least the Vindicators are together again."

"Who are the Vindicators?" Rutledge asked.

"It's the name I came up with for our team," Worsley

explained. "The name Vindicators strikes fear in the hearts of men."

"That is idiotic and easily the worst idea you've come up with," Rutledge declared.

"We'll have to agree to disagree," Worsley said.

Nathaniel awkwardly moved to sit up. "What in the blazes just happened?"

Rutledge turned and leaned against the bars, his strength depleted. "Freya just happened."

"Who's Freya?" Nathaniel asked.

Evie stepped out from behind Reginald. "That's what I want to know, as well," she said.

Rutledge let out a sigh, then lowered his voice. "I recruited Freya to be an agent many years ago. She was a natural, much like you, but she became impatient. She wanted to save England, but she wasn't ready for those kinds of assignments."

Rutledge continued. "She started doing whatever she wanted, profiting off the assignments. I was unable to turn a blind eye any longer."

"What did Merritt say?" Evie asked.

"He ordered me to dismiss her from the agency, saying that she had become a liability," Rutledge replied. "The day I told her that she was no longer an agent, she told me I would live to regret it; but I had no idea she would turn to a life of crime. In hindsight, all the signs were there, but I just didn't believe someone could change that much."

Evie approached Rutledge and crouched down next to him. Her eyes roamed over his bruised face. "How were you able to endure the beatings?"

"The beatings were the least of my concerns," Rutledge replied. "What was worse was knowing that she was targeting you and there was nothing I could do about it in here."

"Why is she targeting me?" Evie asked.

Rutledge leaned his head back against the bars. "She loathes me, and she thinks that you replaced her."

"Did I?"

"I have only recruited three women to the agency," Rutledge said. "One no longer works as an agent, and the other two were you and Freya."

Reginald crossed his arms over his chest. "Now we know who was behind trying to kill you."

"That's a relief," Evie muttered. "Do you know what Freya is planning?"

Rutledge nodded. "She intends to start an insurrection by starting a fire outside of Carlton House," he replied. "When the garrison tries to extinguish the flames, they will storm the building with their pikes."

"But for what purpose?"

"They want to kill the Prince Regent and replace him with his daughter, Princess Charlotte. They blame him for the rising unemployment, the lack of food, and the unsanitary living conditions for the people in the rookeries," Rutledge explained.

"Killing the Prince Regent won't solve those problems," Nathaniel said.

"No, they won't," Rutledge agreed. "She doesn't care which side wins. She only cares about fueling the fire and selling weapons to the highest bidder."

Rising, Evie said, "We need to get out of here to warn the Prince Regent about the impending attack."

"How?" Rutledge asked. "Those guards will kill us if we try to escape."

"Are you proposing we give up?" Evie asked.

Rutledge shrugged. "I have made my peace with the fact that I won't make it out of here alive. I suggest you do the same."

Evie stared at Rutledge in disbelief. Where was her mentor, the one who had taught her to never give up?

"That doesn't sound at all like you," she said. "Is there no fight left inside of you?"

"Not anymore." Rutledge closed his eyes, but not before Evie saw them fill with tears.

───────⌇───────

Reginald watched as Evie paced the cell for what seemed like hours. He knew she was anxious—they all were—but he was growing tired just looking at her.

Hawthorne and Rutledge had their eyes closed as they leaned their heads back against the iron bars, and Worsley was curled up into a ball on the floor. No one was in a mood to talk, and he was fine with that. They were just biding their time until Merritt arrived with reinforcements. That is, assuming Freya's men hadn't found Talbot and killed him before he could get a message to Merritt.

Evie stopped pacing and turned to him, a crestfallen look on her face. "I don't know what to do," she admitted dejectedly.

"None of us do." Reginald patted the ground next to him. "Come, sit for a spell."

Evie shook her head. "I'm not ready to give up."

"I never asked you to give up, but I think you should rest," Reginald said.

"For what purpose?"

"You need to try to conserve your energy for what comes next."

His words must have appeased her, because she came and sat down next to him. Evie's eyes roamed the cell before she asked, "How long do you think it will be before Merritt arrives?"

"I hope it won't be much longer."

Evie looked at Rutledge, and Reginald couldn't miss the pain in her eyes. He could only imagine how difficult it was to see her mentor in such a haggard state, both mentally and physically.

Reginald nudged his shoulder against hers. "It will all work out as it should," he encouraged.

She brought her gaze back to meet his. "This is all my fault."

With a furrowed brow, he asked, "How exactly is this your fault?"

"I should've never been fooled by Freya," Evie replied.

"Need I remind you that we were all fooled by her?" Reginald pointed out. "She was very convincing."

"But if I had seen her for the threat that she was, we wouldn't be in this mess."

"You can't blame yourself for this. It isn't your fault."

Evie gave him a weak smile, but he knew she didn't believe him. Why did she take so much upon herself?

Reginald shifted to face her directly. "You are not alone in this. We will get through it and save the day, because that's what we do."

"I hope you're right."

"Do you not agree?"

"I do, but I'm angry that I allowed myself to get in this situation to begin with," Evie replied.

Reginald eyed her curiously. "Why do you find so much fault with yourself?" he asked. "After all, no one blames you for what happened."

"I blame myself," she said quietly.

"Therein lies the rub, because no one can convince you otherwise," he remarked. "But I urge you to be patient with yourself. You shouldn't blame yourself for the things you didn't know in the past but do know now."

Evie brought her knees to her chest and hugged them. "That's easier said than done."

"For some."

A skinny black rat emerged out of a crevice in the wall and scurried across the cell. No one seemed bothered by their unexpected visitor, and a smile came to Reginald's lips at the thought.

"Why are you smiling?" Evie asked him.

Reginald's eyes remained on the rat. "Do you remember when you begged your parents to let you keep a rat as a pet?"

"I do, but they refused," Evie said.

"As they should have," Reginald teased. "A wild rat would make a terrible pet."

A smile came to her lips. "I see that now, but they didn't like any of the other suggestions I made for a pet, either."

"I do recall you asked for a snake, a badger, a fox, and a squirrel, as well."

"You forgot about the hedgehog."

He chuckled. "My apologies," he said. "I can't imagine why your parents wouldn't want a wild animal in their home."

The light in her eyes dimmed. "I miss them."

"I'm certain you do." Reginald leaned his head against the wall as he mustered the courage to ask the one question that had haunted him over the years.

"What happened between us?" he asked.

She looked baffled. "What are you referring to?"

"Before I left for Eton, I asked you a question," he replied. "Do you remember that?"

Evie pressed her lips together, then looked down and said, "I do."

"I thought we had an understanding between us; I thought you would wait for me." He hesitated. "But you didn't."

"We were young and foolish."

"I don't dispute that, but it didn't change the way I felt about you," Reginald said. "You changed after I left for Eton. Why?"

Evie still wouldn't look at him. "I came to the realization that we would never suit."

"I disagree," he responded, "and shouldn't I have a say in this?"

She looked at their surroundings. "This is not the place to discuss such things," she said.

"Why? Because you have nowhere to hide?" he asked. "I just want the answer to my question, and I would prefer the truth."

He watched as emotions flickered across her face and worried that he had pushed her too hard. Evie did not like to show vulnerability to anyone.

After a long moment, Evie said, "If you must know, it was because of your mother."

"My mother?"

Evie gave the tiniest nod. "She came to call upon me after you left for Eton and informed me that you were betrothed to Lady Agnes."

"Is that the reason you grew distant to me?"

Evie bit her lower lip and didn't answer.

He reached for her hand. "You can tell me."

"Your mother offered me five thousand pounds to stay away from you," she revealed.

Reginald reared back slightly. "Did you accept?"

Evie's eyes grew wide. "Heavens, no!" she exclaimed. "I informed her that you and I were friends, and nothing would change that. In response, she grew upset and said some rather hurtful things to me."

"Which were?"

"I'd rather not say," Evie murmured.

"Please, I want to know."

Evie glanced down at their hands. "She told me that no matter what I do with my life, I will never be good enough for you."

"That's awful, and not true in the least."

"It felt true, and it resonated deeply with me," she said.

"She also accused me of reaching for a title by trying to form an attachment with you."

Reginald tightened his hold on her hand. "What my mother did was wrong," he asserted. "She had no right to say those things to you."

Evie forced a smile to her lips, but it didn't mask the sadness he could see lurking in her eyes. "It doesn't matter now."

"It does to me." Reginald lowered his voice. "My feelings for you have never faltered over these years."

"Neither have mine, but it changes nothing."

"How can you say that?" he asked. "It changes everything!"

Evie slipped her hand out from under his. "Your mother will never accept me."

"I care not."

"But I do," Evie said. "I could never live with myself if I came between you and your mother."

"Even if it was my choice?"

She swallowed. "Even then."

Reginald had pushed Evie too hard, despite wanting to press his point. He loved Evie, and always would! He would do whatever it took to convince her of that, no matter what it cost him.

Evie abruptly rose. "I'm going to check on Rutledge," she said before walking across the cell to her mentor.

Reginald watched as she crouched next to Rutledge and showed him such concern. How could he not love this woman? She had occupied a place in his heart from the moment he'd first laid eyes on her.

The memory of Evie as a child came back to him. She was a scraggly little thing, but she'd had a fierceness about her that had always intrigued him. He knew she was destined for great things, and he wanted to be along for the ride.

Hawthorne rose from his seat and walked over to him. As

he sat down, he kept his voice low. "I couldn't help but over-hear your conversation with Evie."

"You heard all of that?"

Hawthorne chuckled. "How could I not?" he asked. "The cell isn't that big."

Reginald didn't feel like discussing it right now, so he decided to change subjects. "Merritt should've been here by now," he whispered.

"I was thinking the same thing."

"What do you think could have delayed him?" Reginald asked.

Hawthorne heaved a sigh. "I don't rightly know, but we might need to come up with a different plan to escape."

Reginald's eyes shot to the two guards standing back from the cell. "How do you propose to do that?" he asked. "Freya instructed the guards to shoot us if we even attempted to escape."

"Do I have to think of all the good ideas?" Hawthorne joked. "Do you have any weapons on your person?"

Reginald shook his head. "They took them after they hit me over the head."

One of the guards fell to the ground, drawing everyone's attention. Then, the second one fell over, unconscious as well.

Reginald couldn't quite believe his eyes when he saw Mrs. Carter standing there, a pistol in her hand.

"Aunt Nancy!" Evie exclaimed. "What are you doing here?"

"Hello, Evie," Mrs. Carter greeted as she approached the cell. "I'm here to save you." She crouched down, set the pistol on the ground, and removed two pins from her hair. She slid them into the lock and slowly turned them until there was a distinctive click.

Mrs. Carter picked up her pistol and rose. As she opened the door, she said, "Come along, then. We have much to do."

Evie was the first to leave the cell, and she threw her arms around her aunt.

Mrs. Carter returned her embrace. "This is not the time to get emotional, dear," she said. "I promise that I will explain everything later."

Reginald walked over to Rutledge and helped him stand, then wrapped his arm around his back and led him from the cell.

Rutledge met Mrs. Carter's gaze. "It's about time you showed up."

Mrs. Carter smiled. "It's good to see you, too, Adam." She took a step back and informed them, "The building is empty, and Merritt is right behind me."

Worsley exited the cell last and turned to Mrs. Carter. "Would you like to join the Vindicators?"

Mrs. Carter lifted her brow. "What is the Vindicators?"

"It's what we call ourselves now," Worsley replied.

Rutledge groaned. "Get me away from Worsley before I shoot him."

"Gladly," Reginald said, leading him away.

"If you aren't nice to me, I won't let you be part of the Vindicators," Worsley called out after them.

"That's a good thing," Reginald retorted over his shoulder.

Chapter Seventeen

Evie couldn't quite believe what was happening. They had been rescued by her aunt. Aunt Nancy. The same person who always chastised her for not being a proper enough lady. How was this even possible?

"Do close your mouth, dearie," Aunt Nancy advised. "It is very unbecoming of you."

Evie did as she was instructed. "How are you here?"

"I will explain later, but you mustn't let my presence distract you from your mission." Aunt Nancy turned towards Worsley and Nathaniel. "Will you see to bringing these two men upstairs? We need to ask them a few questions."

Nathaniel stepped forward and smiled. "I must admit that I'm surprised to see you here."

"Let's just keep this between us for now," Aunt Nancy said. "We wouldn't want to give Dinah a reason to worry."

Nathaniel tipped his head in acknowledgement before he reached down to pick up one of the men.

Worsley followed suit but staggered as he struggled to put the man on his shoulder. "It would appear this man eats entirely too many biscuits," he joked.

Once the men were headed for the stairs, her aunt clasped

her hands together and smiled. "Run along," she encouraged. "You have a job you need to finish."

"I just don't understand."

Her aunt gave her a sympathetic smile. "Your father wasn't the only spy in the family," she said.

"Why didn't you say anything before?"

"There was no need."

"No need?" Evie repeated. "How can you say that?"

Aunt Nancy stepped forward and rested a hand on her sleeve. "You must put this aside and focus on what's truly important. Can you do that?"

"I can, but—"

"No buts," her aunt said. "Being a spy is in your blood. We do what needs to be done to keep the Crown safe."

Evie nodded. "I understand."

"Good, because I didn't want to explain it again," her aunt said, withdrawing her hand. "It's time to go upstairs."

As they started down the hall, Evie asked, "How did you know we were here?"

"Merritt sent word that you were in danger, and it only took me a moment to realize where my priorities lay."

"You know Merritt?" she asked.

Her aunt smiled. "Of course. Who do you think trained him?"

"You trained Merritt?"

"Well, he certainly didn't train himself."

Evie followed her aunt up the rickety staircase and into the main hall of the building. Hawthorne and Worsley were guarding the two men, who had since woken up. Reginald had found a chair for Rutledge and was standing next to him.

The front door opencd, and Merritt strode into the room with two agents close behind. He turned towards Rutledge and said, "It's good to see you alive."

"Thank you," Rutledge responded.

"Now, where have you been this entire time?" Merritt asked gruffly.

Rutledge winced in pain. "It's Freya. She's trying to start an insurrection."

"For what purpose?" Merritt asked.

Hawthorne spoke up. "She intends to kill the Prince Regent and replace him with his daughter as regent."

"Prinny is having a lawn party this evening," Merritt said, furrowing his brows. "Do you believe she intends to target Carlton House tonight?"

"It's probable," Hawthorne said.

Aunt Nancy gestured towards the two captured men. "Perhaps we should ask these men nicely. They might be able to fill in the pieces for us." She held up her pistol. "I know I might be rusty, but do you mind if I try?"

"By all means," Merritt encouraged.

Aunt Nancy stepped in front of the two men and smiled. "It's simple. Answer our questions, and keep all of your toes." She pointed towards one of the men's boots. "Why don't we start with you?"

The man took a step back and eagerly said, "I'll answer your questions."

"Smart man. Where is Freya?"

"She left to watch the insurrection," the man replied. "She wanted to witness it firsthand at Carlton House."

"How does she intend it to start?" Aunt Nancy asked.

The man hesitated. "There are to be fireworks this evening at the lawn party. That's the signal for people to start marching there."

"Do you know who is marching?"

"There are factions all around Town who've been preparing," the man shared. "They're using the weapons Freya supplied them with."

"Freya mentioned something about a fire," Rutledge interjected.

"The fire will draw the garrison out and the insurrection-ists will use that opportunity to storm the grounds," the man explained.

Aunt Nancy gave him an approving nod. "I knew you were a smart man with survival instincts," she said. "You and your friend may keep your toes."

Merritt gave the group an expectant stare. "What is everyone standing around for?" he asked. "We have an insurrection to stop!"

"I do believe I will sit this one out," Aunt Nancy stated as the two agents with Merritt hustled their captives out. "My spy days are long behind me, and I don't believe I'm needed."

Merritt's eyes crinkled around the edges. "You will be missed."

"That is kind of you to say, but I daresay I would just be in the way."

Rutledge awkwardly rose and said, "I'm ready."

"For what?" Merritt asked.

"To beat Freya," Rutledge replied.

"No, you need to see a doctor," Merritt said. "Let the other agents handle this."

Rutledge shook his head. "I can't do that. After all, this is all my fault. I was the one who unleashed her on England."

Merritt walked over and put a hand on Rutledge's shoulder. "You look like death, and you smell like it, too," he said bluntly. "If you try to go after Freya, she will kill you."

"So be it," Rutledge responded.

"Stay here. There will be other fights," Merritt said.

"But this one is my fight."

Merritt dropped his hand. "No, this is all of our fight," he remarked firmly. "Trust the other agents."

Rutledge dropped down onto the chair and rubbed his ribs. "It would be nice to rest this evening."

"You need it, old man," Merritt joked.

Rutledge chuckled before he turned to Evie, his eyes full of concern. "Be wary of Freya. She'll have no qualms about killing you or anyone else who tries to oppose her."

"I won't let her have the chance to," Evie said.

"She was an agent for many years, and she knows how we operate. In order to beat her, you must think differently, unconventionally, even," Rutledge advised.

"That won't be a problem."

Rutledge looked worried. "Most importantly, do not let her words get to you. She is a master manipulator."

Evie bobbed her head. "I understand."

"I want you to remember something." Rutledge paused. "You are stronger than she is. Just remember what I've taught you, and you can beat her."

"I shall," she murmured.

Her aunt stepped closer to her and extended her weapon. "This was your father's pistol, and I want you to have it."

Evie stared at the firearm with awe. "Do you mean it?"

"I do," her aunt replied. "He kept it in his right boot, just as I am told that you do on occasion. I, for one, think a pistol in a boot is terribly uncomfortable."

Evie accepted the pistol and ran her fingers over the intricate etchings. "I cannot tell you what this means to me."

"I think I have some idea."

Evie slipped the muff pistol into the folds of her gown. "I'll see you tonight."

"See that you do," her aunt said, "and I will ensure the servant's door is unlocked for your return."

Merritt cleared his throat. "I do apologize for interrupting this tender moment, but we have a mad woman insistent on wreaking havoc on London to deal with."

"Go," Aunt Nancy encouraged. "There's a coach out front that will take you wherever you need to go."

As Evie started walking towards the door, Reginald matched her stride with Hawthorne right behind him. "Do you have a plan?"

"No. I was hoping you had one," Evie said as they exited the building.

"We need to stop those fireworks from ever going off," Hawthorne stated.

"How do you propose we do that?" Evie questioned. "It's not as if we can waltz into a lawn party unannounced."

"Why can't we?" Reginald asked, coming to a stop in front of the coach. "There are some advantages to being a marquess."

"But we aren't properly dressed," Evie said with a wave over her simple gown. "And I've seen beggars wear nicer jackets than yours and Nathaniel's."

Reginald opened the door to the coach. "Then we need to find another way in." He offered his hand to assist her inside.

Evie slipped her hand into his and went to step into the coach, but stilled when Reginald leaned close and whispered, "I have not forgotten our conversation from earlier."

"I wish you would."

"I let you go once; I am not about to let that happen again," Reginald said, leaning back to look her in the eyes. The intensity of his gaze was like a welcome, an invitation, a promise of love.

"Reginald, I…" She stopped. How could she adequately express what she was feeling at this precise moment? Frankly, she couldn't even seem to formulate thoughts, not with him looking at her the way he was.

Reginald squeezed her hand and offered her a private smile. "It's all right," he said. "You don't need to say anything now."

Evie took her place in the coach and tried to calm her racing heart. With every word, every touch, she fell deeper in love with him, making it nearly impossible to refuse him. But maybe, just maybe, she didn't want to anymore.

Reginald watched Evie stare out the window. He couldn't believe his mother had the audacity to try to pay Evie to stay away from him. He would have some choice words for her later, but he had more pressing issues at the moment. They needed to find a way to stop an insurrection.

The coach stopped in front of the entrance to Carlton House, and a liveried gatekeeper stepped forward.

Reginald opened the window. "We have urgent business with the Prince Regent."

The gatekeeper appeared unimpressed "Invitation, please."

"We don't have one, but—"

"No invitation, no entrance," the gatekeeper said. "Move along."

Hawthorne leaned forward. "I am Lord Hawthorne and this is Lord Haddington. We need to speak to the Prince Regent at once."

"I apologize, my lords," the gatekeeper mocked, "but if you don't have an invitation, then you will not be admitted. No exceptions."

"The Prince Regent's life is in danger," Hawthorne pressed.

The gatekeeper stepped back. "I assure you that he is well protected within these walls. Now, off with you before I have you arrested for trespassing."

Reginald rapped the side of the coach, and it started to roll away from the entrance. "What do you suggest we do now?" he asked.

Evie's eyes remained on the window. "We climb."

"You can't climb the fence," Reginald said as he followed her gaze.

"Whyever not?" she asked. "I've climbed fences before."

"But you're in a gown," Reginald pointed out.

"That hasn't stopped me in the past."

Reginald frowned. "What if you get caught?"

"I won't," Evie replied. "Besides, we need to get inside to warn the Prince Regent of the impending attack."

"What if he doesn't believe you?"

"I can be very convincing when I want to be."

Reginald turned to Hawthorne. "What is your opinion on this?"

"She's right," Hawthorne said. "While she warns the Prince Regent, we'll need to find the firemaster and persuade him not to light the fireworks."

"What about Freya?" Reginald asked. "She's here somewhere, and I have no doubt she's orchestrating the events."

"Once I warn the Prince Regent, I'll seek out Freya," Evie asserted.

"What are you going to do with her when you find her?" Reginald asked.

Evie tilted her chin. "I'll do what needs to be done. I want her to stand trial for treason."

"Just be careful." Reginald rapped the top of the coach and it came to a stop. "Shall we find a way into the palace?"

They exited the coach and started back towards Carlton House. The palace was surrounded by an iron fence set back from the street. Reginald counted ten guards stationed along it.

"We need a distraction," Hawthorne muttered.

Reginald nodded. "What do you propose?"

"How are your acting skills?"

"I've had no complaints," Reginald replied.

"Do you think you could fake immense chest pains?" Hawthorne asked. "We just need to give Evie enough time to scale the fence."

"What about us?"

Evie gestured towards a gate a short distance away. "I'll unlock the gate when I get to the other side."

"What about the guards?" Reginald asked.

"Let's deal with one problem at a time. Are you ready to climb?" Hawthorne asked Evie.

"I am."

Hawthorne nodded approvingly. "We'll see you on the other side."

The two men continued on for a moment before Hawthorne stopped on the pavement. "This looks like a good enough spot."

Reginald seized his chest and moaned.

"What are you doing?" Hawthorne whispered "You sound more like a wounded dog than a man in pain."

"I'm just warming up," Reginald returned with a glare.

Hawthorne sighed. "Can you speed it along? At this rate, we'll be here all night."

Reginald released a yelp of pain and shouted, "Ah! My heart!"

"Subtle," Hawthorne muttered, gripping Reginald's shoulder as he turned towards the guards. "Someone help me! My friend is in pain!"

A guard approached them on the other side of the fence. "What's the commotion?"

"Did you not hear me?" Hawthorne cried. "My friend is in immense pain and needs help!"

Reginald dropped to his knees and moaned, "Oh, my chest hurts!"

Another guard rushed over. "You need to stop shouting."

"I don't know what to do," Hawthorne whimpered. "I can't lose my friend."

A few more guards trickled over and stared as Reginald overexaggerated his breathing. "I... don't... want... to... die," he said between labored breaths.

The guards whispered among themselves, and one spoke up. "We can't help you. Move along!"

"Move along?" Hawthorne protested. "Do you want my friend to die, here, in the middle of the pavement?"

Reginald fell back, clutching his chest. "I see a light. Someone is there. They want me to walk towards it."

The guards' expressions ranged from disbelieving to disturbed, and some looked frantic as they tried to figure out what they should do.

"What's going on here?" someone shouted from the other side of the fence.

One of the guards answered, "This man is having some kind of fit."

A tall guard with blond hair appeared at the gate and perused the length of him. "Bring him inside," he ordered. "We don't want him to die on the street, not when the Prince Regent is having a lawn party. We wouldn't want the guests to have to step over him when they depart."

He walked over to the gate and unlocked it. "Hurry along, then," he said as he opened it.

Hawthorne reached down to help Reginald, who was still moaning and clutching his chest, to rise, then slipped an arm behind his back and helped him towards the gate.

Once they were through the gate, the newcomer locked it and pointed towards a tree. "Take him over there," he ordered, "and, for heaven's sake, don't make so much noise."

"But I'm dying," Reginald moaned.

"Die quieter," the guard said before turning to a thin, lanky guard. "Turn them loose once all the guests have departed."

"And if he dies?" the other guard questioned.

"Drag his body across the street and send for the coroner," came his unsympathetic reply. "Until that time, I want you to guard them."

"Yes, sir."

"The rest of you, back to your posts!"

"That went better than expected," Hawthorne murmured, practically dragging Reginald to the tree.

"It's because of my superb acting skills."

"You were laying it on a little thick at the end," Hawthorne grunted as he lowered Reginald to the ground and leaned him back against the trunk of the tree. "At least we're inside."

"Do you think Evie made it over the fence?" Reginald asked between groans.

Hawthorne's eyes roamed over the lawn. "I hope so."

The thin, lanky guard approached Hawthorne. "Will your friend be all right?" he asked with apparent concern.

Reginald lifted a hand toward the sky. "The light's getting brighter," he said. "I see my father. He's waiting for me."

"I'm worried it's only a matter of time," Hawthorne lamented.

The guard shifted in his stance. "Is there anything we can do for him?"

"Can you call for a doctor?" Hawthorne asked.

The guard shook his head. "I'm afraid not. I can't leave my post."

There was a rustling in the bushes not far from them, and the guard's alert eyes darted towards it. "Stay here," he ordered.

As the guard investigated, Evie appeared from behind a tree and hit him on the back of the head with the butt of her pistol.

Hawthorne jumped up and ran over to the downed guard, then dragged him into the bushes. "That should buy us some time," he said as he returned.

Evie turned to leave. "I'm going to find the Prince Regent."

Reginald reached for her arm, stilling her. "I'm going with you."

"Why?" Evie asked.

"I've met him on multiple occasions," Reginald said. "He'll believe me if I say his life is in danger."

Evie looked like she was going to argue with him, but thankfully she conceded. "Come along, then."

As Reginald released her hand, Hawthorne said, "I'm going to find the firemaster and try to put an end to this before it even starts."

"Good luck," Reginald responded as he hurried to catch up with Evie. He matched her stride and pointed towards the lights at the rear of the palace. "I suggest we look for him there."

"That's precisely what I was thinking."

They didn't speak as they used light steps to approach the lawn party. They broke through the cover of the trees, entering a large group of people mingling with one another.

A lady with a pointed nose perused the length of them before giving them a disgusted look. It was evident that their clothing did not meet her approval. More people glanced their way, and they were met with more disapproving looks, but it mattered not. They weren't there to earn anyone's admiration.

Reginald's eyes roamed over the lawn until they glimpsed an ostentatious chair towards the rear. It was just the type of furniture the Regent would choose for himself, he mused.

"I know where he is," he said, reaching for Evie's hand.

They pushed through the crowd until they reached the Prince Regent, who was standing near the chair rather than sitting on it. He was conversing with a petite older woman with a thin, diamond-encrusted tiara on her head.

Reginald approached them and bowed. "I apologize for the interruption, your highness, but I must speak to you."

The Prince Regent turned to face him. "Haddington?"

"Yes, your highness."

"I almost didn't recognize you," the Prince Regent said. "Why are you dressed like a pauper?"

"That isn't important—"

"Who did you bring with you?" the Prince Regent asked, his eyes sparking with interest.

"Sir, if I may…"

The Prince Regent put his hand up. "I wish for her to speak," he ordered.

Evie stepped forward. "Who I am isn't important, your highness. We've come to warn you of an impending attack."

"I know you," the Prince Regent said. "You're the late Lord Gladstone's daughter."

"I am," Evie responded as she dropped into a curtsy.

The Prince Regent glanced between them. "Did you think this was a costume ball?" he asked. "That is the only reason I can think of for your wardrobe."

"Sir—" Reginald attempted.

"Now, what is this nonsense about an impending attack?"

"We need to get you to safety first," Reginald said, "then we'll explain everything."

The Prince Regent put his hands up. "Look around you. I assure you that I am perfectly safe here with my guards."

Reginald opened his mouth to respond but Evie spoke first. "With all due respect, your highness, you aren't taking this situation seriously, and we don't have the luxury of time to coddle you."

The Prince Regent's nostrils flared slightly. "Did you forget whom you are speaking to?"

"I know perfectly well who I'm speaking to, but we're here to ensure you live another day," Evie replied. "The moment those fireworks explode in the sky, people are going to start marching here to storm the palace. They want to kill you and place your daughter as Regent."

"They'll never get in," the Prince Regent said haughtily.

"But *we* did," Evie said. "Your palace is not impenetrable, your highness. No structure is."

The Prince Regent eyed her critically. "Why should I believe you?"

Evie squared her shoulders. "You're right. I've given you no reason to trust me," she said. "You can order me to leave, and I will do so, but that doesn't mean I won't stop working until the threat against you has passed."

Reginald held his breath. He wasn't quite sure how the Prince Regent was going to respond to Evie's insubordination, especially since the royal wasn't known for his compassion—or reasonableness, for that matter.

To his surprise, a smile broke out on the Prince Regent's face. "I like you," he said. "You are feisty, much like my daughter, Charlotte." He met Reginald's gaze. "You chose wisely with this one."

"We need to get you inside…" Reginald halted as a boom sounded and a firework exploded in the sky.

Chapter Eighteen

Evie stared up at the fireworks in dismay. The insurrection had started, and there was nothing they could do to prevent it. But that didn't mean they were powerless. They could still ensure the Prince Regent was safe and far away from Carlton House.

Turning towards him, Evie said, "We need to get you to safety, and quickly."

The Prince Regent flicked his wrist, and one of his guards stepped forward. "I have just been informed there is an uprising amongst the people. They intend to march here and overtake the palace."

"I will notify the garrison at once."

"Very good," the Prince Regent said, "and ensure my coach is readied. I wish to depart immediately."

"You're doing the right thing, your highness," Evie remarked as the guard hurried away.

"You'd better be right about this," the Prince Regent said. "I don't take kindly to incompetence of any kind."

"That is something we have in common."

The Prince Regent's eyes roamed over the lawn. "What of all these people?" he asked.

"We will deal with them once you are safely on your way from the palace," Reginald said.

Nathaniel approached them with an apologetic look on his face and quickly bowed. "I arrived too late to stop the fireworks, but I believe I've discovered a way to stop the insurrection in its tracks."

"How?" Reginald asked.

"Freya told us they were going to start a fire to draw out the garrison, but what if there is no fire?" Nathaniel questioned.

"Then the garrison can focus its efforts on protecting the palace," Evie responded.

"Precisely," Nathaniel said. "Now we just have to determine where they intend to start the fire."

The Prince Regent cocked his head. "Hawthorne?"

Nathaniel bowed again. "Your highness," he greeted. "I do apologize for this inconvenience, but I assure you that it couldn't be helped."

The tall blond guard approached them. His glanced between Reginald and Nathaniel and his eyes widened with recognition. He drew his pistol and pointed it at Reginald. "You are under arrest," he commanded.

"Put your gun down," the Prince Regent ordered. "These men are my friends, and you will be answering to them for the time being."

"As you wish, your highness." The guard reluctantly lowered his pistol. "I have come to inform you that your coach is readied."

The Prince Regent nodded in approval, turning away from their group. "Then let us make haste."

As the royal walked off, Evie's eyes remained on his retreating figure. At least he would be safe from the rebels. But their job wasn't done; they still needed to get everyone else to safety and disband the insurrectionists.

Talbot's voice came from behind her. "What did we miss?"

Evie turned to see Talbot and Worsley standing beside Reginald. "How did you get in without an invitation?"

"Merritt's here, and he asked nicely to be admitted," Talbot informed her.

"That doesn't sound like Merritt," Nathaniel remarked.

"Would've been nice to know that was an option," Reginald muttered under his breath.

Worsley grinned. "He can be quite persuasive, and the gatekeeper was no match for him." He held up his arms. "What's the plan?"

"The Prince Regent is on his way to safety, and since we weren't able to stop the fireworks, we now need to stop the fire at the garrison," Reginald shared.

Talbot frowned. "That's your plan?" he asked. "All of it? It's a lousy plan."

"I agree," Worsley said. "It lacks the sophistication of your usual plans."

"We don't have time to argue the point," Nathaniel interrupted. "If we stop the fire, it may curb the momentum of the insurrectionists."

"What if they find another way in?" Talbot asked.

"Then it's up to the garrison to stop them," Nathaniel replied. "But, fortunately, the Prince Regent will not be here."

A movement in the crowd caught Evie's attention, and she turned her head to see a dark-haired woman walking swiftly away from the lawn. *Freya.* She had changed into a maroon gown and piled her hair on top of her head, camouflaging herself as one of the party guests.

Evie started to follow her but was stopped by Reginald's hand on her arm. "Where are you going?" he asked.

"I see Freya," she informed him.

Reginald released her arm. "I'll come with you."

"No," Evie said. "You need to get these people out of here and stop the fire. I can handle Freya. She's only one person."

"I don't know…"

"Trust me, Reginald."

Without hesitation, Reginald wrapped one arm around her waist and pressed his mouth against hers. He leaned back and said, "Go, but make sure you come back to me."

"I will," she responded, feeling breathless.

Reginald dropped his arm. "Good luck, Evie."

Evie turned and raced off in the direction Freya had gone. She pulled her pistol out and cocked it; she didn't want to be unprepared when she confronted the former agent.

She stopped after a short distance away when she realized that Freya had all but disappeared. Where had she gone? Evie's eyes roamed over the side of Carlton House, and she saw an open window on the first level. Would Freya be brazen enough to break into the palace?

Yes.

Evie hurried over to the window and crawled inside. She had just put her feet down when something hard hit the back of her head. She dropped to the floor as pain pulsated through her skull.

"You are far too predictable," Freya mocked above her. "It's pathetic, really."

"You've lost. By now, the Prince Regent is far away from the palace."

"I would imagine so, but he can only run so far before he will be held accountable for what he's done," Freya said.

"What has he done to you?"

"To me, nothing," Freya replied, "but he is killing my countrymen in this godforsaken war."

Evie staggered to her feet. "I thought you wanted war to sell your weapons."

Freya laughed. "You are so narrowminded," she said. "I'm not sure what Rutledge ever saw in you."

"Perhaps he liked the fact that I wasn't inherently evil."

Freya's eyes glinted like ice. "Do you think you're special to him?"

"I do," Evie answered, fighting nausea.

"You're mistaken," Freya spat. "He only cares for himself. He would throw you to the wolves without a second thought if it benefited him."

"That doesn't sound like Rutledge."

Freya walked over to a candle ensconced on the wall and ran her fingers through the flame. "Rutledge recruited me and treated me like a daughter. For the first time, I thought I knew what it was like to have a real father who cared for me. I felt loved, valued."

The ringing in Evie's head was beginning to subside, but she was still shaky on her feet. As much as she wanted to shoot Freya and be done with this conversation, she couldn't risk aiming while her vision was unsteady. She'd probably only have one opportunity; she had to make it count.

Freya continued to play with the flame. "But he took issue with how reckless I am. He wanted me to conform, and when I wouldn't, I was kicked out of the agency."

"Rutledge told me that you started profiting off your assignments."

"That I did. After all, not everyone has an inheritance like you do." Freya smirked. "I know all about you. One doesn't go into battle without knowing one's opponent. Although, you have been a constant disappointment to me. I expected a challenge, but I was always a few steps ahead of you. You just kept playing right into my hands."

Freya removed the candle from the sconce. "It's my fault, really," she said. "You were only just recruited by Rutledge a short time ago, and I've been a spy for years, even after I was dismissed. You see, when England didn't want me, France was more than willing to take me in."

"You're a spy for France?"

"Bravo!" Freya said. "If only you had figured all of this out on your own...then you really would be somewhat clever."

Evie pointed her pistol towards Freya. "Tell me why I shouldn't kill you right now."

"You could," Freya responded, unconcerned, "but you would die, too." She motioned towards bags of gunpowder that lined the floor near her feet. "The spark of your pistol could ignite these bags."

"As could the flame in your hand."

Freya looked amused. "I never did say where the fire was going to be started."

"You would kill yourself to set the palace ablaze?"

"No," Freya replied. "My job was just to distract you."

The wall opened and a man stepped out, holding a pistol in front of him.

Freya's eyes remained on the opening. "If you had bothered to review the layout of Carlton House, you would have known about the hidden corridors the servants use." She blew out the candle and returned it to the sconce. "I hope you don't take this personally, but you must die now."

"You did all of this just to kill me?"

Freya's eyes grew hard. "No, I did all of this to show Rutledge that I was the better spy. Not him! Not you!" she shouted. "He should have never turned his back on me!"

"You betrayed your country."

"My loyalty is to myself," Freya spat. "France made me a very rich woman by setting me up as a smuggler. I knew Rutledge couldn't resist coming after me and my operation. I couldn't have planned it more perfectly."

Freya walked over to her guard and huffed. "Rutledge even tried to save me. Can you believe it? Even after I tortured him for hours, he claimed that there was still good in me." Her eyes hardened and she smiled sardonically. "But he was most despondent whenever I mentioned your name. That's why I knew I had to kill you. You mean more to him than I ever did."

"It doesn't have to end this way," Evie attempted. While

Freya hadn't revealed any weapons, her armed guard and the black powder significantly reduced Evie's options.

Freya gave her an amused look. "How do you want this to end?" she asked. "For us to be friends?"

"No, but we don't have to die."

Freya let out a bark of laughter. "You're amusing, but I can assure you that there is no situation where you don't die," she said. "You may have saved the Prince Regent this time, but I will kill him, even if I have to burn London to the ground to do it."

Evie saw a flicker of movement in the servant's corridor and decided to take the gamble that she wasn't alone—the person there was either friend or foe, and she chose to be hopeful. She slowly returned her pistol to her pocket. "This is your last chance to surrender."

"Look around you," Freya said, putting her hands up. "You've lost!"

Reginald stepped out from the shadows of the servant's corridor and hit the guard over the back of his head with his pistol.

As the guard crumpled to the door, Evie took advantage of the distraction and removed the dagger that was strapped to her leg.

Freya didn't hesitate as she reached down and picked up the fallen guard's pistol. She pointed it at the bags of gunpowder and said, "Get back, or I'll blow us all up."

"You'd kill yourself?" Reginald asked.

"I would!" Freya shouted.

Reginald took a step to the side. "Your death would be in vain. The rebels have already disbanded."

"You're lying!"

"I'm not," Reginald said. "Merritt rallied troops stationed in London and had them positioned along the roads leading to Carlton House."

"They wouldn't have given up so easily," Freya declared.

"There were shots fired, but the insurgents with their pikes were no match for highly trained troops with firearms," Reginald shared.

Freya pursed her lips. "The British people are a bunch of cowards," she grumbled. "They complain about their lot in life, but do nothing about it."

Evie tightened her hold on the dagger at her side. "It's over, Freya."

"Yes, it is," Freya said. "I won't be taken alive. I already know what happens to spies when they're caught."

Freya's finger twitched on the trigger, and Evie reacted. She drew back and released the dagger with a flick of her wrist. It embedded in Freya's chest, and she looked down at it in surprise.

Freya slowly dropped to her knees but kept hold of the pistol in her right hand. "You made the mistake of not killing me instantly," she said.

As Freya aimed the pistol at the bags of gunpowder, Evie ran towards the servant's corridor and dove into it.

Reginald shut the door and piled on top of Evie. His only concern was to keep her safe, not caring if he lived or died as he used his body as a shield.

The powder ignited, and the hidden corridor shook as the explosion rocked it. Debris fell around them, and smoke and dust choked the air. After a few minutes, all was silent.

Evie's muffled voice came from beneath him. "Reginald?"

"Yes?"

"You can release me now."

Reginald glanced over his shoulder and saw that the door was still intact. They were safe. "My apologies," he said as he got up. He offered his hand to Evie and helped her to her feet.

"Thank you for saving my life," she said as she fruitlessly dusted off her gown.

"It only took me a moment after you left for me to realize that I had no intention of letting you go after Freya on your own."

Evie stiffened. "I could have handled the situation on my own. I didn't need your help."

Reginald grinned, finding great relief in the fact that they were both alive. "Why won't you just admit that you're happy to see me?"

Evie's face softened. "I will admit that I do not find you as vexing at the moment, but only because your timing happened to be fortuitous."

"You are a stubborn vixen," Reginald said, taking a step closer to her.

Evie tilted her head to look up at him. "I won't apologize for who I am."

"I wouldn't want you to, because you are perfect just the way you are," Reginald said.

"There are some who would disagree with you," Evie teased.

"I do not care a whit about what other people think; I only care about what you think." Reginald reached out and cupped her cheek. "You are all that I think about, and every day you are the reason I breathe."

"Oh, Reginald," Evie murmured.

"I know you care for me."

"I do."

Reginald leaned closer until his face was just inches away from hers. They stood motionless. He looked deep into her eyes, and he started to see cracks in the barriers she had so carefully erected.

"There is no one else that I want to be around more than you. You occupy my thoughts relentlessly and haunt my dreams. I can no more stay away from you than I can try to keep my heart from beating," he said.

Evie held his gaze. "I feel the same."

"You do?"

"I do, but we mustn't act on our feelings," Evie said.

"Whyever not?"

Evie's eyes became downcast. "Your mother was right about one thing—I would make a terrible marchioness."

"I care little about that," he asserted. "I choose you, and every day I will choose you, over and over, without the slightest hesitation."

Tears came to Evie's eyes. "I know, and that's why I have to let you go."

Someone cleared their throat.

Reginald turned and saw a line of footmen standing there with buckets of water. How had he not noticed them?

The nearest one held his bucket up. "I do hate to interrupt, but the palace is on fire, and you are blocking our path."

Reginald released Evie and stepped to the side. The footmen rushed past him and opened the door. The room was an inferno, and the heat permeated the servant's corridor.

"We should go," Reginald shouted over the noise of the fire.

Evie nodded in vigorous agreement.

Reginald grabbed her hand and led her down the servant's corridor. They didn't speak until they arrived at a door in the rear of the palace.

As Reginald reached for the door, someone shouted from behind them. "Stop, or I will shoot!"

Reginald turned and stepped in front of Evie. Before them was the blond-haired guard from earlier.

The guard approached them but lowered his pistol. "Do you want to explain what happened in there?"

"A French spy infiltrated the palace with the intention of starting a fire to rally the insurrectionists."

"I would say that he succeeded." The guard frowned. "Did he escape?"

"No, you will likely find *her* body once you have doused the fire," Reginald replied. "Why are you not with the Prince Regent?"

"There was no need. He is being escorted to a safe place until the threat on his life has passed," the guard informed him.

"Have the rebels arrived at the gate yet?"

"They have not, but we are preparing for their arrival," the guard replied.

"We are happy to render any assistance that you require."

The guard huffed. "I have seen the help you are willing to offer, and I think we should decline," he said. "Frankly, I preferred you when you were near death."

Reginald chuckled. "Good luck to you." He opened the door and they exited the palace.

Evie glanced over at him. "Why did you lie to Freya about the rebels disbanding before arriving at the palace?"

"I wanted to drain the fight out of her."

"It was smart."

"Was that a compliment?"

"It was."

Reginald's eyes roamed over the palace. The fire seemed contained to one section of the house, and was starting to subside as a line of servants continuously tossed water onto the flames.

Hawthorne approached them. "I see that you both made it out with your lives. Was Freya able to escape?"

"No," Evie replied as she slipped her hand free from Reginald's. "She's dead."

"That's a relief. I did not care for her." Hawthorne flicked his wrist. "Merritt sent me to look for you. He wants to speak to you both."

"This can't be good," Reginald muttered as they followed Hawthorne through the hordes of servants.

Merritt was talking to the guards near the fence. Once he saw them, he stopped speaking and walked over to them.

Merritt motioned towards the palace. "What do you have to say for yourself, agents?" he asked.

Evie opened her mouth, but Reginald spoke first. "It was my fault," he said. "I wasn't able to stop Freya before she started the fire."

Merritt turned to Evie. "Is this true?"

Evie shook her head. "I fatally wounded Freya with my dagger, but it didn't prevent her from igniting the gunpowder."

"Sir, if I may…" Reginald attempted.

Merritt put his hand up, stilling his words. "Next time, make sure your aim is true."

"There will be a next time?" Evie asked.

"Don't sound so surprised; you're a good agent," Merritt said. "You remind me so much of your aunt. She was one of the best agents we had."

"Thank you, sir," Evie said.

A rare smile came to Merritt's lips. "I would be remiss if I did not inform you that you made quite the impression on the Prince Regent."

"That was not my intention."

"Although, I would avoid insulting a sovereign from here on out," Merritt advised lightly. "They tend not to respond very well to that approach."

Evie smiled. "I understand."

Merritt grew solemn. "I will expect a full briefing tomorrow in my office."

Reginald tipped his head in acknowledgement. "Yes, sir."

"It would be best if we departed before the rebels show up," Merritt said with a glance over his shoulder.

"You wish to abandon the guards?" Reginald asked.

"Troops are on their way as we speak and will come up from behind," Merritt explained. "If the rebels are smart, they will lay down their weapons and disband."

Merritt continued talking as he started towards the gate. "I had our coaches brought around. We need to depart at once."

A guard opened the gate and allowed them to exit before he locked it.

Worsley straightened from the fencepost he had been leaning against and exclaimed, "The Vindicators have reunited!"

"Botheration," Reginald muttered under his breath.

Talbot swatted at Worsley's sleeve. "I think it is time that the Vindicators disbanded."

"But we only just started!" Worsley cried.

"Yes, but you're trying to force it now. It's embarrassing," Talbot said.

Worsley tugged at the lapels of his jacket. "Wherever we go, whatever we do, the Vindicators will be there to protect the Crown's interests."

Merritt shook his head. "It's a good thing you're a competent agent, Worsley."

"Thank you, sir," Worsley said. "That is quite the compliment."

"It wasn't meant as one," Merritt remarked.

Reginald stepped up to the coach and opened the door before assisting Evie inside. He followed Hawthorne into the coach, and they sat opposite Evie.

As the coach started moving, Hawthorne glanced between them and asked, "Are you both all right?"

"We are," Reginald replied.

"When I saw the explosion, I was worried that you two hadn't made it out in time," Hawthorne said.

"Freya was no match for both of us," Reginald stated.

Evie bobbed her head. "We make a good team."

"That we do," Reginald agreed, holding her gaze.

Evie broke his gaze and turned towards the window. They all retreated to their own thoughts as they traveled to Evie's townhouse. Reginald stepped down and reached back to assist Evie onto the pavement once they'd arrived.

Evie moved to withdraw her hand from his, but he kept a hold of it.

At her questioning glance, he said, "I will call upon you tomorrow, so we may finish our conversation."

She looked crestfallen. "I wish you wouldn't."

"You seem to believe that you aren't worth fighting for." He brought her hand up to his lips and kissed it. "The trouble is, if you don't risk anything, you risk even more."

Evie's eyes searched his, and he hoped she found whatever it was that she was looking for.

A dog barked. Reginald lowered her hand and stepped back. "It's late."

"Yes, it is," Evie said. "I should go."

"That would be for the best," he agreed.

Evie hesitated for only a moment before she hurried to the servant's entrance and disappeared within.

Reginald stepped back into the coach and sat across from Hawthorne.

"Have you confessed your undying love to Evie yet?" his friend asked.

"In a way."

Hawthorne gave him a knowing look. "The time to be bold is now."

"I don't want to push her if she isn't ready," Reginald said. "I can't risk losing her for my impatience."

"She's ready."

"How do you know?" Reginald asked.

Hawthorne grinned. "She looks at you like a woman lost in love."

"One can only hope."

Chapter Nineteen

Evie locked the door to the servant's entrance and began making her way towards her bedchamber. Her heart was heavy. She wanted nothing more than to fling her arms around Reginald and throw caution to the wind, but that would be terribly unfair of her to do. No matter what happened, Lady Haddington would never accept her.

She desired nothing more than Reginald's happiness. Would he grow to resent her if he had to choose between his mother and following his heart? What if contention plagued them for the rest of their lives, even if mother and son weren't estranged? That was not something she was willing to risk.

As she neared her bedchamber, she saw light coming from under the door and wondered who was up at this late hour. She opened the door and found her aunt sitting on her bed.

Aunt Nancy patted the bed next to her. "Come," she encouraged. "We have much to discuss."

Evie closed the door and joined her aunt.

Once she was situated, Aunt Nancy asked, "How did the mission go?"

"We were unable to prevent the fire and the fireworks

signaling the insurrectionists, but we stopped Freya and were able to get the Prince Regent to safety," Evie shared.

"That is good," her aunt said. "Prinny can be rather pigheaded at times."

"You know him?"

Her aunt nodded. "I've interacted with him on a few occasions. He did threaten to chop off my head once, though."

Evie's eyes widened. "Why would he do such a thing?"

"There was a threat on his life, and he was out drinking with his friends at a pub. I made him leave, despite him not wanting to go," her aunt explained with a twinkle in her eye. "He did apologize afterwards."

"I didn't think the Prince Regent apologized to anyone."

"It is a rare occurrence, but it does happen." Aunt Nancy shifted towards her and said, "I bet you must have a lot of questions for me."

"I do."

"Before you begin, just know that what I've done was designed to protect you and Dinah," her aunt said. "This was a life that I never wanted for you."

"May I ask why?"

Her aunt gave her a weak smile. "Like you, I was a very inquisitive child and wanted more out of life. I noticed your father's antics, and it wasn't long before I suspected he was up to something. I overheard a conversation I wasn't supposed to between him and Rutledge. When I was discovered, Rutledge decided to give me a chance to prove myself at the agency."

"I know how lonely it is to be an agent," Aunt Nancy continued, "because it was years before I told my husband the truth. He was furious that I was risking my life every time I went out on an assignment, but he eventually came to terms with it."

"Why didn't you say anything before now?"

Her aunt sighed. "When your mother and father died, I decided to stop working as an agent in order to give you a normal life." She hesitated. "I saw the path you were going down and how similar it was to mine. I couldn't risk losing you, so I tried to alter your path."

"It didn't work very well," Evie ribbed.

"No, it didn't," her aunt agreed. "I was furious at Rutledge for recruiting you, but I wasn't surprised. Your father taught you everything you needed to be a proficient agent from a young age, despite your mother's protests."

Evie smiled at that thought. "She did not see the need for teaching me how to scale brick buildings."

"No, she did not," her aunt said, "but your mother always knew that you were destined for great things."

"I miss her."

Aunt Nancy reached out and cupped her cheek. "You and Dinah were your mother's whole world. She loved you more than anything else."

"Did she know about Father being an agent?"

Her aunt dropped her hand. "She did, and she confided in me that she hoped you wouldn't follow in his footsteps."

"Why?"

"Being a spy is a lonely endeavor," her aunt said. "You spend most of your time lying or keeping information from the ones you are closest to."

"But I enjoy working as an agent."

Her aunt didn't respond for a moment. "When you first went missing, I suspected you were working on an assignment, and I was so worried about you. I had to pretend that all was well for Dinah's sake, but I knew what kind of dangers awaited you," she said. "Then your sister started following in your footsteps, and I was scared."

"Dinah was only trying to find me."

"Yes, but she was not brought up like you," her aunt remarked. "Dinah is more content with sitting in the drawing room, practicing her needlework and minding a house, than you have ever been."

"That's true, but she is capable of so much more than that."

"I know that now, but you two are all that I have left," her aunt said. "I don't know what I would do if anything happened to one of you."

Evie reached for her aunt's hand. "Nothing will happen to me."

"You say that now, but you don't know it for certain." A small smile came to Aunt Nancy's lips. "Also, you might want to work on your excuses. Some of them were downright terrible."

"I know," Evie said, returning her smile.

Her aunt tightened her hold on her hand. "I am proud of you, and I know your parents would be proud of everything that you've accomplished."

"I hope so."

"Promise me that we will have no more secrets between us," her aunt said.

Evie bobbed her head. "I can do that."

"Good, because I don't know how many more times I can pretend that I don't know you snuck out," Aunt Nancy responded.

Evie smiled. "I would be remiss if I didn't thank you for saving our lives earlier."

Her aunt waved a dismissive hand in front of her. "It was a small thing," she said. "Those guards were easily overpowered. Freya did not do a good enough job training them."

"I can't believe I fell for Freya's innocent act."

"It doesn't matter, because you defeated her in the end," her aunt pointed out. "Don't let your past mistakes define who you are now. You must learn from them, and you will be a better spy because of it."

"I wish it was that simple."

"It can be," her aunt said. "Everyone makes mistakes. The

important thing is that you don't make the same mistake twice."

Evie offered her a sad smile. "I just feel so inadequate at times."

Compassion crept into her aunt's eyes. "You will forever be searching for your own worth and value in other's eyes until you discover it within yourself."

"I know I'm being foolish—"

"You're being human," her aunt overrode. "I just wish you knew how extraordinary you are."

"Reginald said something similar."

"I'm not surprised, considering he's fancied you since you two were little." Aunt Nancy released her hand. "My question is, do you intend to do anything about it?"

Evie winced. "Lady Haddington hates me."

"Lady Haddington hates everyone who doesn't pay court to her," her aunt countered. "I wouldn't take offense. In fact, I might take comfort in that."

"Regardless, I cannot ask Reginald to pick me over his mother."

"What does he say about it?"

Evie moved to lean her back against the wall. "I don't rightly know," she said. "He intends to call on me tomorrow, and I fear he will offer for me."

"Most young women would be elated by an offer from a marquess."

"I know I must sound ungrateful, but I don't want to spend my entire life being at odds with my mother-in-law," Evie said.

Her aunt cocked her head. "How do you know for certain that Lady Haddington doesn't care for you?"

"After Reginald left for Eton, she offered me a large sum of money to stay away from him," Evie shared.

"Did your parents know?"

Evie shook her head. "I was too embarrassed to say

anything. Lady Haddington told me she knew Reginald cared for me, but his interest would wane when he realized what an odd child I was," she admitted. "She said some cruel things to me, and many of her words still haunt me at times."

"That was wrong of Lady Haddington, but I am beginning to see why you've always been so quick to dismiss praise," Aunt Nancy said. "Some people will be critical no matter what you do. You must not take it personally; it has more to do with them than you."

Evie reached for a pillow and propped it behind her. "I've always known that I was different from other young women, but Lady Haddington preyed on my insecurities."

"Do you intend to let her win?"

"I don't think this is a game that has a definitive winner."

Her aunt gave her a pointed look. "You've accomplished so much in your life. Why should the opinion of one person cause you to question everything? Don't give her that kind of power."

Evie pondered her aunt's words. Why had she let Lady Haddington's resentment follow her around for all these years, tormenting her?

Aunt Nancy turned towards the window. "It's late, and I have no doubt that you're exhausted."

The mere suggestion was enough to make a yawn escape Evie's lips, and she brought her hand up to cover it. "I must admit that I am tired."

Her aunt rose. "I hope your dreams are filled with Reginald," she teased as she headed for the door.

As she turned to leave, Evie asked, "How did you know Uncle Andrew was the one?"

"That's easy," Aunt Nancy said. "He loved me in spite of all my flaws and the broken pieces he had to pick up."

"I hope to be as happy as you and Uncle Andrew were."

"We were blessed with a happy union, as were your parents, but it was not without work," her aunt said. "I hate to say it, but falling in love is the easy part. The hard part is making that love last a lifetime through life's varied challenges."

"But is it worth it?"

Her aunt's face softened. "If someone is fortunate enough to find love, and they hold onto it, then their life is indeed blessed because of it."

"You have given me much to think on," Evie said as she removed the pillow from behind her. "I just hope that I'm as strong as you were."

"No." Her aunt paused. "You are stronger." She turned back to the door. "Just listen to what your heart tells you to do."

"Surely, it can't be that easy?"

"It's only as hard as you allow it to be."

After Aunt Nancy left her bedchamber, Evie prepared for sleep. She loved Reginald, there was no disputing that, but she was scared. And—usually—nothing scared her.

Reginald spent his morning at his desk reviewing accounts. Focusing was difficult; his thoughts kept drifting towards Evie. Would she be receptive to his offer of marriage? He didn't know the answer to that question, and it worried him. Furthermore, what would his mother do if they became engaged and then married? Would she come around, or be a continuous thorn in their sides?

He knew Evie cared for him; it was written plainly on her face. But would he be able to persuade her to take a chance on him?

His mother stepped into the room and eyed him curiously. "I was told that you wish to speak to me."

"I do," Reginald said, rising. "Please, come in."

She stepped further into the room. "Should I be concerned?"

Reginald gestured towards the chair that faced the desk. "Would you care to sit?"

His mother sat down but didn't say anything.

Once she was situated, Reginald reseated himself and took a moment to collect his thoughts. He had no doubt that this would be a very difficult conversation, so he decided to just say what needed to be said and hope his mother would be reasonable about it.

"I intend to offer for Evie today."

His mother's mouth gaped. "You cannot be in earnest!" she exclaimed. "Evie would make a terrible marchioness!"

"I disagree."

She jumped up and began pacing. "I know you've always been beguiled by Evie, but you must think of this family's reputation," she asserted.

"I know precisely what I am doing, and I ask for you to respect my decision."

His mother stopped pacing. "I will not."

"If that is the case, I need you to pack your trunks and move into the dowager house on our country estate."

She furrowed her brow. "You wish for me to leave Town?"

"I do, at your first opportunity."

"You would pick that girl over your own mother?" she asked, aghast.

Rising, Reginald replied, "I know that you tried to bribe Evie to stay away from me."

His mother clasped her hands together. "I did that for you!"

"For me?" he repeated. "I think not. You did it for yourself."

"If I didn't step in, then what would have become of you?"

Reginald stepped around his desk and walked to the drink

cart. As he picked up the decanter, he replied, "Most likely, I would have married Evie the moment I finished Oxford, and we would be happy."

"Happy?" his mother scoffed. "That girl got her teeth into you and hasn't let go, even after all these years."

He poured himself a drink and put down the decanter. "I love Evie," he said, "and I will not have you making disparaging comments about her."

"You can't possibly love her," his mother whined.

Reginald picked up his drink but stopped short of bringing the glass to his lips. "I love her with everything I am," he confessed.

"Then take her as a mistress," his mother attempted.

"Absolutely not!" he exclaimed. "I would never disrespect her in such a horrendous fashion!"

His mother went to sit down on an upholstered armchair. "Evie will drag you down, and you will never be accepted in polite Society."

"I do not care a whit about Society."

"But what of Evie?" his mother asked. "Could she handle being given the cut direct?"

Reginald tightened his hold on his glass. "I dare the person who attempts to give my wife the cut direct to suffer both her and my wrath," he growled.

"I do not like this," his mother eventually said with a frown, "but I suppose I can instruct Evie on how to behave like a proper lady."

"You will do no such thing."

"Pardon?"

"Evie is perfect just the way she is, and I do not want her to change to fit your expectations."

"But they aren't my expectations; they are Society's expectations."

"Then Society will need to accept Evie the way she is."

His mother's frown deepened. "It doesn't work that way, son."

"That is the way it will be from here on out," Reginald said firmly.

"You are being entirely unreasonable."

Reginald sat down across from his mother. "Evie told me a little of what you said to her all those years ago, and I was quite appalled."

"Evie has been rather talkative of late," his mother muttered.

"She was just a girl, and you said some terrible things to her."

"Nothing I said was untruthful," his mother said. "I was trying to protect you from her."

Reginald shook his head. "It sounds like I should have been trying to protect her from *you*."

"Reginald…"

He put his hand up, stilling her words. "I love you, but you crossed a line all those years ago when you tried to bribe Evie," he said. "Did Father know what you did?"

"No," she said. "He always cared for Evie. He thought her feistiness was *refreshing*. Besides, with your marriage contract to Lady Agnes signed, he felt there was no danger."

Reginald leaned forward and carefully placed his glass on the table. "Evie didn't want me to choose between you and her," he shared. "Do you know why?"

"I suppose you will tell me."

"The difference between you and her, is that Evie wants me to be happy, even at her own expense."

His mother pursed her lips. "I want you to be happy."

"I don't believe that to be true," Reginald responded. "You want me to fall in line and do precisely what you say."

"It would be much simpler—for both of us."

Reginald sighed. "I will ensure you have a generous

allowance for your household, but I must insist that you leave Evie and my family be."

His mother's eyes grew wide as realization dawned. "You would deprive me of seeing my grandchildren?"

"We shall see when the time comes."

She stared at him in disbelief before gathering herself. "I daresay you are overreacting to all of this," she said. "It isn't uncommon for a bride to not get along with her new family."

"Perhaps, but I will not take any chances."

"What if I promise to change?" Her voice grew panicked. "I'll apologize to Evie, and we will put this unfortunate business behind us."

"I'm not sure if Evie will even agree to meet with you."

"There has to be a way," his mother pleaded.

"I'll speak with Evie, but I can't make any promises."

"Thank you," his mother sighed. "That is all I can hope for."

A silence descended over them, the only noise the crackling of the fire in the hearth. Reginald reached for his drink and took a sip.

His mother pulled a ruby ring from her finger and placed it on the table in front of him. "I want you to give Evie my ring when you offer for her."

Reginald stared down at it. "Are you in earnest?"

"George gave me that ring when we married, and I have never taken it off," his mother said. "I hope that it will prove to Evie that I approve of this union."

"But you don't approve."

"I won't lose you, and if it means that I have to swallow my pride, then so be it."

Reginald put down his drink and picked up the ring. "I am unsure if Evie will even accept my offer."

"She would be a fool not to," his mother said. "After all, you are a marquess."

"That's why Evie is different. She has always judged me for the man that I am, and not for my title."

His mother rose. "I know I haven't been the best mother at times, but I do love you. I see now that she makes you truly happy."

"She does."

"A part of me was always envious of her," she admitted. "I was a lot like her when I was younger. I used to balk at tradition, and would read whatever I could get my hands on."

Reginald had a tough time believing that his prim and proper mother was anything like Evie. "What happened?"

A sad look came into his mother's eyes. "My father ensured I was cured of my incorrigible behavior before I was presented at court. I had little choice but to conform." She paused. "Evie was fortunate to have parents who embraced her uniqueness."

"That she was."

His mother walked over to the door and stopped. "May I stay in Town? For now?" she asked.

"Yes."

She gave him a grateful smile before she departed from the room. Reginald leaned back and admired the ruby ring in his hand. That had not been an easy conversation, but it needed to be done. He knew now, more than ever, that his future was with Evie. Now he just had to convince her of it.

"I do apologize for eavesdropping," Hawthorne said from the doorway, "but I didn't dare interrupt."

"What did you hear?" Reginald asked as he put the ring in his waistcoat pocket.

"Enough."

"Do you think I was in the wrong?"

Hawthorne shrugged. "You're the only one who can answer that," he replied. "I will only say that marrying Dinah was the best decision of my life."

Reginald leaned forward and picked up his drink. After he

took a sip, he asked, "What brings you by this morning?"

"I met with Merritt. He is anxiously awaiting your briefing," Hawthorne revealed.

Glancing at the window, Reginald asked, "Do you not sleep?"

"Hardly," Hawthorne replied as he closed the door. "Merritt wanted me to inform you that the streets are clear now that the rebels have disbanded. They never made it past the gates, and the garrison fought them off with ease."

"That is most fortunate."

Hawthorne came to sit down across from him. "Dinah encouraged me to come speak to you this morning."

"About what?"

"Evie."

Reginald glanced down at the empty drink in his hand. "Why am I not surprised?"

"She wants to know if you intend to fight for her."

"I do."

Hawthorne nodded. "Good," he said. "Do you have a speech prepared?"

"I'm working on one," he reluctantly admitted.

"It might very well be the most important speech you ever give."

"What a demoralizing thing to say." Reginald rose. "I should go. I told Evie that I would call on her, and I want to do so before we report to Merritt."

Hawthorne rose. "May I give you a word of advice?"

"Please."

"Speak from the heart. Nothing else matters."

Reginald tugged down on the ends of his purple jacket. "Were you nervous when you offered for Dinah?"

"Terribly, because I knew what was at stake." Hawthorne lifted his brow. "Do you know what it is you stand to lose?"

Reginald knew precisely what. Evie had taken his fears and reduced them all to one—losing her.

Chapter Twenty

Evie sat in the drawing room as she worked on her embroidery—for once. She could act as a proper lady when she wanted to. Really, she was just biding her time until Reginald came to call. She had yet to come to a decision about what she should do if he offered for her. She knew what she wanted to do, what her heart wanted her to do, but her decision would have consequences, one way or another.

Aunt Nancy's voice broke through her musings. "You're quiet, child," she said, glancing up from her needlework.

"I'm just woolgathering."

"Anything you wish to share?" her aunt asked.

Evie let out a despondent sigh. "I'm still unsure what I'll do if Reginald offers for me."

"Your heart will know what to do."

"You always make complex things sound so simple."

Her aunt pulled the needle through her fabric. "They are. You just overthink it," she said. "But you won't ever get a husband if you aren't proficient in needlework."

"That is not the least bit true."

"May I see your handkerchief?"

Evie held it up. "It isn't my best attempt," she admitted.

Aunt Nancy furrowed her brow. "Why does it have an elephant on it?"

"It isn't an elephant! It's my initials." Evie turned the handkerchief towards her and studied it. "Perhaps I was more distracted than I thought."

"I would save that one for Reginald," her aunt said with a smile.

"It's far more interesting than the ones I usually stitch," Evie said, abandoning the handkerchief on the table. "I do not see the point in needlework."

Aunt Nancy shifted her gaze towards the door before she lowered her voice. "I assure you that needlework does come in handy, because you never know when you will be required to alter your clothing to change your appearance or stitch someone up."

"Have you stitched someone up before?"

"I have," Aunt Nancy replied. "We were in France, and one of the agents took a bullet. We couldn't seek out a doctor for fear of being captured, so I stitched his wound."

"When were you in France?"

"Which time?" her aunt asked as her eyes twinkled with amusement. "I've been there many times over the years."

Evie leaned forward and matched her aunt's hushed tone. "Do you miss being an agent?"

"I did at first, but my priorities have shifted over these years," Aunt Nancy said. "Now my sole focus is to ensure you are properly settled."

"But what about the adventure of it all?"

Her aunt lowered her needlework to her lap. "I must admit that I did experience a thrill when I rescued you, but those guards were hardly a match for me."

Barnes stepped into the room and announced, "A Mr. Rutledge has requested a moment of your time."

"You may send him in," her aunt said.

Evie couldn't help but notice that her aunt took a moment to smooth her coiffed hair. Interesting.

Rutledge stepped into the room and her aunt gasped. "You look terrible, Adam!" she declared.

He chuckled. "Thank you, Nancy, but I assure you that it looks worse than it really is."

Evie gestured towards an upholstered armchair. "Would you care to take a seat?"

"I would," Rutledge said as he walked over to the proffered chair. "I just wanted to ensure you were both all right."

"That is kind of you, but we are both quite well," Aunt Nancy responded.

Rutledge nodded before turning fully towards Evie. "I wanted to personally apologize to you about Freya. I was going to tell you about her on that day we were supposed to meet, but I was abducted the night before."

"You have no reason to apologize," Evie said. "You could hardly have known that Freya was so unhinged."

"I should have known."

"Don't blame yourself for something you had no control over," Evie said. "That isn't fair to yourself."

Rutledge gave her a peculiar look. "That's odd advice, coming from you."

Evie laughed. "I suppose Reginald has started to wear off on me."

"I believe that's a good thing," Rutledge said. "Haddington is a good agent, and an even better gentleman."

"Would you care for some tea?" Aunt Nancy asked, waving her hand over the tea service.

"No, thank you," Rutledge replied, rising. "I have work I need to see to."

"You work too hard," she chided lightly.

"Maybe I need a distraction," Rutledge said, holding Aunt Nancy's gaze.

Evie saw a blush appear on her aunt's cheeks before she ducked her head.

Rutledge turned towards her. "I hope you don't mind, but Merritt asked me to be there when you and Haddington brief him about what transpired with Freya last night."

"I don't mind at all."

"Take care of your aunt," Rutledge said with a wink, "and don't pester her with too many of your questions."

With a parting glance at Aunt Nancy, Rutledge departed from the room.

Evie gave her aunt an expectant look. "Would you care to explain what just transpired?"

Her aunt was the picture of innocence. "I don't know what you're referring to."

"Rutledge was flirting with you."

"Poppycock! Adam is just a good friend."

Evie wasn't going to let her aunt off that easily. "There's nothing wrong with letting Rutledge pursue you."

Aunt Nancy poured herself a cup of tea. As she retrieved the cup, she said, "Rutledge and I had a brief flirtation before I met Andrew. We decided that it would never work between us because we were both agents."

"But you aren't an agent anymore."

"Yes, but I'm afraid that too much time has passed." Her aunt took a sip. "We both married other people and moved on with our lives."

Evie gave her a knowing look. "You're lonely, and I know Rutledge has been very lonesome since his wife died."

"That's most unfortunate, but a marriage must be based on more than the participants' loneliness."

"It can be the start of a conversation."

Aunt Nancy set her cup down on the saucer. "I am content with living through you and Dinah."

"Aren't you always telling me that I must follow my heart?"

"That is hardly applicable here," her aunt asserted. "Adam and I simply have a shared past and we are friends."

Evie put her hands up in surrender. "I promise I won't bring it up to you again."

"Thank you," her aunt said.

Barnes returned to the drawing room. "Mr. Wymond has come to call," he said. "Are you available to receive him?"

"I am," Evie replied.

A moment later, Mr. Wymond stepped into the drawing room, looking unusually earnest. His gaze caught Evie's immediately.

He smiled, but it didn't quite meet his eyes. "I was hoping to speak to you privately."

Evie glanced at her aunt for approval, who tipped her head in agreement. "We can take a tour of the gardens."

She had a sneaking suspicion what Mr. Wymond wished to speak to her about, but she wasn't repulsed by the thought. He was a good man, and she had no doubt that he would make a woman very happy—but it wouldn't be her.

Mr. Wymond approached and offered his arm. "Shall we?"

Evie accepted his arm and they departed the drawing room, continuing towards the rear of the townhouse and stepping out onto the veranda. A footman followed them outside and stood by the door.

Once they were walking down a path, Evie slipped her hand off his arm and put a little space between them. She didn't wish to be rude, but she didn't want to encourage him, either.

Mr. Wymond looked up at the sky. "It's a lovely day we are having, is it not?"

"It is," she agreed.

He stopped abruptly, and his boots ground on the gravel as he turned to face her. "I didn't come today to discuss the weather or the state of the garden," he admitted.

"What would you care to discuss instead?"

Mr. Wymond hesitated. "May I speak freely?"

"I would prefer it."

Shifting in his stance, he said, "I believe I have done a sufficient job of making my intentions known towards you."

"You have," she agreed.

Mr. Wymond took a step closer to her. "I care deeply for you, and I hope that you return my affections." He held his breath in anticipation of her response, which Evie found charming.

"I do care for you, but not in the way you are hoping," she said. "I consider you a friend."

Mr. Wymond's face fell. "Did I do something wrong?"

"No," she rushed to assure him. "I'm afraid my heart has already been claimed."

Understanding crossed his features. "I must assume that Lord Haddington is the lucky man."

"He is, and has been for a very long time."

"I feared that was the case, but I had to try to win your affections, anyway."

"I'm glad you did, because it gave me an opportunity to become better acquainted with you."

Mr. Wymond reached for her gloved hand and brought it up to his lips. "You are an extraordinary woman, Miss Ashmore," he said. "You deserve a lifetime of happiness."

"As do you, Mr. Wymond."

"You are kind," he said, "but I do not believe I am destined for happiness. I'm afraid I have done too many things that I'm not proud of."

"Haven't we all?"

Mr. Wymond released her hand but remained close. "I do not know what regrets you could possibly have."

"You would be surprised," Evie said. "No one gets through this life without scars. Be proud of yours, because they helped define who you are."

"My scars run quite deep."

Evie placed a comforting hand on his sleeve. "You are not alone in that."

"I feel alone," he murmured.

Evie was about to reply when she saw Reginald approaching them, a thunderous look on his face.

———————

Reginald knew the polite thing to do was to allow Evie to converse with Mr. Wymond in private, but that all changed the moment he saw how close they were to one another. He refused to let Mr. Wymond snatch Evie from right under him.

Evie removed her hand from Mr. Wymond's sleeve and turned to face him with a bemused look. "Reginald," she asked mildly, "whatever is the matter?"

Halting before them, he announced, "I have come to challenge Mr. Wymond to a duel."

"Do be serious…" Evie attempted.

"I accept," Mr. Wymond said.

Frowning, Evie glanced between them. "There will be no duel."

"Name your seconds," Reginald demanded.

Mr. Wymond opened his mouth to respond, but Evie interrupted. "Can I speak to you, Reginald?" It was clearly not a question, but a demand.

Reginald put his hand out, indicating that she should go first. He knew he was being ridiculous, but he didn't like the way Mr. Wymond looked at Evie. He took a moment to glower at him before he turned to follow her.

Evie walked a short distance away and spun back around to face him. "What do you think you're doing?" she asked in a hushed voice.

"I think it's fairly obvious," he replied. "I challenged Mr. Wymond to a duel, and he accepted."

"You'd kill him!"

"We don't know that for certain."

Evie put a hand on her hip. "This is not you," she declared. "You aren't reckless with your life."

He shrugged one shoulder. "I guess you don't know everything about me."

"I know everything I need to," Evie said. "You are a good man, and I know you're better than this."

Some of his anger dissipated, but he still couldn't abide Mr. Wymond. That man was a thorn in his side.

Evie dropped her hand from her hip. "Will you please tell me what has you so upset?"

Reginald shuffled his feet. He couldn't lie to Evie; not when she was looking at him like that. "I'm afraid I got jealous when I saw you with Mr. Wymond."

"I see; and you thought a duel was the way to solve it?"

Reginald winced. "It may not have been my brightest idea."

"No, it wasn't." Evie turned back towards Mr. Wymond and announced, "There will be no duel."

Mr. Wymond looked disappointed. "I understand," he acquiesced with a bow. "I shall bid you good day, Miss Ashmore."

As Mr. Wymond left, Evie turned back to Reginald and arched an eyebrow.

"I've never known you to be jealous before," she said. "It's not a good look on you."

Reginald sighed. "This isn't how it was supposed to go."

"What are you referring to?"

With a glance back at the townhouse, he replied, "I've been practicing a speech all morning, but now that I'm here, I can't seem to recall a word of it."

Evie eyed him curiously. "Why don't you start at the beginning?"

He reached for her hand. "Evie," he said, then took a deep breath, "I want to marry you—no, I *need* to marry you."

"Was that part of the speech you were rehearsing?" she asked with a twinkle in her eye. "It didn't seem too complicated to me."

He shook his head. "No; I'm trying to speak from the heart, but I'm afraid I don't have very much practice at it."

Evie gave him an encouraging smile. "If you can stare down a French spy without blinking, I daresay you can properly express your feelings for me."

Reginald hesitated for only a moment before saying, "I love you, Evie, and that will never change. I love everything about you. Even the things I don't like, I love. And I want you with me, always. I love you, and I hope that you love me, too."

"Do you truly love me?" she asked.

"Yes, wall-climbing and all," he replied. "You make me a better man, and a better agent."

A small smile appeared on her face as she beamed up at him. "I love you, too, no matter how hard I fought not to."

"I hoped that you loved me, but I didn't dare to presume."

"I've loved you since we played at the creek and you made me mud cakes on the banks," Evie said.

"You remember that?"

She laughed. "How could I forget? You were the only one who would go swimming with me and face our parents' wrath."

Reginald took a step closer. "I know that I'm imperfect, but I humbly stand before you and hope you will take a chance on me."

Evie cupped his cheek in her hand. "I love you, not because you're perfect, but because you're perfect for *me*. You have always taken me as I am."

"Will you marry me, Evie, so I never have to go a day without you again?" he asked softly, nuzzling her hand.

Evie's eyes filled with tears as she lowered her hand from his face. "I want to, but what of your mother?"

"Oh, yes, my mother," Reginald said as he fumbled around in his waistcoat pocket for the ring. He held it up to her. "This is my mother's ring."

"I don't understand."

Reginald lowered himself down to one knee. "My father gave this ring to my mother on their wedding day, and she's never taken it off... until now."

"But why would she do such a thing?"

He smiled. "Because she wants you to know that she approves of us marrying."

A line appeared between Evie's brows, and she looked quite concerned. "Did you threaten her?"

"No," he replied with a nervous chuckle. "I told her that I love you more than anything else and I wouldn't rest until you agreed to be my wife." He left out the part about asking his mother to move to the dowager house and limiting contact to his family. They could discuss it later.

"She may approve of this wedding now, but what about in the future?"

"We will take it one day at a time."

Evie looked unsure. "What about me working as an agent?" she asked. "Will you take issue with it once we are wed?"

"I do not wish to change one thing about you."

"And what of my aunt?" she asked. "Because I will not leave her behind."

"Your aunt will always have a home with us."

"May I get a dog?"

Reginald huffed. "I will buy you whatever your heart desires if you say yes," he replied. "It is deucedly uncomfortable down here, I might add."

Evie's eyes darted towards the ring. "I will agree to marry you on one condition."

"Anything."

Bringing her gaze to meet his, she said, "You must promise me that you will always kiss me goodnight."

Reginald rose. "I will, gladly."

A grin stretched across her face and a giddy laugh escaped her lips. "Then I will marry you, Reginald."

Without waiting another moment, he removed the glove on her left hand and slipped the ring onto her finger. "It's official now," he said.

Evie's smile turned mischievous. "I do believe it isn't official until you've kissed me."

"My pleasure," Reginald said as he stood. He gently wrapped his arms around her and slowly inched forward, having an immense desire to engrave this moment onto his heart. This was a memory he would treasure forever, the first time he kissed his betrothed.

Evie's eyes closed and she melted against him. Needing no further encouragement, he kissed her on the cheek first, then her lips. This was no chaste kiss; he kissed her long and deeply. He hoped that she could feel the promise in his kiss—that he would hold her just like this forever. Now that she was in his arms, he had no intention of ever letting her go.

Reginald reluctantly broke the kiss and leaned his forehead against hers. "I could get used to this."

"As could I," she said breathlessly.

"I propose we post the banns tomorrow and be married as soon as they're done being read."

"I am in agreement."

Reginald grinned. "I do hope you will be this agreeable during our marriage."

"Not likely," she responded, closing her eyes and resting her head on his chest.

Hawthorne's voice came from behind them. "I must assume that this means you two are engaged."

Reginald released Evie and turned around to face his friend. "It does."

"Finally!" Hawthorne exclaimed as he clasped his hands together. "And not a day too soon."

"I beg your pardon?" he asked.

Hawthorne smirked. "We've been placing bets on when you two would end up together, and I just won."

"You're an idiot," Reginald muttered as he reached for Evie's hand.

"Perhaps, but I am now twenty pounds richer," Hawthorne remarked. "Also, Dinah and Aunt Nancy have a special dinner planned this evening to celebrate your upcoming nuptials. All of our friends are invited."

"When did they plan that?" Evie asked.

Hawthorne gave her an amused look. "They started months ago," he replied.

"That seems rather presumptuous," Evie said.

"Not when everyone could recognize that you two belonged together," Hawthorne explained. "We just had to wait until you figured it out."

As the couple walked hand in hand back to the town-house, Reginald couldn't quite believe that he had done what he'd set out to do. He had won Evie's heart—and that was something he would never take for granted.

Epilogue

Three weeks later

Reginald tried to keep the wiggling puppy on his lap as the coach bumped over the road. The black pup was far more interested in looking out at the passing scenery than settling down.

Hawthorne watched with an amused look. "You should have gone with diamonds for a wedding gift."

"Evie didn't ask for diamonds; she asked for a dog," Reginald said, turning the puppy to look at him. "I wouldn't dare disappoint her, since I still need to get her to the church tomorrow."

"That's wise, but I do hope Dinah doesn't get any ideas."

The puppy lunged at Reginald and licked him on the lips. "Bleh! Not the lips," he ordered as he wiped his mouth on the sleeve of his jacket.

Hawthorne laughed. "Yes, I do believe he understood you."

"I've never had a dog before," Reginald admitted, holding

the pup at arm's length. "I'm not quite sure what to do with one."

"You should've thought about that before you bought one from Worsley and Talbot."

"It's highway robbery, what they charged me for it," Reginald grumbled.

Hawthorne eyed the animal. "How do you think your mother will do with your new addition?"

"She'll no doubt hate it," Reginald replied, "but she'll have to come around when I tell her it's for Evie."

"Has your mother finally come to terms with the two of you?"

Reginald lowered the dog to his lap. "She's apologized to Evie, on multiple occasions, for her past behavior, and has vowed to change."

"Do you believe it's genuine?"

"I do, because she wants to be in our lives," he said. "She doesn't want to miss out on her grandchildren."

The coach slowed to a stop and dipped to the side as the footman stepped off his perch. The door was opened, and Reginald struggled to keep the puppy in his arms as he stepped outside. He turned and handed it off to the footman.

"Will you see to the dog while I'm gone?"

"Yes, my lord." The footman gently lowered the puppy to the ground and held tight to the leash as it tried to dash for the street.

Satisfied that the dog would be cared for, Reginald brushed himself off and stepped inside White's. His eyes roamed the usual corner for his friends, but he saw no sign of them.

"It would appear that we are first to arrive," Reginald said.

Hawthorne headed for their table and pulled out a chair. Reginald took the seat next to him, catching the eye of a passing by servant and indicating that they wanted drinks.

The server tipped his head in response and went to fetch them.

"Do you think Hugh will make an appearance today?" Hawthorne asked.

"I don't rightly know," Reginald replied. "I haven't seen much of him since he returned from his wedding tour."

"Neither have I, and we live in the same house."

"He does seem happy, though."

"That he does." Hawthorne's eyes strayed towards the door. "Don't look, but Mr. Wymond just stepped inside the club."

Reginald shifted a little to watch as Mr. Wymond step further into the main hall. "I see they allow everyone in nowadays," he remarked dryly.

Hawthorne grinned. "Didn't you challenge him to a duel the last time you saw him?"

"That would be correct."

"Do you still hold animosity towards him, considering you won the contest for Evie's heart?"

Reginald turned back to face Hawthorne. "I still find the man to be quite irksome, but we fortunately do not run in the same circles."

"He's approaching our table."

"Botheration," Reginald muttered under his breath.

"Lord Hawthorne," Mr. Wymond greeted with a tip of his hat.

Hawthorne responded in kind. "Mr. Wymond."

He turned towards Reginald. "Lord Haddington," he said shortly.

Reginald had no desire to converse with Mr. Wymond, but it would be rude of him not to at least acknowledge him. He met his gaze and tried to make his voice sound somewhat cordial. "Mr. Wymond."

The man looked as uncomfortable as Reginald felt, and he shifted his gaze quickly back to Hawthorne.

"I just came from visiting my sister and Lord Hugh," he revealed. "He wanted me to inform you that he will be a little late, but he still intends to come."

"Thank you," Hawthorne responded.

Reginald hoped that was the end of it, but it seemed he was not so lucky. Mr. Wymond turned back to him. "I wanted to wish you congratulations on your upcoming nuptials with Miss Ashmore."

"Thank you."

"I do hope that we can let bygones be bygones and be civil to one another in the future."

Reginald frowned. "Frankly, I hope to see very little of you."

"That is something we both can agree on." Mr. Wymond started to turn but stopped himself. "Promise me that you will take good care of her."

Reginald was prepared with a snide remark, but the sincerity in Mr. Wymond's eyes gave him pause. "I promise," he said.

Mr. Wymond nodded. "I did notice that you bought her a dog," he remarked. "That was brilliant."

"I did, but how did you know?"

Mr. Wymond's lips twitched. "It tried to relieve itself on my boot, but your footman pulled him back before he was able to do so."

"I knew he was a smart dog," Reginald joked.

Mr. Wymond tipped his head and headed towards a hall off the main room, passing a server, who came and placed two glasses on the table in front of them.

As Reginald reached for a glass, Grenton and Graylocke approached, looking perplexed.

"Did I just see you speaking to Mr. Wymond?" Grenton questioned as he pulled out a chair and sat down.

"You did," Reginald confirmed.

"Didn't you challenge him to a duel?" Graylocke asked, sitting next to him.

"I did, but Evie called it off," Reginald sulked.

"Smart woman, considering duels are illegal," Graylocke pointed out.

"Only if you get caught," Reginald said, lifting his glass to his lips.

Grenton shook his head. "Am I to assume that you are on friendly terms with Mr. Wymond now?" he asked.

"No; we barely tolerate one another," Reginald answered.

The server returned with two more drinks, and Graylocke reached for one. "I propose a toast to Haddington," he said, smiling and raising his glass. "He is finally succumbing to the parson's mousetrap like the rest of us."

Grenton raised his glass. "To Haddington."

After they toasted, Hawthorne announced, "Marrying my wife was the best decision I ever made."

"I feel the same way," Graylocke said. "I have never been happier since I convinced Beatrice to marry me."

Grenton pushed his glass away. "I need a clear head," he explained, "because Georgie and I are attending Lady Clonbrock's ball this evening."

"How dull," Graylocke muttered.

"She's agreed to be a patron of the orphanage," Grenton shared. "With any luck, more of her associates will follow suit."

"The orphanage appears to be thriving," Hawthorne commented.

Grenton bobbed his head. "That it is," he confirmed. "Georgie has made sure of that, and she has been most grateful for your wife's help."

"Dinah has grown quite fond of the girls," Hawthorne said.

As Reginald took a sip of his drink, Lord Hugh approached, a solemn look on his face.

Hugh stopped beside him and leaned close. "Miss Ashmore is outside, and she wishes to speak to you."

"Evie is here?"

"She is, and I daresay you must not keep her waiting," Hugh said. "She's garnering some attention."

Reginald shoved his chair back and strode to the door. As he stepped outside, he saw Evie crouched down, petting the puppy, who appeared elated at the attention. Her lady's maid was standing close by, but she refused to meet his gaze.

Evie glanced up at him. "What a darling puppy!" she gushed.

"I'm so glad you approve, since I bought him for you," he shared, "but I had hoped to surprise you later when I came to call."

A bright smile lit Evie's face. "I love him!" she exclaimed as she picked up the animal. "I shall call him Sir Jasper."

"That's a terrible name for a dog."

Evie brought the animal's face close to her own. "What do you think, Sir Jasper?" she asked. The pup attempted to lick her face, and she laughed. "I do believe he likes his name."

Reginald took a step closer. "Not that I'm complaining, but may I ask why you are standing outside White's?"

"Because I needed to speak to you at once," Evie said as she put Sir Jasper down and stood up.

Now she had his full attention, and he waited for her to elaborate.

"Merritt has an assignment for us."

"Can it not wait until after our wedding tomorrow?" he asked.

"I'm afraid not," she replied. "There's talk of a meeting tonight at the Crowned Owl. Merritt wants us to attend and see if this group poses any real threat to the Crown."

"I assume there is no chance I will be able to talk you out of going."

Evie placed a hand on her hip. "I think not," she said. "Besides, you were the one who insisted on being partners with me."

Reginald saw the determined tilt of her chin and knew he was fighting a losing battle. They would have to go to this meeting in the rookeries and report back to Merritt before their wedding at noon the next day.

"All right, we'll go," he conceded, "but don't think for one second I'm not going to marry you tomorrow."

Evie's face softened. "I am counting down the moments."

"As am I," he replied.

Reginald wished they were any place but here in the middle of town, because he wanted to take Evie into his arms and kiss her senseless. But that would cause a scandal, and that was something neither of them wanted.

"I love you," Evie said softly.

Reginald reached for her gloved hand and brought it up to his lips. "You have my heart, Evie," he murmured. "I hope you know that."

"It's only fair, since you have mine."

He kissed her hand, his lips lingering. "After tomorrow, we will never be apart again," he said as he reluctantly released her hand.

"What a wonderful thought." The dog barked and jumped up on Evie, drawing her attention. "It would appear that Sir Jasper is excited by the prospect, as well."

Reginald reached down and picked up the squirming youngster. "I have a feeling that Sir Jasper will require a lot of training."

Evie leaned forward to pet the dog. "We'll get along just fine, won't we, Sir Jasper?" she asked. "We'll be one big, happy family."

Family.

There was no one he would rather form a family with

than Evie. She was his everything, the very measure of his dreams.

The End

Mr. Stephen Wycomb is utterly miserable as the unrelenting grief of his past failures in the Royal Navy continue to haunt him. After a failed attempt at a courtship, the only thing keeping him in London is to ensure his sister is happily settled with her new husband- a man whom he has an uneasy alliance with. He has sworn off marriage, but his determination sways when he is introduced to a strikingly beautiful young woman.

That beautiful young woman, Gemma, the Countess of Hawkinge, has been invited to spend the Season with her family in London now that she is finally out of mourning for her late husband. She jumps at the opportunity, hoping this trip will give her the reprieve she so desperately needs.

As Stephen and Gemma develop an easy friendship, she begins to wonder if there might be more happiness to life than she had previously thought. Yet nothing is as it seems. When the couple find themselves caught in a web of greed and deceit, they must determine whether they are willing to risk everything for a chance at true love.

Also by Laura Beers

Proper Regency Matchmakers

Saving Lord Berkshire

Reforming the Duke

Loving Lord Egleton

Redeeming the Marquess

Engaging Lord Charles

Refining Lord Preston

Regency Spies & Secrets

A Dangerous Pursuit

A Dangerous Game

A Dangerous Lord

A Dangerous Scheme

Regency Brides: A Promise of Love

A Clever Alliance

The Reluctant Guardian

A Noble Pursuit

The Earl's Daughter

A Foolish Game

The Beckett Files

Saving Shadow

A Peculiar Courtship

To Love a Spy

About the Author

Laura Beers is an award-winning author. She attended Brigham Young University, earning a Bachelor of Science degree in Construction Management. She can't sing, doesn't dance and loves naps.

Besides being a full-time homemaker to her three kids, she loves waterskiing, hiking, and drinking Dr. Pepper. She was born and raised in Southern California, but she now resides in Utah.